I0669507

Bayou Brides

by

Linda Joyce

Fleur de Lis Series, Book Four

Bayou Brides

Cover Art by *Kim Mendoza*

The Wild Rose Press, Inc.
PO Box 708
Adams Basin, NY 14410-0708
Visit us at www.thewildrosepress.com

Publishing History
First Champagne Rose Edition, 2017
Print ISBN 978-1-5092-1770-0
Digital ISBN 978-1-5092-1771-7

Fleur de Lis Series, Book 4
Published in the United States of America

His mesmerizing blue-gray eyes
drew her farther through the open window. A sensual smile slowly rose on his lips. He winked.

A bluesy 12/8 beat thumped in Nola's chest. The entire world melted away. A daydream took over. Just the two of them promenading down the long drive, like it was in antebellum days. He, in cutaway tails, and she, twirling a parasol and coyly giggling at something clever he said.

The illusion was abruptly shattered. Her sister grabbed the back of her shirt and yanked her inside the room. "What!" Her daydream had popped like a string on an overplayed guitar.

"Get in here."

"Why?" Her perfectly wonderful dream had been cut short.

"You were about to fall on your head. I gotta go." Biloxi headed for the door. "I want to meet this guest."

"You're a married woman. A mother of three," Nola hollered at her. "Hussy! Strumpet! What will I tell my nephews and niece?"

"Darlin', a woman can look. Come with me? You're single. You can *touch*," she teased.

Touch him? No. He was too…vivid, too real. Virile. Oozed with sensuality. Just too male.

The man made her hear the blues. In the best possible way.

Praise for Linda Joyce

"With her rich imagery and complex characters, Linda Joyce captures the flavors and rhythms of modern southern romance. Her books go on my keeper shelf so I can return to them again and again, like dear friends."

~Melissa Klein, author of Out of Bounds

~*~

"When I read Linda's books, I am swept away. Linda writes with such emotion and clarity, you can't help but fall in love. Her books are a refreshing escape!"

~Taylor Anne, author of Smoke and Mirrors

~*~

"Southern writers have their own unique vibe; Linda Joyce conveys that oh-so-genteel, tradition-bound warmth and familiarity with her Fleur de Lis romance series…"

~Susan Coryell, author of A Red, Red Rose

~*~

"Linda Joyce is the master of emotional impact and epic storytelling."

~Kathy L Wheeler, author of Color of Betrayal

Dedication

This book is dedicated to my mother,
Chieko Fukuhara Brannan.
She was a mix of Macy Lind and Deidre Dutrey,
and though she was Japanese,
she spoke perfect English...
well, maybe with a hint of a New Orleans accent.

Acknowledgments

No book of mine is published without the help from supporters. I am extending a BIG thank you to Mr. Allen Cruthirds, a firefighter at NOFD Fire Station Engine 35, for the information he provided about how the City of New Orleans decommissions and sells off old fire stations. Not only is he a fire fighter, but he's worked his way through the City's process and owns such a property. I also understand he's an artist, and I look forward to seeing his work the next time I'm home. Just so you know, in Bayou Brides, the community center Nola is leasing from Emile is that of retired fire station.

Author Goldie Edwards is always kind to me, beta reads to keep me on course, and supports me in so many ways. Thank you, Goldie. I value your friendship very much.

I am very grateful for author Melissa Klein and author Rachel Jones for their constant support of my writing. We meet once a week to trade pages and critique. Their input has helped improve my story and help me grow as a writer.

To Cheryl Walz, my behind the scenes support, with her Chicago Style book and English Teacher background, thank you. Also, she catches some of my funky word choices and challenges me with, "Are you sure that's the word you want? Here's the meaning…" and she's always right. I appreciate that she helps me continue to learn.

Linda's Lovelies, my street team, who share on social media and help other readers to find my books, Big Hugs!

To Barbara Hackel and Linda Bass for their continued support of reading, reviewing, and spreading the word about my writing, I am very grateful for your continued support.

Hugs and gratitude to author Gina Hooten Popp. We met when I was first learning to write and she's always been cheering in my corner...and cheering me up through the challenging times in my life.

There are three men and a "boy" in my life who do so much behind the scenes for me. I rely on them and appreciate their continued encouragement. The "boy" is General Beauregard, my writing buddy, cookie mooch, and constant reminder that sometimes I must get up from the computer and stretch my legs—of course, that means he wants to take a stroll outside. As for the men, one is Gene Horton. He and his wife, Carolyn, whom we lost in December 2016, have been good friends for many years. Thank you Gene.

To the man who's known me all my life and still tells me he's proud of me. Thank you Calvin Brannan. I love you very much.

The final man is my darling husband, without whom, I would not be able to do all that I am able. He attends to all sorts of details, like keeping my website functioning, joining me at events, even serving up food at book signings, and his patient and undying love is what makes my life so full. I'll love you forever.

True American Music

Saxophone wails,
washboard scratch,
drums beat percussion.

Dobro twang,
bass guitar licks,
harmonicas howl.

Juke-joint piano,
spoons click,
fiddles and accordion groove.

Soulful hollers evolved into lyrical sound,
Sex, hunger, work, love—
life's rhythmic celebrations.

Three-chord progressions
in endless improvisation.
12-bar blues.

~Linda Joyce

Chapter 1

Irritated, Nola Dutrey grabbed a pillow and flopped on the padded bench in front of the floor-to-ceiling window in her bedroom to catch a breeze. Sitting, she scanned the sheet music for "The Look of Love" and kept a one-eyed lookout for Momma who insisted they visit all the vendors at the Bridal Extravaganza taking place on the grounds of Fleur de Lis. Momma had said, "You're twenty-eight, and at that age, the first female in the family with no marriage prospects." That wasn't exactly true—there had been a couple, but she just hadn't found "the one."

Reading the song lyrics on the page, she paused. "Will the right man ever look at me just like that?"

Sighing, she reached for a freshly fried beignet dusted with powdered sugar on the plate beside the bench. "Well, until then, I have you." As she licked her lips, the lecherous grin of Emile Broussard popped into her mind. She shuddered, refocused on the sweetness of her treat, and then sang a few lines of the lyrics.

A cool March breeze rippled the sheer curtains in the bedroom, reminding her of stories about swishing petticoats from antebellum times. Musical notes floated on the air from the string quartet playing in the gazebo on the side of the house. Dappled light through the trees and the blooming spring flowers added the perfect touch of romance to day one of the event. Her sister and

1

Cousin Branna had selected the best time to host the event—after Mardi Gras and before Easter.

Below on the lawn and extending down the long driveway, white tents dotted the landscape like white-capped mountains—a foreign landscape in southwest Mississippi. Florists, photographers, musicians, and wedding planners showed off their wares and services to prospective brides. One area had been reserved for food vendors, and they drew in the crowds. Aromas of garlic, sausage, and fried shrimp tickled her nose. She took a second bite of the beignet, savoring the melt-in-your-mouth flavor.

Nola sighed. She was home to do her family duty, but wishing she were in the lounge at Arceneau's rehearsing for her upcoming tour—a summer of festival hopping and singing with different bands—rather than hiding in her room with the stink of Momma's words wafting around her. A pang of envy hit her. "Just look at them. Brides-to-be, their mommas, their entourage. Giggling like drunk cackling hens." They mingled and sipped champagne in their pastel Sunday finest. The bridal show could pass for an Easter-hat parade, given the extravagance of many.

But most of them came because they had a groom on a string attached to their engagement ring and a wedding loomed in their future.

She sighed. Maybe her family was right. Maybe she was the problem. All around her the connection of true love beat as palpable as any living heart. She wanted that. Forever love that could weather anything.

But no man had entered her life and evoked within her the same deep emotion as when she sang a love song—like the one she had to finish rehearsing to sing in just a bit.

"Damna—" She stopped when Great-Grandmother Grace's *tsk!* floated on the air. Though the older woman had passed about ten years ago, G.G. Grace reached down from heaven to keep her in line whenever she visited Fleur de Lis. "I apologize. No cussing. Got it." She never dared back talk to the ethereal spirit.

Stuffing another throw pillow behind her back, she squirmed to get comfortable. "But G.G. Grace, why spend buku bucks on a fancy shindig to hitch yourself to a man when there's barely a fifty-fifty chance of marriage success?" Never would she stand a chance of winning *that* debate with anyone in her family. There hadn't been a divorce in the family yet. That put a boatload of pressure on her to choose well. So what if *all* the other women in the family had married by twenty-eight?

Until her time came, she chose music. Romantic love and the ballads written about it were songs she thoroughly enjoyed singing. She hugged the sheet music to her chest. Love songs had triggered a deep yearning that had stayed with her since she was sixteen. Over the years, she'd tripped into "like"—G.G. Grace had called it "puppy love." Twice she'd landed in "infatuation land." But never had she met a man that enflamed a smoldering burn deep inside her. She wanted to fall in love. Deeply. Madly. The kind of love that churned up her life the way a hurricane churned up the sea. Southern breezes hadn't blown that man in her direction yet.

If and when she ever fell truly in love, it would be forever. Like a swan, she would mate for life—but her family didn't know that about her. They called her a butterfly, flitting around, never landing anywhere for long, but she didn't see the need for wasting time developing a relationship with a man when intuition told her it wouldn't last. And she didn't do one-night stands.

Nola closed her eyes. It would take a game of truth or dare before she admitted she was jealous of the brides visiting Fleur de Lis today. To avoid Momma and the swath of envy pricking her conscience, she had snuck upstairs to hide. Momma's invitation was a command, not a request. Deidra Dutrey, always a force to be reckoned with, usually got her way. Why hadn't Momma set her sights on Linc to settle down? He was older. He would carry on the family name.

If only life were a musical...

Downstairs, the screen door slammed and drew Nola's attention.

"Nola. Bridgette. Dutrey. You can't hide from me!"

Wrapping her long hair in front of her, Nola melted onto the floor between the bench and her bed. Angels willing, she had a chance of avoiding her sister, even if it was only one in a million.

Biloxi stomped up the stairs. "I know you're in here." She opened the door, and the hinges squeaked. "I came to remind you to be at the café before three to sing."

Nola held her breath as she watched her sister's Louboutin shoe-clad feet step in her direction.

"Ohhhh," Nola groaned, looking up from the floor. "Okay. You found me."

Biloxi pointed to her watch. "It's two now. You have less than an hour. This is your contribution to

Fleur de Lis. When people hear you sing, they'll see the added value of hosting their party here—we have the famous Nola Belle singing to melt hearts."

"But I'm hiding from Momma." She pushed to standing.

Biloxi raised an eyebrow.

"I didn't mean to lie. I wanted her to leave me alone, stop groom-shopping for me. I only said I had an *interest* in someone, and she got it into her head that this unnamed someone is about to give me a ring. Now she wants to promenade me through the bridal show."

"No, sister, you blurted out that you were interested in getting engaged."

Nola shrugged. She'd made the audacious announcement under pressure. It was a dim-witted idea that popped into her head, and then the words came flooding out of her mouth. "She thinks finding my soul mate is like any other kind of shopping."

"I'll try to keep Momma occupied, but you *have* to show up to sing. She'll know where to find you at three."

"What do I do? Momma doesn't care who I marry, just as long as I get a ring on my finger, set a date, and walk down the aisle that ends with an 'I do.' I'll tell her the man has met another woman and says I'm not"— she lifted her fingers, making imaginary quotation marks—"the one."

Biloxi shook her head. "Don't involve me in your lies. I won't be a party to your deceptions. Now get—" She walked to the window and stood to the side, out of view. She pointed to the black limo pulling in front of the house by the fountain. "Wonder who that could be. The limo companies participating in the show are already here." After puffing out a soft whistle, she said, "Look at that."

Amused by her sister's gawking, Nola sank down on the bench, flipping her waist-length hair over her shoulder. Framed by the bedroom window, a man in a well-fitted, dark peacock-blue suit exited the limo after the driver—she recognized her neighbor—opened the door. He stood inches above the driver, making him taller than six feet. Several women mingling near the fountain cast long appreciative looks in his direction— they practically drooled. Nodding slightly, he smiled and then adjusted his pink striped tie, taking a moment to flirt with the women. The fact that he wore a pocket square caught Nola's interest, a man who paid attention to small details. Nice.

Or had someone dressed him that morning? Like a girlfriend or wife.

Sauntering in the direction of the house, he radiated relaxed ease. His smooth stride reminded her of the majesty of a fine stallion. Male grace and full of strength. Light shone on his blue-black hair. "Fine looking," she murmured as a warmth ignited in her chest. Maybe he'd be interested in helping her out of her mess. After one look at him, anyone in her family would believe love had—at first sight—caught her in a cast net. For a second, she considered shouting for her father to grab his gun for a shotgun wedding. Yes, the man was that hot. Could give a girl the vapors.

She stretched and leaned out the window to catch the last glimpse of him as he began climbing the front steps of Fleur de Lis.

He paused and looked up.

Their gazes locked.

His mesmerizing blue-gray eyes drew her farther through the open window. A sensual smile slowly rose on his lips. He winked.

A bluesy 12/8 beat thumped in Nola's chest. The entire world melted away. A daydream took over. Just the two of them promenading down the long drive, like it was in antebellum days. He, in cutaway tails, and she, twirling a parasol and coyly giggling at something clever he said.

The illusion was abruptly shattered. Her sister grabbed the back of her shirt and yanked her inside the room. "What!" Her daydream had popped like a string on an overplayed guitar.

"Get in here."

"Why?" Her perfectly wonderful dream had been cut short.

"You were about to fall on your head. I gotta go." Biloxi headed for the door. "I want to meet this guest."

"You're a married woman. A mother of three," Nola hollered at her. "Hussy! Strumpet! What will I tell my nephews and niece?"

"Darlin', a woman can look. Come with me? You're single. You can *touch*," she teased.

Touch him? No. He was too...vivid, too real. Virile. Oozed with sensuality. Just too male.

The man made her hear the blues. In the best possible way.

****

Stepping in front of the screen door of Fleur de Lis, Rex Arceneau observed a woman coming down the stairs. She appeared to float more than walk in a flowing flowered dress and high heels. Elegant. Classy.

Nice legs.

7

But a pang of disappointment hit him. She wasn't the same woman who'd stared at him from the window upstairs. Too bad. *That* woman he wanted to meet. An air of sensuality swirled around her even from a distance. His breath had hitched, just for a second. Her sultry expressive eyes whispered to him the way melodic music tells a story. He wanted to hear the full score of her melody. An image of her lips barely caressing his flashed in his mind. Hot emotion surged through him. The urge to close his eyes and follow the sensual scene to conclusion pushed hard. She'd planted a seed of strong desire, something he hadn't experienced in a long time.

"May I help you?" The woman in the flowered dress opened the door.

Rex straightened and pulled a business card from the inside pocket of his suit coat. "Arceneau." He cleared his throat. "Rex. I believe my sister has a booth here. Could you point it out to me? I need to speak with her."

"I'm Biloxi." She took the card and scrutinized it. "X. Rex Arceneau. I'm one of the organizers of this event. What's the X for, Rex?"

"Xavier." She raised an eyebrow, and he smiled. He was used to people's reactions to the rather old-fashioned name. "But no one calls me that." His mother had, but no one else.

"Ahhh," she said in a way that he couldn't decipher whether or not she considered it good or bad. "I'll be right back. I'll ask *my* sister to escort you to find *your* sister. Arceneau's. Great French Quarter restaurant."

She left him standing outside on the porch. He hoped the sultry-eyed beauty upstairs was her sister.

Turning to face the fountain and the circular drive in front of the house, he tried to distract his mind away from the daydream of her almost-kiss. He scanned the tents. No way to tell one from the other. In the future, if his sister participated in this kind of event, he'd insist on some sort of flag to identify her tent from all the others. Attention to detail set Arceneau's apart from the competition.

Clasping his hands behind his back, he rocked back on his heels. He'd been clear with Kayla earlier in the week. In their conversation, she'd agreed to abstain from this event—all events—until he finished going through the account books of the restaurant and until her full month as head chef ended. But Kayla had lied and participated anyway. The lying part was something new for her.

The businessman in him squelched his anger because the big brother in him understood she would say anything to placate, smooth the way, and try to please him. Her pattern of behavior since she was a child. Since their mother had died.

"Rex?"

He turned when the screen door opened behind him.

"I'm sorry. I can't find my sister. She must have taken the elevator down and scooted out the back door." Biloxi looked at a tablet in her hands. "I have the layout here, and I'll be able to direct you to your sister." Her finger rubbed against the touch screen. "It's the fourth tent"—she pointed to the right side of the driveway—"from the far end."

"Thank you for the directions." He started down the stairs to the driveway.

9

"She's attracted a lot of guests today. Your sister didn't just bring food for sampling, she's hosting cake decorating demonstrations, too."

Rex turned back at the bottom of the stairs. Raising an eyebrow, he asked, "And what, pray tell, is she cooking?"

Biloxi sniffed. "Do you smell that? Oysters roasting. Served on the half shell. With three different toppings. Also oyster artichoke soup."

Lifting his chin to sniff as Biloxi directed, he caught sight of the woman with the sultry eyes inching along on the upstairs gallery, her back against the house. Obviously, she hoped to remain unnoticed. Carrying her shoes and a hat, she made a three-step dash and disappeared around the corner. Curious behavior.

"Kayla is a fine chef." He redirected his gaze to Biloxi.

"We were honored she decided to join this event. And I'm remiss. My condolences on the passing of your father. It's great to know your sister will carry on the family tradition at Arceneau's."

"She is talented."

But she, like Papa, hasn't a clue about the bottom line. Red isn't good. Red means STOP.

Biloxi tilted her head. "Is there anything else I might do for you?"

"Yes." He paused and cast a glance up to the spot where he'd last seen the captivating woman. Disappointment pricked him. She wasn't peeking around the corner at him. "Does your sister have long, dark wavy hair, bedroom eyes with a fiery flash in them?" He didn't mention her feminine curves in the navy blue, body-hugging dress.

"Ah…" Biloxi stammered.

"What's her name?"

"Nola Bridgette Dutrey."

"Thank you. I'll find my sister now."

Ohh…the famous Nola. Now I have a face to go with a name.

A moment later, he heard the tap of Biloxi's heels on the wooden gallery above him.

"Rex."

He turned and looked up at her.

"You might know her as Nola Belle."

He lifted a finger in salute.

I know all too well about her.

Chapter 2

"No." Nola gripped her cell phone tighter and stepped into the shade of a large oak tree on the front lawn at Fleur de Lis. The late afternoon delivered the full taste of fresh spring to southern Mississippi, but the conversation triggered a rage washing over her as bold as hot sauce made on Avery Island. "Non-negotiable."

"Nola, your tone suggests you think I'm asking for something beyond the boundaries of decorum." The voice belonged to a man who flirted with one foot in purgatory and the other in hell.

"It's Ms. Dutrey to you." She had a mind to give him a good shove, sending him to Hades. He was making her life miserable.

After forcing a smile and nodding politely to a passing guest, Nola moved farther away from the crowds at the bridal show. The fair-like atmosphere at her family's antebellum home was surreal compared to her sordid conversation. The businessman and New Orleans councilwoman's staff member for Constituent Relations made her itch like poison oak.

"It's not uncustomary for me to meet with community members on weekends, or even before or after standard working hours. Everything will look respectable."

"Mr. Broussard—"

"Sweetheart, we've got history. We're past

politeness. After all, I still have those photos of you, you know."

Nola flipped her long hair back and squared her shoulders. Never before had the urge to slap a man welled so strongly. If she didn't fear hurting her hand, she'd punch an oak tree, but the poor thing hadn't done anything. It didn't deserve her wrath.

"Emile—" she said sweetly, changing her tactic. Her momma hadn't raised a fool.

"Now that's better."

"I am *not* going to meet you for drinks at the Carousel Bar at Hotel Monteleone." He'd called it "their" place since the noted establishment was where he insisted she sign the lease agreement for the space she rented from him. At the meeting, he tried sliding his room key into her hand. But again, her momma hadn't raised a fool. Had he really thought she was a member of the twenty-five-dim-watt club?

"Oh, sure you will," he purred. "You want to keep that converted fire station as headquarters for your band."

"That's blackmail," she snapped. The words tumbled out of her mouth before she could stop them. Okay, so she wasn't a fool, but too quick on the draw when faced with an unsavory situation. As her daddy occasionally pointed out, her mouth tended to engage before her brain. But it was because she lived life from her heart. Passion should've been her middle name. "There's a special place in Hades for people like you, Mr. Broussard."

"This is business. I have other community groups that would kill for the use of that space…if you're not willing to cooperate."

"Politics has made you seedy."

"The fact of the matter is to keep the space—you have to meet with me."

Fury roiled inside her. Nola stormed toward the back of the house, lest her mouth have another blurt-before-brain moment. The control-hungry, power-abusing, douchebag's "meet" had connotations that made her see red. Hot. Bloody. She couldn't stomach him, but she needed to keep the lease on the space.

Leaning against a black ornamental fence post, Nola drew in a slow ragged breath as a soft breeze whispered across her bare arms. She grabbed for the crown of her wide-brim hat in case it took flight. The hint of coolness caused an involuntary shiver. Releasing her breath slowly, she planned her next move in this chess game of wills. To save her kids, to save her band, she had to suck it up. Make nice with Emile. After all, as he'd said, it was business. Nothing personal. The man was lucky she preferred to fight her own battles, otherwise her cousins-in-law, Jared and James, along with her brother-in-law, Nicholas, would make gator bait out of Emile. As much as the man needed to learn some manners, she needed to keep the use of the building more.

"I will agree to meet you." She pursed her lips, while trying to decide which public place would have the right ambiance. "Not at a bar. Remember, I'm working with children. I want to maintain a respectable appearance."

Deep throaty laughter on the other end of the phone reminded her of what had first attracted her to him at a karaoke contest the night they met years ago. His *joie de vivre* intrigued her and that led to a date, but never again. Instead, she mentally made a list of expletives she could mutter about him—they would shock the saltiest tugboat captains on the Mississippi.

"That's rich! Remember, I was there when Nola Belle made her burlesque debut."

"You jackalope!" Pushing off the fence, she stalked to the parking area on Loblolly Lane. She couldn't risk anyone overhearing. "It was a dance show. I never took off my clothes. I shimmied fully dressed. That was a charity event. I had just turned eighteen." The man would make a good reporter for a sleazy tabloid.

"And what a night to remember. Luscious breasts. Creamy. White. Small waist. Rounded hips made—"

"You have an extraordinary imagination. I was covered head to toe. You could make communion with the Pope sound tawdry."

"Yes. I. Can." His voice was low and gravelly like Barry White. Coming from someone else, it would be sexy.

"Mr. Broussard. I will have coffee with you at Jolt. Tuesday, the week after next." She smiled. He wouldn't be caught dead in the grunge coffeehouse.

"Not Jolt. And this week. It's important."

Dang his countermove!

"I'm working at Harbor House."

"I know. Perfect. Tuesday it is. I'll take you for a late supper afterward. We can talk. By the way, I love hearing you sing. Sultry and angelic. Satisfying in the best way."

The innuendo made her skin crawl. As soon as she ended the call, she would need a shower. Mentally, she ran through a list of nouns and adjectives for his epitaph. Her G. G. Grace had a plethora she'd taught the girls in the family because she strongly objected to twenty-first-century potty mouth. *Lecher* fit Emile Broussard as well as his custom-made shirts, just enough room around the collar to hang him.

"Nola, I look forward to seeing you at Harbor House."

She ended the call, but between now and then, she had time to come up with a plan to ensure Mr. Broussard stayed far away from her in the future.

Maybe she could convince the hot guy with the pocket square to act as her date on Tuesday night to squelch any ideas Emile might have.

In the meantime, she had to take the Fleur de Lis Café stage in ten minutes, then hightail it back to New Orleans. The best nights of the week were when she sang at Arceneau's. And Kayla promised she'd finally get to meet her older brother.

****

Fuming, Rex stepped into the limo. Sometimes his sister could irritate him like a loose tooth. He hated deception. Especially from her.

"You okay?" Marquis, the limo driver, asked. He navigated around the fountain and headed down the long driveway to the main road taking them to New Orleans.

Rex sighed. "Yeah. Let's go back to the city. All this country air is too much... So, tell me who was fool enough to give you a license, let alone a limo to drive?"

"My day job." Marquis adjusted the rearview mirror. "Besides, somebody's got to carry your sorry ass around while you're here. Might as well be me. And look at you! Last time we broke bread, man, you were wearing a white chef's coat splattered with finger-lickin' good sauce. That cool New York chef style at your place, 29N & 90W."

"That's only one of my three restaurants. You'll have to try the others next time."

"Like I was saying. Never seen you dressed like this"—he flicked his wrist—"like you're ready for a wedding. You're so pretty, you could be a groom. You cleaned up again just to come south?"

"Naw, I did this just to see you." Rex laughed. The suit had been a gift. He'd worn it for a photo shoot that morning. He'd been reluctant to accept it, but the tailor had insisted because the garment had been custom fitted just for him.

"The hell you say. You're not my type. I like curves." Marquis waved his hands, outlining a curvy silhouette. "Got my eye on one."

Rex fidgeted with his cuff links and wondered where he might find his father's missing gold pair. "No doubt. But I thought you musicians had a woman in every town."

"Don't believe the rumors. That's how words become lies."

Rex raised an eyebrow.

Not the only way.

Rex rolled down the window as they reached East New Orleans and breathed. How humid air managed to smell distinctly unique was amazing. A tingling sensation spread through his body as though oxygen in his blood carried shouts of "welcome home." The scents of brackish water and spices filled him. The Cajun and Creole influences found in the cuisine remained a hallmark of the city. Almost drunk on it all, he realized how much he needed recharging. New Orleans provided an energy he soaked up and carried with him everywhere he traveled.

"Sorry about your old man," Marquis said, as he changed lanes.

"Thanks, but I'm glad the funeral is out of the way." Was it only three weeks ago? Digging through all his father's personal and financial affairs had required more time than he anticipated. Daily phone calls to his sister wore him out. It was as though he were fighting a war with her all to ensure she got exactly what she wanted. Why she continued to see him as a threat was baffling. He'd come home for a face-to-face, hoping to preserve his relationship with her.

"How long are ya stayin' this time?"

Rex shook his head. "That will be determined by several factors. At least a few weeks. Maybe a month."

"Then I'll see you in June when you're back in New York."

"Yeah? You got a gig?"

"Studio work on a few records. One's for our hometown piano player. I really appreciate you introducing me to people when I was up there last."

"Least I could do. Your playing is impeccable. Let's not wait until then. Let's have dinner at Arceneau's one night while I'm here. I'll introduce you to my sister, the chef."

"Why have I never met her before? I *have* seen ads for that sultry thing singing in the upstairs lounge. She's singing tonight. I'm gonna try to make it by to hear her one night—we can have dinner then. She's a neighbor of mine."

"You could only be talking about Nola Dutrey."

"Sweet thing, that one. Fiery. Doing some good stuff in the community."

Rex fought from refuting Marquis' assessment of the female in question. Once he began reviewing his father's accounting records, he discovered *the* Miss Dutrey was associated with some questionable entries. The restaurant paid the woman nearly double the amount listed in her contract. A reason for the improprieties? Regardless, it contributed to the bleeding of the business and Arceneau's debt. Kayla hadn't even been aware of the amount of red in the books.

He had a mission. After he fixed the business issues, but before he returned to New York, he had to tell his sister the truth about Papa, and he prayed like hell she wouldn't slam the door in his face forever.

As the limo traveled surface streets, Rex noticed familiar houses flipping by like pages in a picture book. Purple with white gingerbread trim. Green accented with yellow. He wondered who lived in the pink one with lime-green shutters. Only in New Orleans.

As they drove farther, the neighborhoods transformed from colorful shotgun houses to stately and large homes. The familiarity of home dispelled some of the apprehension lodged in his chest. He loved his childhood Garden District neighborhood. Cherished it. Kayla couldn't be serious about selling. Their mother's touch remained everywhere. He needed that connection, the same as he needed the energy from the city, especially now.

"Arceneau family residence," Marquis said proper-like, pulling to the curb.

"Appreciate the ride." Rex climbed out of the limo.

"Come by the 12/8 one night when I'm playing."

Marquis leaned against the driver's door and pushed up the brim of his chauffeur hat. "It's a new blues bar."

"Maybe."

"I'll bring you up on stage. You can play backup for me."

Rex shook his head. "Not sure I'm good enough anymore." He hadn't picked up his trumpet in six months. Enough time for rust to set into his fingers. But the offer was tempting. There was no feeling as complete as performing in front of a live audience. Maybe if he practiced he could rehab his playing.

"Man, modesty don't become you. You got it goin' on."

"No promises." Rex waved goodbye, then lifted the latch on the decorative wrought iron gate. The irony of the symbolism made him chuckle. It was created to keep some out and to keep others in. Did he have any right to want to stay in the house? Kayla, on the other hand, wanted out—a decision he feared she would regret in years to come.

Crossing the threshold brought a rush of uncertainty. What incentive could he offer his sister? If he invested in the business, he couldn't afford to buy out her half of the house. If he refused to invest in the business, he'd be destroying his promise to his mother, and Kayla could be out of a job.

His sister had never made life easy for him.

"I'm home," he shouted, entering the foyer.

No response. Kayla was at the bridal show. Papa...buried. Momma gone for years. Not even an insouciant cat to greet him.

Rex called Kayla on her cell phone.

"Rex?" Kayla answered.

"I'm calling to let you know I'll be in to help you with the rush tonight."

"No."

"What do you mean, no?"

"You gave me a month on my own. A month to prove myself. I still have another week. Back the hell up. Don't show your face in my kitchen unless you want to come in after midnight and clean."

Rex remained silent for a few breaths.

"Rex?"

"You're right, little sister. You have another week. I've almost finished going over the books. Just know when your week is over, the first thing we're cutting from the budget is the singer."

"No."

Letting go of an exasperated breath, Rex asked, "What do you mean, no? This reminds me of when you first started talking. 'No' was your favorite word. Are we regressing?"

"Not only no, but fuck no. Don't be a jerk-wad. Just because you run an operation in New York City, don't think you can bring your salsa down here and toss it around. We'll talk in one week. And by talk, I mean, we'll discuss everything and come to a mutual consensus. Nothing changes until then. Arceneau's is *not* a dictatorship with you in control."

Rex sighed. *Well, maybe it needs to be if you want to succeed.*

"I'll be by later tonight," he told her, mostly to aggravate her, but he'd respect their agreement. "Catch you then."

He ended the call with her cussing at him and shouting something about Nola Belle. He would get to the bottom of the inconsistent accounting, but why was Kayla willing to bleed the business dry for that singer? The beautiful Nola Belle couldn't be all that.

Chapter 3

Saturday morning, Nola trudged the block from her apartment to the coffee shop. The temperature was warm, yet the humidity low. A perfect spring day. Two days down and two days to go on the bridal show.

"Hey, girl. You're here early," the cashier called out as Nola entered the old house. The woman hollered to a barista, "Skinny *decaf* mocha."

"Thanks." Nola pushed her sunglasses on top of her head.

"You weren't here for the last two days. What's up? I set my calendar and clock by you. You're here Monday, Wednesday, and Friday at nine. Never on a Saturday before noon. It's only eight. In the morning. You know that, right?"

Chuckling, Nola said, "I'm that predictable?"

"Yes. Especially about the skinny, the decaf, and the mocha. Anything else for you today?"

"Any ham and cheese croissants left? I need one to go. Headed back to Fleur de Lis again today."

"I hope to make it over there tomorrow. I can't wait to see your family home. And, if I'm lucky, someday Mr. Right is going to marry me there." The woman clasped her hands to her chest, closed her eyes, and smiled dreamily.

"Better than Mr. Wrong." Nola pulled a chair out and sat at the nearest table.

23

"Oh, I already had him. He's long gone. I'm holding out for Mr. Next-To-Perfect."

Nola smiled. So she wasn't the only one waiting for someone special. Her family repeatedly accused her of being too picky. Attraction was a funny thing… Her thoughts drifted once again to the man with the blue-gray eyes who made her heart beat in 12/8 time. He set her imagination running wild. Images of them flipped through her mind like a kaleidoscope—walking along the Mississippi River holding hands under a full moon while musicians played, her singing for him and only him in a dimly lit club, and then sharing breakfast at a café while they read the Sunday paper together.

What would he be like in bed?

Unexpectedly, her body thrummed with excitement.

She shook her head to ground herself in reality. He was just too much.

Her sister had told her to flirt more, and now appeared to be in cahoots with her mother about finding her a man. She planned to avoid them both until her three p.m. show by hanging out with Remy, Biloxi's oldest boy, who preferred going flying with Uncle Linc than fishing on the bank of the Pearl River. Her nine-year-old nephew agreed to spend time with her only after she promised to let him help her pick out a new kayak for Fleur de Lis.

"How are things with the band?" the cashier asked, interrupting Nola's thoughts. "My nephew has a crush on you. Says you sing like an angel."

"Well, I don't know about that…but he's learned a lot in three months. I'm so proud that he's practicing."

"He and a few of his friends have a corner staked

24

out on Royal Street. They play for the tourists. Make a few dollars. Here's your heated croissant. Coffee up in a minute." The woman turned to take the order of a newly arrived customer.

Pulling out her phone, Nola checked a website selling band uniforms. When she'd been in marching band, uniforms were not even a second thought. She wore what she was told. Now she poured over pictures of coats, bibbers, hats, and gauntlets. The drum major would need a cape and gloves in addition to the rest of the uniform. Did they need spats? Special touches and details on a uniform helped set a band apart from the rest, but what could she afford? Mentally adding in her head, she counted the price at nearly three-hundred dollars a student. Multiply that by thirty…the cost was staggering.

With coffee in hand, she pointed the rental car east and headed back to Fleur de Lis. Rolling down the windows, she enjoyed the wind in her hair and the quiet of no radio.

Her cell rang, and she pushed the button on the steering wheel for the hands-free speakerphone in the car. "Hello?"

"Miss Dutrey, I'm Allen Sikes. Chef Allen. You've probably seen me on TV. It's come to my attention that the space you're leasing for your band may be available in the next thirty days."

"What?"

"Is there any possibility that you could vacate sooner? I could make it worth your while, financially, of course. I would like to be up and running with my cooking school as soon as possible."

"Mr. Sikes. Chef Sikes, I have no idea what you're

talking about. I have a one-year lease of the premises with an option for a second year."

"So I hear, but I also understand that you're having financial difficulties and won't be able to make the balloon payment that's been deferred."

How did this man know so much about the nitty-gritty of her lease? What was Emile trying to do? Seething, she worked to control her temper. The man had no clue about the inner workings of the manipulating mind of Emile. But she planned to talk with the councilwoman about him. This had to be, at the very least, a conflict of interest. Could be more criminal—like extortion or blackmail.

"Chef Sikes, I have no intention of giving up the space or reneging on the lease agreement. So, no. You may not provide me financial remuneration to have early access to the space. It's. Not. For. Lease." She held the end-call button down and cut him off.

Why in the world had she ever decided that Emile could be trusted?

First time, shame on him. Second time, shame on me.

She'd been blinded by his offer to help her make her dream come true.

"Deep breath." She attempted to calm herself. After pushing in a CD, music filled the car. She rolled up the window and caught the groove of Tab Benoit singing "New Orleans Ladies."

Images of the Tab at the last concert she'd attended drifted to images of the man with the steely blue-gray eyes. The peacock-blue suit color was growing on her...only a little.

"Suck it up, girl. Just ask Biloxi who he is."

At the very least, maybe he would agree to be her date for her parents' anniversary party.

Maybe.

****

After Rex returned home from a late afternoon run, he shook his head, unable to push away the images of Nola Belle and her captivating eyes. He entered the house. Stillness surrounded him as he walked through the rooms on the main floor. A momentary draft made him shiver. An ethereal presence. He caught a whiff of his mother's perfume, and he couldn't shake the sadness hanging in the air reminding him of Papa.

Everything remained as Rex always remembered it—freshly cleaned by their longtime housekeeper and looking as though Kayla lived elsewhere. Had she finally outgrown her sloppy teenaged ways?

The room was so neat it belonged in a magazine spread. Antiques. Aubusson rugs. Momma had been an only child, and she inherited many of these belongings from her wealthy parents. Otherwise, he and Kayla wouldn't have grown up with such fine things.

"Grandfather, you were wrong when you said Momma married down." Rex hadn't understood those words then, they were lost on a young boy. "Momma had married a diamond in the rough when she married Papa."

And honestly, Kayla was like Papa. With some mentoring and if only she'd listen, Kayla possessed the skills to run the restaurant on her own. But only if she'd take advice and direction. Part of what had made him successful was taking on business partners. They shared the risk and the reward. And three minds proved better than one. His sister needed him as a business partner.

"Kayla," he said aloud, trudging up the stairs. "Even from a distance, all of your life, I've been protecting you. Since you arrived home from the hospital. I was four. Your silly gurgling smile captivated me."

Twenty-eight years later, he still watched over her. She showed tenacity. That quality made her a wonderful pastry chef. All those intricate decorations were something he had no patience for. Those same attributes would make her a great executive chef. Yet at the same time, Kayla's stubbornness rivaled Papa's. As did her temper *and* her foul mouth.

"If I didn't know how much you loved me and truly valued my input, I'd be offended by your off-color vocabulary and personal jabs," he said aloud.

In his bedroom, Rex changed into faded jeans, a hole worn through on the thigh, then pulled a dark purple sweater over his head. Every sound—drawing back the drapes, his feet on the wooden floor, opening a drawer—brought an awareness of what family used to feel like in this house. The love Momma had wrapped around them. The boisterousness of Papa was like a triple shot of espresso. Rex mused. Worry wasn't part of his vocabulary back then. Now it was the legacy left by both parents.

He'd helped raise Kayla, acting as both father and mother after Momma died with Papa immersing himself in the restaurant. Rex missed Kayla's laugh. He used to tell her jokes to stop her from crying over some little-girl drama he didn't understand, like the color of the laces for her sneakers needing to be mint green, not neon orange. These days, serious and somber best described him. It was to be expected. Important decisions had to be made, yet he didn't want to lose the love and adoration of his little sister. Didn't want her to cut him out of her life, even halfway.

"Snap out of it. Have a little faith in her. Hell, have a little faith in yourself." He reached for the remote, turning on the CD player on his desk. Wynton Marsalis was his go-to horn player when he needed inspiration. Playing an air-trumpet, Rex's fingers showed their muscle memory as he accompanied his idol. Maybe he would take Marquis up on his offer to jam after all.

Buoyed by the music, Rex opened the closet door and turned on the light. Three trumpet cases sat on a shelf right where he'd left them, only his best one moved with him to New York. After dragging a chair to reach high overhead, he pulled down the oldest case. His first practice trumpet. A Yamaha. He'd cleaned it not long ago. The kind of break he needed from all the funeral arrangements and related events.

Gathering a small blanket from a drawer, he removed the trumpet and wrapped it, then placed it in a backpack.

"It's Saturday night. Let's see if I still got it goin' on." Rex turned and locked the door before heading out to catch a streetcar. At his stop on Canal, he hopped off and headed into the French Quarter. Often, kids played on Royal Street, a favorite place for tourists.

Energized, Rex glanced from side to side at the shops. On his last trip down—Papa's funeral—he hadn't visited the Quarter. Since The Storm, every time he came home, a new shop had popped up, though several longtime businesses had closed permanently, unable to survive the down years after Katrina. Aromas of fresh baked French bread and andouille sausage filled his senses. Hot frying oil. Gumbo. Soaking in the scents, he continued his search, heading toward a favorite area where anyone could find street musicians; there had to be a group who'd let him jam. The stretch between 300 to 800 Royal was his target.

Stepping off the sidewalk onto the brick street, he avoided a crowd on the corner watching a mime—white face, white gloves, and traditional black beret—trying to get out of a box. Soulful licks from a guitar drifted to him as he continued his trek. Ahead, he found his spot, or rather the sound he sought. A band. Near the police station at Royal and Conti.

A small crowd blocked his view. People clapped to the beat of the music, and Rex slowed to listen. Five instruments. He maneuvered his way through the throng of people to stand on the front line of the semicircle of spectators. Five kids, all around twelve years old, played "When the Saints Go Marching In." Their ensemble included a snare drum, two saxes, a trombone, and a trumpet. Their timing hit the mark, evidence that they practiced together.

As the group finished playing, the girl with the saxophone raced up to the crowd beginning to disperse with a hat in her hand. A few people tossed in bills, but mostly it was the clinking of coins as the audience thinned.

"Hey there," Rex said, addressing the group. "I've got a deal for you."

"What kinda deal, mistah?" the drummer asked.

Rex pulled out his trumpet and tossed his backpack against the building. "I want to jam with all y'all."

The drummer, clearly the spokesperson for the group, eyed him up and down. "You're an old dude.

We don't need your help."

Nodding, Rex said, "I completely agree. I need you. I'm willing to pay each of you twenty bucks to let me play the rest of the night with y'all."

"I gotta be home by nine o'clock," the trumpet player grumbled, his brow furrowed with concern.

"We've got almost two hours." Rex pointed to his watch.

"You're gonna pay *each* of us twenty?" the girl with the sax asked.

"Yes."

"We need to talk for a minute," the drummer said. The young musicians huddled around their leader.

"That could be a big donation."

"But he's an old dude."

"Money talks. Bullshit walks."

"Okay, old dude," the drummer said. "Show us the green, and it's a yes."

Fishing money out of his front pocket, Rex fanned out five twenty-dollar bills. The girl saxophonist snatched the money from him. "It's all here." She pulled up the hem of her jeans, folded the bills, and stuck them into her sock. "Let's play."

The drummer called time and started the beats for another rendition of "When the Saints Go Marching In." Rex took a spot in the back, wanting the kids to be highlighted and for people to see and hear how good they were.

The crowd grew and thinned with each new tune they played. As eight thirty approached, the drummer said, "Time."

The other members of the group began to pack up their instruments.

"We gonna give him"—the drummer flicked his thumb in Rex's direction—"a cut of the take?"

It took a moment for the comment to sink in as Rex wrapped his horn in the soft blanket. "No, dude," Rex said. "I got what I needed. We're good. Thanks for letting me hang with you."

"Perfect," the girl sax player said. "The money isn't for us anyway. It's for our marching band. Miss Nola's gonna be real surprised when she sees our donation."

"Miss Nola?" Rex hefted the backpack on his shoulder. "Nola Dutrey?"

"She's our music and band teacher."

"At school?"

"Naw," the drummer said. "We belong to a community band she started. I think she teaches part-time, though."

"She teaches smart kids at a private school," the girl added.

Rex nodded. Interesting information. "Catch y'all another time." Rex waved goodbye to the group of kids.

"For an old dude, you're not bad. You playing upped our take. We're here every Saturday night. Come see us again."

Waving, Rex headed toward Arceneau's.

The story of Miss Nola grows increasingly interesting.

The siren with the sultry eyes, long hair, and lovely curves. His thoughts had drifted repeatedly to her, but he always shoved them away. She was an employee of Arceneau's, and any involvement would be a bad idea. But it wouldn't hurt to catch her act tonight.

Don't get involved with a problem. Fix things for

Kayla and go back to New York.

He shook his head. Maybe checking out Marquis at the 12/8 Blues Bar was a better idea.

But one thing was certain, Kayla still needed to understand—it was the business or Nola singing. Both couldn't occupy the same financial books and the business still succeed.

He prayed Kayla wouldn't make good on her threats.

Chapter 4

"Yes, I *promise*. No, I'm not lying. While I've been working on the songs for the tour, I've also practiced the songs you requested for Momma and Daddy's party. It will be a memorable thirty-fifth wedding anniversary."

Barefooted, Nola paced back and forth in the courtyard of her New Orleans apartment. Early morning coolness from the brick seeped into her feet and invigorated her pace. She lengthened her stride and walked circles around the courtyard pool. A turquoise and white cotton caftan brushed against her legs creating a sensual sensation of freedom. But the feeling chafed against the bonds of family tradition. Fleur de Lis represented security. A home to always return to, but the rules...they squelched creativity. She wasn't a proper southern miss like her sister. Bossy Biloxi carried her Keeper of Fleur de Lis role with aplomb, while Nola had forged her own path.

Stopping abruptly, Nola shook out her hair and wiggled her shoulders, hoping her sister's imaginary death grip would release its far-reaching grasp. They'd gone over the details just yesterday after the bridal show. Her patience with Biloxi was paper-thin. She sighed. "Most of the songs you picked aren't my genre, but... I'll make it memorable."

"In a good way, I hope. Everyone's putting their

talents to use. We're counting on you and yours."

"Yeah. Yeah." She waved at Kayla Arceneau entering the courtyard with two cups in hand. Rarely did she see her friend out of a white chef's coat and black slacks. But it was Monday, the only day of the week the restaurant closed. Kayla appeared relaxed in faded jeans and purple t-shirt with a fleur de lis in glittery gold.

"I've got to go," Nola told her sister as her neighbor began his morning trumpet practice before catching the streetcar for work. "I have a voice student arriving." She ended the call. It amazed her how easily lies slipped from her lips these days. Somewhere in heaven, an angel put another mark under the "lies" column on the scorecard of good and bad deeds all the while shaking his head.

Little white lies don't count if no one gets hurt.

"How's the tour pulling together?" Kayla sauntered toward her like a graceful giraffe. Tall, golden blonde, and long-legged.

"Pretty good, I guess. I'm not going to sweat the small stuff. The manager is paid to worry. I just show up on schedule. Everything works out in the end. My responsibility is to sing my best." Nola looked up to meet Kayla's gaze.

"So, you met my brother at Fleur de Lis." Kayla handed over a white cup with a famous New Orleans coffee company logo. Nola sniffed the aroma filling her senses and willed the muscles in her shoulders to relax.

"And before you ask," Kayla continued, "it's decaf, skinny mocha. I made sure they didn't slip up and give you *real* coffee this time. How you don't drink caffeine and go all day and most of the night is beyond

35

me. Bitch."

"Caffeine gives me nightmares. As you know." She raised an eyebrow to make her point and flashed an ornate silver cross dangling from a silver chain around her neck.

"I thought it was a joke when you called screaming in the middle of the night about vampires taking over New Orleans."

"You hung up on me!" Nola hadn't yet forgiven her.

Kayla grunted. "Hey now. I answered the phone. I *did* give you advice."

"Butcher. Baker. Candlestick maker," Nola snarled.

"That's the best you've got? Geez, you swear like a nun. You really are a Damn-Good-Catholic girl. Anyway, I'm a caffeine junkie. I admit it. The smell of coffee wakes me up daily. The only thing I need a man for—besides the obvious tension reliever in the bedroom, and you need to give me a gold star for not saying the f-word—is to bring me dark roasted brew in bed every morning." Kayla grinned as a dreamy expression settled on her face.

"Bring your caffeinated self over here, you junkie, you." Nola pointed to the edge of the pool. After taking a big sip, she set her cup on the brick patio, then hiked up the caftan to her knees, and sat, her legs dangling in the barely warm water. "And, no, I didn't meet the famous Rex Arceneau."

Kayla sat facing her, legs folded cross-legged. "No? Hmm, I thought you had. Rex is being heavy-handed about cutting expenses. Shit. I had hoped if he heard you sing, he might understand why we need you."

"Your brother came to the Bridal Extravaganza?"

"Yep, he arrived unexpectedly, just to shame me—his preferred method of control. I thought the two of you had met."

Nola shook her head. "Unless he was in the audience when I sang one of the days, he didn't introduce himself to me."

"Funny. He described you down to the shoes you wore."

"He probably saw my picture somewhere."

"The navy-blue dress is a new one. The $29.99 special. Remember, I helped you shop for it at that consignment store." After taking a long, slow sip of coffee, she added, "He always has a way of getting under my skin. He's got this all-knowing sense, or he has spies or something."

Nola added up the details her friend provided. "Did he have on a dark peacock-blue suit? Pink tie and pocket square? Looking fine, but like he could be somebody's pimp?" The image of the man with the hypnotic steely blue-gray eyes made her pulse quicken. But the rapid spike tumbled as she finished the sum of the equation.

That was Kayla's older brother?

She sipped her coffee, waiting for her friend to say more. Was he like a corporate seagull? An influential person who dropped in, crapped all over everyone, and then flew away—in his case, back to New York City. Back to his glamourous restauranteur life as the managing partner of a group owning three prestigious locations. Yes, she'd read up on him after the way Kayla had waxed gloriously about his success. But what she really wanted to know was if the man was a good kisser…not that his sister would have any intel on that.

"So you did meet him. He did a photo shoot for *New Orleans Eats* magazine before hightailing out to Fleur de Lis to catch me in the act. The magazine stylist selected the outfit for him, and the tailor insisted he keep it, or so he said. Something about the color being a new trend for grooms."

"I didn't know pimps were getting married these days."

Her trumpet-playing neighbor hit a smooth high note. Nola applauded while keeping her gaze fixed on her friend.

Kayla narrowed her eyes. "I'll admit he's being an ass, but he's still my big brother. He's always looking out for me."

"I didn't meet him." Nola leaned over, and with her hands cupped, scooped up some water from the pool, flicking it at Kayla. "Wake up. He's not your big brother. He may be your older brother, but he's your business partner. Absent one at that. What gives him the right—"

"He owns the lion's share." Kayla shook her head. "The last time Papa talked to me about ownership, he, Rex, and I each owned the business as equals. That conversation took place when I turned eighteen. I assumed Papa would leave the restaurant to both of us equally." A sad resignation tinged her words.

"Even though Rex doesn't do anything?"

Kayla rolled her eyes. "He's still an Arceneau. He helps from afar. And I just learned Uncle Henri owns ten percent of the restaurant. I'm not sure how he finagled that. And Papa left fifty percent to Rex, making him the largest percentage holder. The worst part—I need him here. Not in New York City. He's an excellent chef. Creative. I'm a chef, but my talents are more sugar based. How do I get him to stay on? Again. F-me."

"That sucks duck eggs." Nola shook her head in disbelief. All Kayla's dream to take the restaurant to the next level, along with a remodel, had to be crumbling.

"Watch that mouth, sister. The fans of Nola Belle think she's a classy dame."

"And Nola Belle is. However, she is only one part of me."

"I don't know why Papa did what he did…sadly, I'm here to say, my *business* partner's plan will impact you, too."

"How?" Nola fixed her stare on Kayla as her mind whirled with one threatening scenario after another. A shadow of fear made her shudder. She'd worked hard at juggling many plates in the air to help her special project. If one plate wobbled too much, the whole set could come crashing down.

"It's not personal, ya know. He says we're paying you too much. While we regroup, reorganize, and slightly rebrand, music has to go."

The trumpet player blew a loud, sharp note off-key.

Nola blinked. The man with the hypnotic steely blue-gray eyes just bypassed the silver cross around her neck and drove a stake through her heart.

The sound of plates crashing rang in her ears.

****

Morning light slanted through blinds covering the single window in the third-floor office above the restaurant. Rex leaned back in a leather, executive-office chair, rested his feet on the desktop, and pretended to inspect his black Salvatore Ferragamo loafers. Moving his hands behind his head, he didn't want his uncle to mistake, not even for a second, who was in charge as the executor of Papa's estate. Not Kayla. Not Uncle Henri, but him. Xavier Rex Arceneau. "You want to buy me out." He flicked a piece of invisible lint from his gray Italian-wool slacks.

"I had discussed this plan with your papa before he passed. We never got around to finalizing the paperwork." Uncle Henri removed his sport coat and then settled back in the upholstered wingback chair. He looked younger than his nearly sixty-five years despite the silvery gray of his hair. Maybe his youthfulness came from spending a day every week on his fishing boat. All that sunshine gave him a glowing tan. Then he loosened the knot of his tie. The light caught the gold rim of his cuff link drawing Rex's attention like a spotlight.

How did he get those?

Later, he would have yet another talk with Kayla, but this time if she lied, he would pin her to the freezer door with a stare and browbeat the truth from her. Had she given them to Henri?

"And what will happen to Kayla?"

"She'll continue on"—he shrugged—"as always."

"You'll allow her to run the kitchen? Not just be a pastry chef?"

Uncle Henri paused. "I will do what is best for business."

"And you want to keep the name of the restaurant?"

"But of course! I'm an Arceneau, too." Wide-eyed, his uncle leaned forward and locked stares with him—a direct challenge. Warily, Rex sifted through the wave of energy hitting him. His uncle's bold declaration carried a hidden message of deceit. But which part was he lying about?

To prevent giving away his thoughts, Rex sighed and reached for the documents his uncle had presented. "Cash buyout?"

Uncle Henri nodded, his eyes lighting with eagerness.

"I need time to think about it."

"My offer is more than fair. It's generous. You could be on a flight back to New York tonight."

Time would reveal the truth of the premonition hammering in Rex's head. But how much time would he need to spend in New Orleans to uncover his uncle's true intent? Here everything vibrated more intensely. Light glowed brighter. Music sounded richer. Food tasted better. He chuckled. Orgasmic came to mind whenever he looked at a plate of roasted oysters.

An intimacy existed with the city that was hard to explain to any outsider. New York demanded much less for him to survive. There he got lost in the crowd, enjoying anonymity. Yet the sights and scents of New Orleans overwhelmed if he didn't take care to protect himself energetically.

His mother had passed a tiny portion of her gift of second sight to him, his inheritance, she'd told him. He tried to shut it out, but it wouldn't be denied—like sometimes knowing when people lied. The benefits of the gift were particularly strong whenever he stayed in New Orleans. For instance, the attraction to Miss Nola

Belle haunted him last night. He tuned in to her. She was more than curious about him, felt the attraction, too. The magnetic pull wasn't something he could act on while she remained on the Arceneau payroll. But he seriously doubted she would consider dinner with him after he cut her from the golden-goose-producing paycheck. A kiss or something more intimate, like a place beside him in bed, could only be a whimsical dream.

"Rex? Daydreaming about what you can do with all the money?"

Rex sighed, picked up the phone, and pressed a button. He would no more reveal his plan than his uncle would admit the truth about his motives.

"Kitchen. Yes, Mr. Arceneau?" Kevin's voice sounded through the speaker.

"Kevin, please bring two coffees with setups to the office."

"Would you like some beignets, too?"

"If it's not inconvenient, that would be nice." He set the phone back in its cradle.

Uncle Henri nodded. "Beignets are always welcome, and coffee would be good."

Keeping a steady gaze on his uncle, Rex took in the older man's body cues, preferring to rely on evidence rather than the interrupting energy of something he didn't always understand. Being empathic had been a hindrance as much as a gift.

Uncle Henri rose, went to the file cabinet in the corner, and opened the bottom drawer. Rex steadied himself to be passive. The overfamiliarity of his uncle's knowledge of things in the office triggered a niggling irritation.

"Here it is." Beaming, he clutched a box displaying the name Rémy Martin XO Excellence.

"Cognac. My father kept alcohol in the office?"

"I gave this to him as a special gift when we signed the papers for my share of the restaurant. After you and I complete our deal, we'll open the bottle and toast to your father. May my brother's soul rest in peace. He knows I'll look after my nephew and niece."

"I'm curious, Uncle, why you want to bother with Arceneau's. You have three restaurants, and as you said before, you've signed a partnership deal with a celebrity chef to launch a new eatery at the casino. This would make five establishments. What could you want this place for?"

A nearly unperceivable tic flexed in his uncle's jaw.

"I want to preserve the Arceneau name. This is the longest running business in the family. Kayla will always be involved."

Lies.

Rex stood. His uncle handed over the box. He set it on the desk and lifted the bottle from inside. A crystal decanter caught the light, and the topper cast rainbows in the room. "You've always enjoyed the finest of things in life."

"*Humph.* You mean I pilfered money away on extravagances. I know what your father thought of me."

Rex lifted an eyebrow. "The differences you and my father experienced are none of my business. He's gone. I won't discuss him with you in that way."

A knock sounded at the door.

"Enter."

One of the sous chef's apprentices brought in a

tray.

Rex slid the expensive bottle to one side, allowing the tray to be placed on his desk.

"Thank you," Rex called to the young man exiting the office as quickly and quietly as he'd come.

Uncle Henri reached for a cup. "Ahh, coffee with chicory."

"One of the things I miss when I'm in New York."

"You're eager to go back, I'm sure. Let me help you with that. Sign the papers, let's crack the seal on the bottle, and we'll conclude our business quickly. In fact, take the bottle with you." Henri sank into the chair, crossed his legs, resting the cup and saucer on his knee.

Rex studied his uncle and allowed a slow, half grin to rise. "One would think you're in a New York rush. I prefer to take things slower down here." He didn't intend to share his findings from his review of the business accounts or his plan to attract more customers, putting the business back in the black—for Kayla. But first, he had to secure her buy-in about his ideas before investing his own money. "I've scheduled some time off to relax. Kayla and I have Papa's personal estate to deal with."

"Keeping or selling the house?"

"Why? Do you want to buy that, too?"

Uncle Henri chuckled. "No, boy. Too much of your mama lives in that house, even after all these years."

And you were never welcomed there…

"I'll be staying for a while." Rex sat and sipped his coffee, savoring a familiar flavor of home. He hadn't made the decision to stay a while until he'd spoken the words. "I'm looking for some inspirations to carry back to New York—besides I've got my eye on something."

Uncle Henri laughed. "A someone, I'll bet. A woman, no doubt."

Rex allowed his smile to widen. "You know me so well." Except his uncle didn't know him at all.

They'd rarely been in the same room since his mother had died. After college and then culinary school in New York, he'd stayed. Dealing with his father's ego and insistence on his French style of cooking didn't mesh with the newfound independence Rex had discovered up north. There, he couldn't depend on the family name, wouldn't be accused of riding his father's coattails.

Instead, he'd struck out on his own with meager financial support from Papa and built a partnership as well as a reputation in a city known for celebrity chefs.

Thirteen years of hard work.

After finishing his coffee and listening to Uncle Henri catch him up on all the extended family gossip, stories about people, all who had shunned Kayla over the years, he stood. Lucky for him, Henri took the hint.

"Well, Rex, I'll leave you to think about my offer." He walked toward the door, but paused and turned. "I should ask Kayla to plan a family reunion. We haven't held one in a few years."

"Good luck with that idea." Rex chuckled.

"Yes, she's great in the kitchen, but not much of a social hostess." His tone was wistful, as though he recalled a better time from the past—the gala parties and fundraisers his mother had hosted.

"I'll be waiting for your answer." Henri disappeared down the stairs.

Rex placed the crystal decanter on the shelf behind

the desk to keep the trigger of his anger in plain sight. He refused to discuss his mother or her life with his uncle. Not after all that had happened. Yet, Uncle Henri was partially right about him, too. He did have his eye on a particular woman, but it wasn't for the reason Uncle Henri imagined.

Chapter 5

"Does your brother have a heart?" Nola rose from the side of the pool and paced. She swallowed against momentary panic. A calm head always prevailed in a crisis, a fact she had learned from her sister in the aftermath of Hurricane Katrina. Fleur de Lis flourished because her sister had taken the helm. Drawing a deep breath, Nola blew it out, letting peace wash through her.

"I promise he does."

"You swear on Julia Child's grave?" Nola narrowed her eyes at Kayla after invoking her friend's cooking hero. "You know my band kids are counting on me. Maybe I could make him see reason. What if I talk with him? It's not like he's the king."

Kayla sipped coffee. "Oh, but he now is the King of Cuisine at Arceneau's. Trust me. Let me work this out with him. I have an idea we can talk about over lunch."

"Why didn't you say so! Get your skinny derrière in drive. I haven't had anything but coffee today."

Looking at the morning sun lifting in the sky, then at Nola, Kayla shook her head. "It's too early. Mae's isn't open yet."

"I should've guessed we'd head to Tremé. Her fried chicken is your crack."

"That's where we're going for lunch because you insist I do yoga. Besides, I've something to show you.

47

My plan is not a one-hit wonder, but something I think might keep you on the charts."

Nola squeed. "I love it when you use music biz analogies. But seriously, if you've got a plan, I'm willing to listen. I'll do anything to help my kids. The band *will* march for Mardi Gras next year. 'Do not go where the path may lead, go instead where there is no path and leave a trail.' "

"I do know more than cooking, drinking, and men. I know Ralph Waldo Emerson when I hear him."

"Well, Miss Smarty Chef, who said, 'Between two evils, *I* always pick the one I never tried before'? Tell me that."

"Mae West. I love old movies. Interesting that you should quote a diva. Nola Belle is a combo of bohemian and sassy, very sensual on stage, but in real life, you're—"

"A typical Taurus. Daddy says I'm a butterfly. Organized Earth Mother is what Momma calls me. I'll never fit into her mold. She's accepted that. I'm not like Biloxi and Linc with their southern halos. They're the target market for *South by Southern Accents* magazine."

Nola headed to the stairs leading up to a landing and her apartment. What kind of woman attracted Rex? The look in his eyes when their gazes locked stole her breath away. She had a definite interest, and if they played spin the bottle, she'd discover just how deep his interest in her went. But she wasn't about to ply Kayla with questions about him—too creepy. She hated it when women tried that with her about her brother. Somehow she had to gain insights about Rex to chip away at his royal decree. Did they have any friends in common in New Orleans who might have influence with him?

"You understand family and expectations. He was always Papa's favorite. Firstborn. And a son." Kayla dropped the empty coffee cups in the trash at the foot of the stairs. "I have to navigate this situation expertly. I need him to stay, but I don't want him helicoptering around me."

Kayla's calm confidence stalled her fears. Maybe her income wouldn't dry up. The small trust fund Great-Grandmother left her provided enough money each month for her to pay rent. Her teaching job paid the rest of the bills. The singing gigs at Arceneau's and Harbor House supported her band kids, outfitting them with instruments. But uniforms were still needed. Her summer tour could cover that expense.

There's got to be a way to convince Rex to continue the music. Think!

A new plan began to take shape in Nola's mind. One that involved the steely-blue-gray-eyed Rex. If she mapped it out with precision, he would be saying "yes" before he could even think "no." If ever she needed to amp up her powers of persuasion, now was the time.

"I see the gears turning in your head."

"Learning something from me, aren't you?" Nola climbed the stairs. "Clearly you came with a plan for the day. What's on the agenda?"

"Go change. We're taking the bicycles. Near the river. Marigny Street."

Behind her, Kayla raced up the steps. When Nola stopped, Kayla bumped her from behind.

"Good morning, Marquis." Nola batted her lashes at the trumpet player. "Nice horn practice. Have a good day." She enjoyed the playfulness between them. But though he played the blues, her heart never beat 12/8 time over him.

Marquis tipped his hat at her. As she turned, she caught his flirty wink at Kayla. "Mornin'."

Her friend stared as he descended. As he started to turn back, Nola quickly entered her apartment, pulling Kayla inside to keep her from openly gawking at the man.

"Hire *him* for your tour."

"What?"

"I'll come on the road as the band's chef. I swear, that man could be the twin of Brown Sugar on that crime program on TV."

"Starstruck, darlin'?"

"Well, he makes my panties wet, you know what I mean. He's as hot as asphalt in the middle of summer in Louisiana," Kayla drawled.

"And he plays a mean horn, too." Walking toward her bedroom, Nola thought of a plan to bring the chef and musician together. She pulled her caftan over her head to change, then hung it in the closet.

"Shit, Nola, I know we're really close, but girlfriend, you're way too…"

"What?" Nola reached for the clothes neatly laid out on her bed.

"I'm just sayin'…"

"What!" She pulled on walking shorts over lace panties, then slipped on a bra from her favorite store in the French Quarter. Once, she took a burlesque dance lesson there during a lingerie party. The store trashy in its name, yet their merchandise was anything but. They carried elegant imported lace, silk, and satin garments. What woman didn't want that kind of luxury next to her skin? It was her one weakness in life. Other women were shoe whores, like her sister, or bracelet mongers like her cousin Evie. She'd take sexy lingerie any day.

"The whole nudity thing...bothers me. I'm not comfortable walking around naked. Like you do."

Nola walked back into the living room of her tiny apartment fully dressed. "You don't like being naked, or you don't want to see me naked?"

"Yes."

"I wasn't naked. I had on a caftan."

"But—underneath. And then you took it off."

"Are you really that self-conscious? Or is your potty mouth a cover-up for your prudishness?" Nola pulled on her socks and reached for her sneakers.

"Apparently so."

"Lordy, when you grow up with so many women around—"

"But that's the point. I didn't. Momma got sick when I started school. She died when I barely finished second grade. Rex was about twelve. Papa worked all the time. Most of what I learned about being a girl, I learned from magazines or Rex—my aunts and cousins never had much to do with me. I grew tall and gangly quick. Imagine shopping for your first bra and your brother waiting by the escalator at a department store praying he won't be seen by anyone he knows."

Inwardly, she chuckled at the image of a young Rex awkwardly hanging out. "That's what girlfriends are for." She stood straight, bent over, and placed her palms flat on the floor, shifting her weight from side to side to stretch.

Kayla shrugged. "I didn't really have any. I spent

most of my after school and weekend time at the restaurant. Ask me about grills, ovens, and fryers. Those I can tell you about. Rex was lucky. He took music lessons. Guitar, trumpet, and piano."

Nola straightened suddenly. "He what?" Her heartbeat quickened.

"Took. Music. Lessons. How do you sing when you don't hear well? He's musically talented. I'm not. I only took piano because he forced me."

"He plays?" Her pulse spiked. Warnings pinged in her brain.

"He says he jams at a bistro next to one of his restaurants in New York. Guitar or trumpet. He gave up piano because it wasn't portable. But I've only been to New York once to visit him, so I can't vouch for what he says, just about his years of lessons."

"You and your brother are *full* of surprises."

"You haven't known me all that long. He and I are as dull as a machete after hacking sugar cane."

Nola grabbed her backpack.

He's a music man.

She had no choice but to avoid Rex now. Whenever the blues called, her infatuated heart listened. Not this time. She would shut it down. A guillotine couldn't drop faster. No interaction with Rex equaled no further attraction. If he intended to fire her, he would have to do it over the phone. She would avoid him until her performance on Saturday night. Arceneau's had been a great gig—paid better in tips than any place she'd worked, but she would pull on her big girl panties and soldier onward. A bit of resourcefulness and creativity had landed her that gig. Another opportunity would materialize if she meditated about it. Otherwise, she'd have to walk on her hands and knees over glass to beg her sister to host a fundraiser for her kids. A band wasn't complete without uniforms. Family involvement was only a very last resort—she preferred independence. To do it all on her own. But for her kids…she might have to suck it up.

"So I guess I should get used to the idea of being fired." But that didn't stop her burning curiosity about him from blazing brighter.

"Don't go singin' the blues just yet, sister. Just wait until you hear my plan." Kayla stepped out of the apartment onto the landing.

"I'll go quietly." But her unyielding heart took on angel wings and fluttered in her chest.

Double dang him!

Nola turned and locked the door to her apartment before bounding down the stairs. Kayla waited at the bottom. Shutting out all thoughts of Rex, Nola turned to her friend. "Honestly, you're not dull, you're busy. But all work and no play…what if I get you a date with Marquis?"

"I don't know…work comes first."

"I'm not saying you should marry the guy"—an image flashing in her mind of Rex's lips close to hers, so close they barely touched in a light kiss, stunned her—"I'm talking a date. Let me find out which club he's playing and we'll go—at midnight after the restaurant is closed. You can check him out and decide."

"I'm not really good at dating. Starting a relationship…I just lost the greatest man in my life…loss of my father…but I can dream about the future. Let's go see this place I want to show you.

Follow me."

Nola stayed close behind as Kayla took off on the bicycle. "This is liberating." Nola lifted her arms and rode without her hands on the handlebars as she used to do on the long driveway at Fleur de Lis. "Krewes need to have a bicycle club in their Mardi Gras parades."

The ride took them from Burgundy Street toward Marigny Street and the river. Cries from seagulls and blasts from a calliope on a riverboat docked at the end of Canal Street filled the air. Not far away the rumbles of the streetcar added to the mix. All purely New Orleans.

"This is it." Kayla pulled up in front of an old brick building restored and segmented into condo units per the sign advertising them for sale. Nola slid her bike onto the rack and locked it beside Kayla's.

"I heard about this place." Nola pointed to the vacant lot across the street. "Look, the ugly metal building is gone." The once industrial area had an urban vibe with a touch of New Orleans history. Still, her heart ached over washed away traces of old.

"Wait until you see the view from the rooftop deck."

The concierge at the desk greeted them. "Miss Kayla, I've been waiting for you. Here are the keys to the unit. Take your time. I'll be here when you're done."

"This way." Kayla crossed the lobby to the elevators. Her sneakers squeaked against the polished concrete floor.

"You've been here several times?" Nola whispered. The place was nearly tomb-like. Cold. Rigid. The tall ceilings and windows with only modern furniture reminded her of a mausoleum. But she could imagine fantastic acoustics if she belted out a song.

"I've got a plan. I'll tell you, but first, let's look at the unit I want."

Kayla opened the door to the condo on the fourth floor, and Nola stepped inside. "Nice. They kept the integrity of the old brick. It has a charm that transports you back decades ago."

Kayla pointed to an opening on the left. "This is the first bedroom. Is it big enough? It doesn't have an attached bath, but the one next to it is large, modern, and private."

Nola scoped out the space. "A queen bed will fit in here nicely. There's a whole wall of closet space. A girl's dream shoe closet." Even at Fleur de Lis, there wasn't a room with a closet as large as that one. Her sister would faint.

"This bathroom is three piece. A shower, but no tub. There's a tub in the attached bath in the bedroom I want."

"You're going to actually move out of your family home?" Nola asked, astonished Kayla could consider the idea. "It's a lovely mansion." A coveted address on a quiet street tucked away behind a black cast iron fence with fleur de lis finials. Plus, a pool.

"Your parents sold theirs."

"It wasn't the showcase you live in. But we have Fleur de Lis. It's more like it owns us than the family owning it. It takes so much work and attention to keep the house and the grounds in top shape. The Garden District house was rarely used."

Continuing down the hall, Nola sensed Kayla's excitement as she followed her when she turned left.

"Ta-da!" Kayla waved her arms in an open area a few feet from a bank of pristine white cabinets that made up the kitchen. "I'll need to add an island here with a small fridge. I'll move that fridge out. Put in a big commercial one over there."

"I'll ask Marquis to be *my* date when you host your first dinner party. Then he's sure to ask you out. Hey, that's a view of the river!"

"I'll put a big TV with a long couch over there. An antique trestle table with seating for eight. Benches on either side. Chairs on the ends. I will bring furniture from home. Plus, I have china passed down from my great-great-grandmother."

"I can see your vision. Maybe add some interesting industrial lighting over the table—maybe some gaslight fixtures converted for electric. This is an awesome place." Nola turned slowly in a circle to take in the details of the large open-concept area. She stopped her twirl, took in a breath, and sang, *"The city is my oyster…no place else could cloisterrrrr…meeeee."* The acoustics weren't perfect, but better than some of the small clubs she'd been booked in.

Kayla lowered herself to the floor in front of the floor-to-ceiling windows. "Do you think you could live here, too?"

"Live here?"

"Yeah. Roommates."

Nola quirked her mouth to one side. "Why?" The happy plus of Fleur de Lis—there was always family in residence there. The negative of Fleur de Lis—there was always family in residence there. After growing up with a large extended family, she loved them to pieces, but craved her own space, which was why she rented a tiny apartment—plus it was all she would afford. All extra money went to her band kids.

"You need to move. The owner of your building is selling, right?"

"Turning it into condo units, which I can't afford. I'm waiting to see if a new owner might rent to me."

"I want out from the weight of my father's house, to strike out on my own—like you. I told Rex I want to sell the house and buy this."

"He agreed?"

"Not exactly. But I offered for him to buy me out. Then you could live here."

"What?"

"It's a perfect solution. I buy this place. You pay only nominal money, nearly rent-free—because I know of your independent streak. With the extra money from my portion of the sale of the house, I can be a benefactor to your kids' community band."

"You're joking. You just want me to go bra shopping with you."

"I'm quite capable of buying bras...but you could help me with *lingerie*."

Nola laughed. "It's not like I know what Marquis' preferences are, but the way he looked at you—no condiments needed."

"Well, maybe just some whipped cream." Kayla blushed.

Nola grinned and nodded as images of Rex's wink flashed in her mind. What would grab his attention? A flirty move or an enticement of something more?

"Hello? Nola, phone home. Where did I lose you?" Kayla waved her hand.

"Oh. Sorry. My thoughts drifted. Somewhere..."

Was there a voodoo potion to keep Rex out of her head? "You want to be a benefactor? You don't like pint-sized people under the age of eighteen."

"But I want to help. I don't have to *do* anything. Just give money and show up at events. It will be good for my exposure, too. And living here is a win-win for both of us."

How did she delicately decline Kayla's offer? It wasn't just the condo or the roommate part, but Kayla's sibling that came as part of the package. Rex would turn her world upside down. She could fall in love, and he would leave. Return to New York. A place she could never live.

The risk was too great. Rex Arceneau had to be out of bounds.

"Say, yes." Kayla pouted.

"You can try to convince me while we're at Willie Mae's." Food would distract Kayla. "Then I want to go to Arceneau's and rehearse. I'll announce the end of my run at this weekend's performance. Rex isn't kicking me out of the club until after this Saturday night, I hope."

"Yeah, well…you water that little seed, and we'll see what grows. Who knows the mind of my brother? 'Hope springs eternal,' as they say. But I'll pull every string I've got."

Would helping talented kids matter to Rex? Kids who loved music. Kids in need of a safe place and a guiding hand. Could Rex understand? If so, could she find the chink in his armor…and still protect her heart?

Chapter 6

The warning buzzer caught Rex's attention. He glanced up from the computer screen. A door to the restaurant had opened somewhere. Faint giggles floated up through the air duct system. Seconds later the buzzing stopped, which meant Kayla turned off the alarm before it sent a message to the security company. She had no way of knowing he was sequestered in the office on the third floor. Staying out of sight might provide him with useful information, since clearly his sister wasn't alone.

Tucking a folder into the bottom desk drawer, he locked it. Kayla had never seen his birth certificate, and he wanted to keep it that way. His mother had given it to him after she became seriously ill, explaining all the ramifications for him and Kayla and all the reasons he had to keep it a secret. Then he'd been too young to understand all she said, but the uncomfortable truth had grown on him as he got older the way kudzu covered a hillside in the south.

If his father had ever seen the document, he hadn't examined it thoroughly. His uncle? Surely not. Had they known, their egos would've destroyed the family. As fathers, they hadn't concerned themselves with the welfare of their children until their children were of an age to work in restaurants and help build the family legacy. Papa and Uncle Henri each vied to be the best chef and launch their businesses to celebrity status—it mattered not that they pitted cousin against cousin along the way. Thinking about the dysfunction started a burn in his gut every time. The shame of the truth was something he hoped to keep from Kayla. However, the truth of their parentage didn't obliterate the fact that they were still siblings. Still Arceneaus.

A click of the mouse closed the open spreadsheet on the computer. With the last of the accounting books forensically reviewed to his satisfaction, he had worked on a plan to give his sister what she needed professionally—and financially—plus a way for him to keep from losing money if he invested. The financial decline of the restaurant was worse than expected. Yet, barring some unprecedented downturn in the economy, he could make it rally *if*—and it was a big *if*—Kayla agreed to his changes. Otherwise, she would be on her own. He wouldn't invest a dime. In six months, she'd be shut down. Yes, there were other jobs at nearly any restaurant, but not as an executive chef. She'd be forced to leave New Orleans, which would crush her artistic creativity with food.

It would scar him forever if his sister lost her legacy.

Never would he allow his uncle to take over Arceneau's.

He sighed. Shucking oysters barehanded would be easier than obtaining Kayla's cooperation. Her independent streak was long and wide. A definite Arceneau trait.

"Champagne," Kayla shouted from below.

He walked to the office door, opening it farther. Footsteps on the back wooden stairs leading up to the second floor sounded out a beat. A burst of laughter from the lounge urged him to check on Kayla, but he stayed glued to the spot when he heard his sister call out, "Nola, I think I've got it bad for that horn blower."

Horn blower? Who? What were his sister and Miss Belle up to? He listened intently.

"I *have* to rehearse." Nola sounded insistent.

Maybe chitchat between his sister and the illustrious Nola Belle would give him a clue as to why Nola received such a large paycheck every other month. The accounting records provided no description. What services did she render? Could it be blackmail money or extortion of some kind? Instinct made him shove that idea aside. Nothing as sinister as that. He would've sensed that about her immediately, the way a dog could sniff out drugs. Yet still…how well did anyone really know someone else? His parents were a prime example. Family secrets buried deep. But just as the tides rose and fell in the bayous, clues to secrets always rose to the surface—all it took was time.

"One more toast. To my big brother. Let's hope he finds a woman and gets laid. He's wound so tight if he were a guitar, his strings would break."

In the quiet of the building, Rex heard every sound floating up. Glass clinked.

"Again," Kayla said.

"No more. I've already had too much to drink." Nola giggled.

"Or not enough."

"Whaaat?"

Someone fingered piano keys. Nola's image popped into his mind, and he imagined her standing before him, reaching up, and running her fingers through his hair. His scalp tingled from her touch. He shook his head to clear away the intense reality, but the sensations lingered.

"What do you think about my brother?"

"Think? Not a thing."

"You said he looked like a pimp."

A pimp?

"Don't be offended. He's a fetching-looking fellow."

"Where did *that* description come from?"

"My great-grandmother. That's how she would've described him."

Fetching-looking fellow? He raked his fingers through his hair and rolled his eyes.

"I think the two of you could be good between the sheets."

He smiled. *Yes, they could be good in bed.*

"Has the bubbly popped your brain cells?"

"I heard you were seeing that Emile guy— politically connected. That's how you got the space for the band. But I've never seen you with him. Let your ha-ya down, Nooola." Kayla slurred her words.

"It is. And for the record, I've never had a relationship with Emile."

Rex's fingers itched to stroke her long wavy hair. The idea of another man doing the same left a bitter taste in his mouth.

"No, girl. I mean…the levee you have around your heart. Let it wash away. Momma always said the fastest way to a man's heart—"

"Through his stomach?"

"But Momma was wrong. I've fed a lot of men in my short life. In and out of bed. I've not found the right one. I think music might bring me better luck. Like with that horn blower."

"Kayla. You're drunk."

"That's okay. Keeps me honest. It's the only time I truly say what I feel."

"So what's on your mind?"

"Will you act as my priest and hear my confession?"

Rex's heart seized. Kayla's tone dripped with sadness. It had to be the alcohol. Kayla never drank before five p.m. and never at the restaurant—a rule he'd taught her after reading it in some book about manners. What kind of bad influence did Nola Dutrey have over his sister? He quietly stepped into the hall to hear more of their conversation.

"Sober up and ask me again later," Nola answered.

Rex frowned. If Kayla was drinking during the day, her judgment had to be impaired. Maybe he needed to rethink his plan. Did she have a problem she had hidden from him? Investing in upgrades and branding only to have her make stupid mistakes as a result of overindulging with alcohol would be a waste of money. He had to be sure she was capable of running the restaurant after he left. One thing was certain—his sister had changed.

He folded his arms and leaned against the wall. Worry and concern beat a steady thrum in his chest. Last night was the perfect example. His sister had argued against keeping Papa's house. Too big. Too much upkeep. Too quiet. She hadn't said too lonely, but he'd felt a rush of mournfulness from her. It was more than grief from the passing of their father.

He wanted her to live fully. Have a life—not just

the restaurant. He couldn't recall her last boyfriend. Maybe he needed to hit up his friends and fix her up. She'd laugh at that suggestion. He couldn't blame her. During her high school years, he'd done everything to keep guys away from her—including lying about her having an STD. He pleaded stupidity when she discovered the lie he'd told in a panic. It was years before she forgave him after suffering through the humiliation.

But he did it to protect her.

Now she wanted to cut family ties and buy a condo? A converted warehouse facing the river just outside the French Quarter. As soon as Papa's house sold, she intended to move. The Garden District home they'd grown up in no longer held any appeal. She wanted freedom to have a new life. Besides, she'd argued, she was never home to use the pool, let alone try to seduce a pool guy. She threw out a lecherous grin, and he swallowed a laugh.

"Everything I've read about grief says making a major life decision in the first year isn't a wise move," he'd told her.

"You've been reading about grief?" She lifted an eyebrow. "Since when?"

"There's a lot you don't know about me, Kayla."

"Maybe so, but there's a lot you don't know about me. You're the one who left for college and never came back. I've been here with Papa all these years. I have to get out of this house!"

He'd sighed. If he wanted the property, which he did, he'd have to buy her out. That could be dicey if the truth he was hiding ever came out. The idea of remaining tightly tethered to his New Orleans roots came into sharp focus, and the urge to stay tugged as hard as the urge to return to New York.

Then Kayla had announced Nola Dutrey would be her new roommate at the condo.

"Why share a place with someone else? If she's in need of your help so badly, let's lease her a room here—we've got five bedrooms."

Glaring at him, nostrils flared, fists straining to strike, Kayla had shouted, "She won't take charity. *And* she's going to continue to sing at the restaurant if I have to pay her from my share of the sale of the house. She's involved in a project that needs funding, and I intend to help."

Below in the lounge, feedback from a microphone squealed. Rex's attention snapped to his sister and her friend. It sounded as though Nola prepared to sing. He'd heard a lot about her talent, but reserved the right to make his own judgment until he heard her voice. The CD of hers he'd purchased from a gift shop on Royal remained unopened in his bedroom.

But what was the real scope of the project Nola was involved in? She drew his sister like a tourist to Marie Laveau's grave. He'd never seen Kayla so attached to anyone. Nearly devoted. Nola had changed her from a quiet mouse to…this crazed tiger about to pounce. Was voodoo involved?

No matter. He'd get to the bottom of it.

He locked his jaw. Emotions warred. If Nola was all *that,* maybe he needed to leave Kayla in her hands. Sell the house. Let little sister fend for herself while he flew back to his comfortable, well-organized life in New York. Go back to where emotions didn't slam him to the wall. Where scents and sounds didn't upend his life at every turn. New York was safe.

Then a realization hit him hard.

Nola has replaced me as Kayla's confidant.

His sister had always looked up to him. The feeling banging around inside him was more than overprotectiveness with a swath of jealousy. Was Kayla unplugging from their family ties? He needed to get close to Miss Nola Dutrey and discover her secrets.

As though on cue, Nola crooned the first line of "The Look of Love." The sultriness of her tone rolled through him the way warm honey oozed.

Her voice could melt sugar.

A flush of desire gripped his body as she continued to sing. He made fists and then relaxed his fingers. He pictured her sensual eyes, heavy-lidded, and gazing at him. Licking his lips, he imagined tastings hers, full and luscious.

All his senses heightened. The curse of New Orleans. He ached to satisfy the burning want she created within him.

Hearing her wasn't enough.

He needed to *feel* the melody of Nola Dutrey.

Quietly he removed his shoes, and with them in hand, descended the stairs. Stopping on the bottom tread, he leaned against the wall all the while hypnotized by the silkiness of her voice. It cleansed his soul, filling him with newfound peace along with hot desire. Every word she sang fused with the fibers of his being.

Quiet settled in the room as she finished the song. He slipped on his shoes. What did a mortal man say to a woman who sang like an angel? Not a pickup line. Something thoughtful and intelligent, but he couldn't think intelligently now. He had no words for the feelings she evoked within him.

"Oh crap! I've got to run. Kayla, wake up! Let's go to my apartment. You can sleep there while I have band practice. Come on, girl."

"Leave me here," Kayla groaned. "I'll call you."

"Fine. Ringy-dingy later," Nola said.

When Rex stepped into the room, he saw the last of the back of Nola's head as she descended the stairs to the first floor. He went to the closet in the corner of the lounge and pulled out a clean black tablecloth to cover his sister. Kayla snuggled it around herself without waking up as she lay sprawled on the red tufted bench. He would deal with her later. Right now, his attention remained on the songbird of New Orleans, and he wasn't going to let her fly away.

****

Nola shuffled into the community center an hour later after leaving Kayla to sleep off the effects of too much champagne. Later tonight, she hoped to drag the chef over to see that trumpet player blow at The Warehouse. After all, their philanthropic mission of providing musical instruments to schools and after-school programs sparked her decision to start a neighborhood marching band. For a fleeting moment, she considered asking Kayla to invite Rex tonight, but a nagging feeling stopped her. He wanted her fired. Wanted her gone. She was happy to get in and out of Arceneau's today without seeing him. Best to keep a low profile. At least until the show on Saturday night. Just maybe, her singing would give him a new perspective about her. If she couldn't change his mind, she had to trust that another job would land in her lap.

Have faith. But jobs with the flexibility that Arceneau's offered were few and far between—not many places would leave a standing gig open like they did when she'd toured all summer last year.

Dropping her purse on a desk, she clapped her hands. "Hey there!" She tried to get the attention of her rambunctious students. "Settle down."

Her pleas blended with the noise bouncing off the white cinder-block walls, and she flipped the overhead lights off and on several times to signal for their attention. She counted twenty-three of the thirty-five students in attendance. If she couldn't gather more of them together for each practice session, she might have to sanction the less dedicated ones. It wasn't fair to the rest of the band, who worked so hard three times a week on marching formations and music, to be brought down by those not putting in the time and lacking performance luster.

She positioned herself in front of a music stand before the group. "Take your seats and hang on my every word. We're going to pick a drum major in May. That person must demonstrate"—she counted off on her fingers—"dedication, leadership, and musical knowledge. So be thinking of who among you fits that criteria. But know, this isn't a popularity contest and I reserve the right to veto and pick my own."

"We need a name for the band," a trumpet player called out.

"Marigny Marchers," someone else shouted.

"I think alliteration is catchy." Nola nodded.

"What's al...al-litter-ation?" one of the saxophone players asked.

"Al-lit-er-a-tion," she sounded out the word. "Like

Marigny Marchers. Both begin with the 'm' sound. Alliteration is when the same sound happens to closely connected words."

"This is marching band. Not English class," another student groaned.

Nola flashed a smile. "Maybe so, but see how education is catchy? Good start to deciding on a name. We'll finalize it before fall. In the meantime, let's focus on the music. The name will come."

"Miss Nola." A girl waved her flute in the air. "When are you leaving to go on tour? My cousin says you're famous. Wants your autograph on a CD."

Nola cocked her head to one side. "I'm not famous. Just trying to pursue my musical dreams like you." She wanted to be a good example for them. Working on her craft showed them, instead of telling them, to stay focused on their aspirations.

"Yeah, but you've been on stages where people have paid to hear you sing," a young man in the drum section shouted. "Like at festivals and sh—stuff." The drummers all clicked their drumsticks together in unison, affirming the statement.

If only they showed that precision during practice.

She allowed the smile on her face to grow. "Each of you"—she pointed to several students—"is here because you love music and are taking the time to study it and learn to play an instrument. You have no idea the places music can take you. Yes, I'm heading out on tour, but not until after school gets out in May. A couple of my friends along with the drum major will handle summer practices. My dreams haven't been handed to me. Like y'all, I'm working hard on mine, too. I just came from a rehearsal."

Which reminded her, she had to pull music for "Unforgettable." Her sister had texted that a bride had selected that song for the father-daughter dance at her wedding the first weekend in May at Fleur de Lis. She hadn't performed it before, and it would take some practice to make it perfect.

"Let's get started," the bass drummer boomed out his command.

"I agree," Nola said. "Tenor drums. One. Two. Three. Four." She pointed, and the drummers began to play.

Tat. Tat. Tat. Tat.

The sound filled the community center, echoing around the room. The rest of the band members tapped their feet in 4/4 time.

She clapped out the beats. "Snare drums." After keeping time for a full six measures, she pointed to the bass drummer to add his percussion sound.

When they were all finally in sync, Nola pointed to the brass section and with an upward swipe of her finger, the trumpets, trombones, and a single tuba chimed in. A moment later, she stood in front of the woodwinds. "Ready. Set. Let's. Go." Saxophone notes were mixed with notes from a couple of flutes and a clarinet.

The level of improvement since the beginning of the year astounded her. These students were thriving in the program. Musically, they'd be ready for Carnival season next January, but they needed uniforms. Needed a trailer to haul instruments to events. Traveling added additional expenses. Backing a marching band had cost way more than she had imagined. Her expense planning proved to be slightly lacking. But each student had their own personal instrument—that in itself was a huge accomplishment. Her heart swelled with admiration for each of the students in the band.

The practice session lasted two hours. Tired in the best way, she laid down her baton. "Great job! I'm so proud of you." They'd finally polished "When the Saints Go Marching In." Maybe she had finally reached them. The kids were obviously practicing together outside of classes—a big accomplishment since she put the band together less than a year ago.

"I'm going to select a few other signature songs for us to learn, now that you've conquered the anthem of New Orleans." She would pick one with a definite level of difficulty. One that would make folks take notice of this troupe at Mardi Gras. Most bands were the offspring of a school with a fight song, but her band rose from the middle school children whose parents couldn't afford the additional expenses of instruments, music lessons, and uniforms.

"See ya," the students said, pushing through the chairs and music stands and making their way to the door.

She scanned the room. Her nerves rocked on the very edge from the chaos of clutter. Nola began on one side of the open space and moved the chairs and music stands into place, matching them up to small colored dots she'd placed on the floor to maintain the organization of the room. Everything in its place and a place for everything. G.G. Grace had instilled that in her.

Once finished, Nola stood back and took in a deep breath, relaxing as she let it go.

A timer buzzed on her phone.

"Oh crap. I'm going to be late."

She grabbed her purse, turned off the light, and opened the door, running into a broad chest.

Startled, Nola looked up. "Sor—"

"Whoa." He smiled wide. Her breath caught. Her gaze locked with his. She noticed the twinkle in his eye. He found her funny?

Shaking her head, she tried to clear the daze washing over her. Her heart thumped faster.

The Rex Arceneau smiled at her.

Chapter 7

She looked lovely in twilight, Rex mused, memorizing the contours of her oval face.

"Are you okay?" He reached for her shoulders to steady her, fascinated at the quickly changing emotions in her eyes and the heat flowing from her body through his hands and into him. Involuntarily, he massaged the smooth skin of her arms, savoring the connection. After the soul-moving experience of hearing her sing, he had to know her better. Her hypnotic voice floated in his mind, and it was as though everything else in the world were just background noise.

"I'm fine." She jerked away. "Back up." She pushed on his chest, but he didn't budge. "I need to lock the door. Wouldn't want your thousand-dollar suit to get soiled."

Her protests were a smoke screen. Whenever she touched his chest, her heart quickened. He intuitively sensed her confusion about her feelings. She might try to deny they had a connection, but it would be a lie.

"Could we go inside and talk for a minute?" He gestured toward the door.

"No. I have an appointment." She stared at him, lips pursed, then she turned her back on him to lock the door.

Rex stuffed his hands into his pants pockets to keep from reaching for her again and rocked on his heels.

Something was happening between them. Something besides a clash of wills. All of his senses said he'd be a fool not to dig deeper to discover the depth of the pull of desire. But first, he'd have to convince her brain of what her heart had already started to feel.

The hard part would come later…like how to make her understand that any personal connection between them could not thwart his business plans for his sister. "As an employee of Arceneau's—"

"Which I understand from Kayla, I won't be much longer."

"You're angry before you even hear the facts?"

She held up her finger. "Fact one, I need the job at Arceneau's. Fact two, Arceneau's needs me—I pack the lounge every Friday and Saturday night."

"Did Kayla tell you how much debt the restaurant is in? Cut me a break. I'm trying make the business viable before I hand it off to her."

"So you are a seagull." She spat the accusation.

"Don't worry. At some point soon, I head back to New York. Everyone will be happy. So if you'd spare me a few minutes…" He reached for her. He'd said the part about New York to gauge her reaction. Outwardly, she hid her emotions. Yet the rapid pounding of her heart and the magnetic attraction she felt for him couldn't be more clear than if she'd posted it on a billboard on Canal Street. He possessed an unfair advantage. At times like this, his gift was a sweet blessing. She experienced the magic between them even if she failed to acknowledge it. It had a hold on her, same as him.

"Your schedule doesn't dictate mine," she snapped, pulling away. "I have a job this evening. Another employer who pays me to work on Monday nights."

How many jobs did she have? Was she in financial trouble? Did she pilfer money away, like gambling at the casinos? Those things he couldn't sense about her. "I'll walk with you, and we'll talk."

"Suit yourself."

In all the bios and interviews he'd read about her, none mentioned a stubborn streak as long as the Mississippi River. However, he enjoyed a challenge. Never backed down after setting his course on a specific path. He had to make Nola understand, when it came to his sister, his goal wasn't to hurt her or rob her of something, but to restore balance to her world now that their father had died. Even more than that, Nola needed to understand that the relationship developing between her and him couldn't be denied by money or other friendships.

After locking the heavy, solid front door, Nola jerked on the accordion security gate and set it into place. With a *click*, she snapped a padlock closed.

"That's not a meaningful deterrent to anyone who wants to get in," he said as two rowdy pubescent boys passed them in the street on bicycles nearly weaving into pedestrians and shouting lyrics to a song he couldn't understand. A block away, a car horn blared, sharp and quick. In response, another driver laid on his horn. The approaching nighttime shadows didn't always bring out the best in people. "Good bolt cutters and that lock is meaningless."

She ignored him. Twisting her long hair, she piled it on her head, pulled a clip from her bag, and secured her mane. Then she walked away, leaving him standing on the sidewalk as though they hadn't been having a conversation.

He jogged a few steps to catch up with her. The cadence of their footsteps fell into place in a comfortable rhythm as they walked the next block together. She didn't bolt. A slight thing. He sensed a bit of yielding of her hostility.

"How did you find me?" Nola asked quietly. "This isn't exactly your part of town."

"Marigny. I'm familiar with it." Back in the day, he'd played in clubs on Frenchman whenever someone turned a blind eye and let a teenager jam. New Orleans was *his* town. "I heard you leave the restaurant earlier, and I needed to talk with you, so I followed."

"Followed me?" It was an accusation.

"Yeah."

"Were you skulking around outside during band practice for two hours?"

"The two-hour part, yes. I don't skulk."

She huffed out an exasperated sigh and picked up her pace. "A brilliant vocabulary from a man who's noted to be so accomplished. 'New Orleans' Own Conquers New York.' Wasn't that the headline in *Restaurant Guide* last week?"

He smiled. She *had* taken an interest in him. He'd seeped into her thoughts, not just into her heart. Did he have a right to be pleased? He began to whistle. Beside him, she quickened her stride. If it was a race she wanted, he'd have no problem. Her short legs were no match for his long ones. She could never hope to win. "Are you always running off to somewhere?"

She stopped.

He took a step past her, then turned about-face.

"What's that supposed to mean?"

Around them, twilight deepened into dark. Traffic pulsed with people returning home from work and others heading to restaurants and clubs for the evening. The clang of the streetcar bell rang out in the distance. "The first time I saw you, you were upstairs on the gallery at Fleur de Lis and escaping from your sister."

"No. Silly man. That might be your conclusion. Again, facts are involved, and you don't have a clue as to why I did what I did."

He was missing many factual notes about her, which was the reason he wanted to talk, but he had her number on her emotional dial—that she could take to the bank. "Earlier, when you left the restaurant, I started after you. I'm certain you heard me, but you put earbuds in and chose to ignore me instead."

She twisted her mouth to one side and rolled her eyes.

Score a direct hit.

"I was in a hurry. I didn't know it was *you* bellowing." She folded her arms over her chest and chewed her bottom lip. "I don't respond to strangers screeching at me on the street."

Screeching? Now she was baiting him for a fight. There was more than one way to do battle with a stubborn female. "Fair enough." He smiled and nodded. "However, the fact is, I didn't want to interrupt your class, so I waited until it was over." He'd told the truth. Well, not all the truth. He waited, and listened, not only waiting for her to sing again, but also just in case he could uncover clues to the mystery of why she received so much money from the restaurant.

"Mr. Arceneau. You're a spy. If you want to speak with me about your business, then please have the courtesy of doing so at the restaurant. After Saturday night." She continued down the street. "You could make an appointment."

"You're doing it again."

"What?"

"Running away."

Raising her arms, she flicked her hands and held up her palms at him, energetically stopping him. Then she turned, and with a long stride, walked away.

If she thought of getting rid of him, soon she'd learn his tenacity outstretched her own—he was the next logjam in her life. She hadn't yet accepted that fact. "Don't think this is over, Nola," he muttered to himself. "Stop!"

As he waited for her to halt and turn back to him, he enjoyed the sweet sway of her hips, and he imagined her dancing salsa with him. Sassy and sexy.

Only feet ahead of her, a car suddenly turned at the corner, blocking her path. The pair of kids on bicycles he'd seen earlier came around the car. The larger boy grabbed Nola's purse, yanking it off her shoulder. The smaller one kicked her in the hip. Nola lost her balance, stumbled, and went down.

Rex's throat constricted. He raced for her, his heart pounding in his chest.

The boys pedaled toward him.

He jerked on the handlebars of the larger kid who carried the purse, grabbing it from him.

The bike's front wheel turned perpendicular. The kid tumbled onto the pavement. The bike crashed on top of him. The smaller boy took off, leaving his groaning friend behind. The car at the corner squealed away. Nola still lay on the ground.

Reaching her was his only concern. With her purse, he raced to her and knelt down, placing her bag between them. Her expression was dazed, eyes confused. Most of her hair had fallen loose from the clip. After brushing her hands together, she rubbed them on her pants.

"Are you okay?" he asked. Her delicate hands were scraped, but not bleeding.

She looked up, appearing to be searching for something in him. "I don't know," she stammered. "I think so." She tugged on the clip, removing it. The rest of her hair tumbled down in waves of silkiness. She rubbed the back of her neck.

"Do you need a doctor?" He dragged his attention from her hair to her face. Brushing her hands away, he massaged her neck searching for signs of blood. His hands then moved down the length of her arms. As he felt for injuries, he experienced jolt after jolt of connection with her. The intensity of which, he'd never encountered before.

"Let me get up."

As he helped her rise, a commotion sounded behind them. They turned. The purse-snatching kid picked up the damaged bicycle and hurled it into an old car in a driveway. The alarm sounded against the backdrop of city noise. Porch lights flicked on.

"Asshole!" the boy shouted. "Look for me." He beat his chest. "I'll be back!"

"We need to call the police." Rex watched the kid run away and disappear around the corner.

"I need to go home and change before I go to work."

He placed his hand in the small of her back to

steady her. "It wouldn't hurt you to get checked out." He felt the effects of adrenaline shooting through her body—a pulsating current. His own heartbeat synchronized with hers. She was shaken and unsteady over the shock of the attack, yet no serious harm had been done.

"I *need* to go to work."

"You *need* to call the police."

"Are you deaf? I have to go to work." Her insistence was just shy of hysteria.

"Then I'll walk you." He couldn't leave her to fend for herself. She needed him whether she understood that or not.

"Home to change?"

"Is it far?"

She shook her head. "I live on Burgundy."

He slipped an arm protectively around her shoulder, and she leaned a bit into him. "I'll take you wherever you need to go." He sensed her weariness and focused on sending healing energy into her body. As they walked a block farther, reaching Elysian Fields, Rex raised his hand. A cab pulled to the curb. He opened the door and motioned for Nola to get in. She cocked her head in protest.

"Get in, or I put you in."

Her shoulders sagged. The pout on her lips begged to be kissed, but he restrained himself. If he kissed her senseless, it would distract her from the shock, but kissing had to wait for another time. If he started, he wouldn't want to stop.

Settled in the cab, she leaned forward and gave the driver her address, her voice barely above a whisper.

Rex reached for her hand, his fingers rubbing over

her palm. She pulled away. "It's sore."

"After I get you home and I've talk with the police, I'll get some ice for it. Maybe the cops can find the kid from the bike he left behind."

"I know who he is."

"What?"

"I know him."

"What's his name?" Rex snapped. "I'll have the police meet us at your home. That was assault." He pulled out his cell phone, but she placed her hand over his and squeezed.

"No. Please. I'm trying to get Leon into the band." She sighed. "It's ugly, but the only way I might be able to save him is to hold this incident over his head. Force him to join us."

"Why?"

"Could we talk about this later? My head hurts."

Rex remained silent during the remainder of the cab ride. What was it about her band of kids that made her take such risks? Kids like that needed discipline. If their parents weren't doling it out at home, then society had an obligation to do so. Nola had to file a report and have this kid picked up—stop him from trying to steal from someone else. Doing so could save his life.

Arriving at their destination, Rex paid the fare and then helped Nola out. Nearby, someone practiced scales on a trumpet. He recalled Marquis saying Nola was his neighbor. If it was him, maybe the two of them could talk sense into her.

Nola slid her hand between two slats of wood in the fence, and a gate opened. A soft glow from lights around the courtyard pool provided enough illumination to make out a set of stairs. "I live there." She pointed to a door accessible through a second-floor landing.

The wooden stairway was wide enough for him to walk beside her and assist. He couldn't protect her if she tripped, but he could keep her from tumbling backward. Her pace lagged as she climbed, the soles of her shoes scuffing on each step. He sensed fatigue setting into her body, the aftershock of the attack.

"Lord knows, I never imagined *this* when I started out this morning," she said, more to herself than to him as she reached the upstairs landing.

"Ditto that." It wasn't his place to demand that she not go to work, or insist she crawl into bed. Maybe if he could convince her to sit calmly for a little while, maybe nap, her spiking pulse would settle down.

In front of her door, she pulled her purse off her shoulder and rummaged around. Her hand shook as she tried to slide the key into the lock.

"Here, let me."

He unlocked the door and opened it. She took two steps inside. Following behind her, he closed it and took in the surroundings. A single nightlight lit up the tiny apartment. She made it to the couch and collapsed. Rex joined her. Sitting beside her, he pulled her into his arms to offer comfort and moral support. Helplessness hit him hard as tears slid down her cheeks.

What could he do for her? What wouldn't he do to erase the pain and sadness washing through her.

"I want to save them all," she groaned. "I've worked so hard." Her voice wavered.

"Shh." He pressed his lips to her forehead, kissing her there.

She's more concerned about her attacker than herself? Could she be in shock?

The pads of his thumbs wiped away her tears. Protectiveness surged within him so compelling it shocked him. Pulling her to him, he hugged her tight. She clung to him as though she needed him close as much as he needed to hold her.

Her eyes searched his face. It was as if she saw him, truly saw him for the first time. Her eyes grew wide. She must have come to some sort of realization. It surprised him when she placed her scraped palm over his heart.

He sensed her growing connection with him. It ran like an electrical current binding them together, as though they were within a solid force field. She lowered her chin, and he planted kisses down her nose.

Her breathing grew more labored. She wrapped her arms around his neck and resettled herself in his lap. There was no way she couldn't feel his erection, the physical impact she had on him was as hard and strong as the emotional one he had with her.

The room was quiet. Soft sounds from a trumpet filtered in as if playing just for them. The longer he held her, the less he heard anything beyond short little puffs of her breath. She licked her bottom lip. Then the tip of her tongue glided over the peak of her upper lip. Mesmerized, his gaze followed her every subtle movement. It triggered a powerful hunger. He fought to contain his impulses.

****

"Rex," Nola said softly, intoxicated by the feel of him. Had the assault weakened all her defenses? She wanted to feel alive and safe, and the only person giving her that had his fingers tangled in her hair and his gaze glued to her mouth.

83

"Yes?" His eyes remained transfixed on her lips like a starving man staring through the window at Central Grocery. He nodded only slightly.

Her mind screamed for her to stop and consider the consequences.

I could've been seriously hurt!

Reason fled. Logic evaporated. Her emotions listened to no one. Need flooded so strong that only a straitjacket might restrain her from reaching for him—but she doubted even that would do it.

Moving, she straddled him. Energy flowing between them made her body crave a deeper connection with him.

Logic pounded, trying to prick a pinhole in the barricade of her runaway emotions.

No mixing business and pleasure.

Forget that!

She'd never made love to a man on a first date, and this wasn't even that. Maybe it was adrenaline? Maybe it was the need to connect with him after that awful scare? Bringing her lips to his, she pressed hers to his in the barest of kiss. "Rex, I'm really going to kiss you now."

"Are you sure about this? I don't think I can stop if you push this any further."

"I want you."

The moment the words slipped from her lips, longing urgently demanded satisfaction. Desire surged. Her brain shut down. Emotions flared bright and hot. So hot, she needed to be out of her clothes. She yanked her shirt over her head and tossed it. His gaze transfixed on the swell of her cleavage. Her breathing deepened when she witnessed his raw desire.

He cupped her face. Warmth radiated from him into her. He slanted his head and began to devour her lips. The electric jolt between them startled her.

Craving took over.

She moved off him and stepped back to remove her pants. He followed her lead. It was as though a southern springtime storm raged in her tiny apartment. The only thing that mattered—she wanted him. To please him. To feel all of him. To hear him moan with pleasure.

To make him feel what she felt when she sang a love song.

Naked, she stood before him. He reached for her.

Nola pushed him back to the couch and straddled him again. Her gaze remained glued to his. As she undulated her hips against him, he drew in a sharp breath. She wanted a deeper connection. He cupped her ass, then lowered his mouth to her breast. A rosy bud beaded under his kiss.

Nola moaned softly, "Ohhh…yessss…."

He rocked with her, his hardness pressing against her, but he made no further move. She understood he was allowing her to set their pace, to show him what she wanted. Lifting a bit, she slid over him, settling herself and joining them together. Tension inside her coiled tighter.

Slowly, she moved rhythmically. Holding her hips, he pumped up and back. He licked his lips, and her desire urgently flared. She rested her hands on the tops of his shoulders and held on, arching to give him greater access to the most intimate part of her body. He thrust. She contracted her pelvic muscles around him, not wanting him to completely withdraw. Their movements transformed into perfect timing.

But she wanted more. Tension twisted tight in her core. She feared she'd explode.

"Ohhh," she moaned. "Ohhh…Reeex," she groaned as he thrust deeper, bouncing her butt against his legs. She wanted all of the ride.

His thrusts quickened to 4/4 time. He tweaked one of her nipples. "Feel good, baby?"

The sensations were so exquisite, she could barely nod. "Don't…stop."

All sense of everything left her. She closed her eyes and focused on the inexplicable rocketing of her soul. "Yes!"

"Now, darlin'?" Rex asked.

"Yes!"

Three hard pumps followed. The tip of his manhood thumped a spot in her and sent waves of pleasure. She'd only read about a G-Spot. Hadn't been convinced she had one.

"Ahh…" Her coiling tension shot upward. Her breath caught. She reached a pinnacle. Joyous bliss exploded into waves of silkiness and velvetiness washing through her body, the likes of which she'd never experienced. She rode the emotions flooding her body and senses, savoring the euphoria.

"Yes, woman," Rex growled. His body tensed beneath her. He thrust upward and froze. His hands tightly grasped her hips.

In awe, she watched as the tenseness in his expression lifted away and the sweetness of pleasure etched his face. Eyes closed, he smiled sensuously.

He opened his eyes again, and his gaze locked on hers. Captivating. Hypnotizing.

The last of her elation joined with his. Together

they rocked slowly, a sensuous dance. She leaned into him, her breasts pressed to his chest, and she rested her head on his shoulder. The afterglow of physical love warmed her. She cherished the feeling of their bodies joining. Heaven couldn't offer more than what she'd just experienced with this man.

Rex turned his head slightly and kissed her nose, then sighed deeply. She smiled. Their contentment was fully in sync.

"We could move to my bed and do this again," she whispered.

His chuckle rumbled in his chest and radiated through hers.

"Darlin', I'll do it anytime and anywhere…with you." He wrapped his arms around her, enveloping her in a sense of security.

Bang. Bang. The door opened.

"Ringy-dingy!" Kayla shouted.

Startled, Nola looked at Kayla, then to Rex. She hid her face in the crook of his neck. Oh, God, what must Kayla think? Peering, she caught her friend standing with her mouth agape. Rex grabbed for his shirt and covered Nola.

"Holy fuck!" Kayla backed out of the door and then reentered. "No. No. No." She dropped to her knees.

Footsteps on the landing outside sounded heavy but quick.

"I heard shouting. Everything okay?" Marquis burst in.

Kayla made the sign of the cross, folded her hands in prayer, and closed her eyes. "I promise, God, I'll never swear again if I open my eyes—I'll even do it one at a time—if you make it so what I saw before was just an illusion."

Nola started to rise, but Rex held her close to him. "Shh," he whispered. "Just wait a moment before you move."

"What the hell?" Marquis said.

"Rex?" Nola asked.

"Let's see if God will grant her wish."

Was he crazy? Making love with him was as real as it got. Not sure what to do, she scrunched her face. Her brain ticked off all the reasons why making love to Rex couldn't happen again. Still, she hated the idea of moving out of his embrace.

But crazy couldn't be repeated again.

Chapter 8

Rex kissed the top of Nola's head. "I want to reaffirm my promise to you. Anywhere and anytime." He ignored his sister's repeated *"harrumph"* and the trumpet player's growl. As long as he believed in his wish, the intruders were a figment of his imagination. They weren't fools, at least not the unintelligent kind. They could take a hint. In a moment, they'd leave.

Or he'd throw them out.

Then he and Nola could resume their "getting to know you" dance. He could give her more of what she wanted. Hell, he'd do anything to hear her moan his name.

He looked up again. Kayla and Marquis had their arms folded over their chests. Lips drawn thin. He could understand Kayla being mad, but what was stuffed up Marquis' ass?

Rex sighed. Until the second Kayla burst through the door, his brain was conjuring delights he could bestow upon Nola's luscious body and his anatomy wholeheartedly agreed. To have her gaze at him with sultry bedroom eyes filled with adoration and joy brought forth an urge of desire that even uninvited visitors couldn't quell. He adjusted her in his lap. He had to get them to leave. Now.

Mere feet away, Marquis lifted a pink blanket from the only chair in the room and threw it. Rex caught it and then covered Nola and himself more.

"You're demented." Kayla's voice rang with condemnation. He couldn't be sure if her scorn was directed at him or Nola. Or both.

"Man." Marquis shook his head. "I told you about the curves."

Marquis had a thing for Nola? He'd never put a name to the curves.

I can read energy sometimes. I don't ever read minds.

"She's practically a sister to me." Kayla narrowed her eyes at him.

"That's enough." Nola rose, pulling most of the blanket with her. She reached and tugged off his shirt, throwing it in his lap, saving him from the prying eyes of their intruders and a possible view of his half-mast erection.

Wrapping the blanket around herself like a sarong, she pointed to the door. "Ringy-dingy means call me, not burst into my apartment, Kayla. And *you*, Marquis, I don't understand the judgmental scowl on your face. Both of you, thank you for your concern. Now. Get. Out."

"Wait a minute," Kayla began. "I demand to know what the fuck you and my brother are doing together...fornicating! He's going to fire your ass. This gives new meaning to sleeping with the enemy."

Marquis furrowed his brow. "I told you she was doing good things in the community, and you're gonna fire her? Shit. You're not the man I thought you were." Marquis shook his head and turned, leaving the apartment. After he crossed the threshold, he turned back. "Miss Arceneau, let me get you a drink.

Something strong. I'm in the apartment at the end of the landing."

Kayla threw her hands up. "I'm outta here. I'm gonna get drunk to wipe away the vision burned in my brain of the two of you." She pointed at Rex. "You want to throw your hands into the business? Tomorrow's a great time. I'm sure I won't make it to work. Not after the night I intend to have." She stormed out of the apartment, slamming the door behind her.

"Finally," Rex said, raking his fingers through his hair. "Come over here, woman."

Nola shook her head. She moved silently around the small living room gathering up his clothes strewn around when their haste to sate their desires had taken control. As though watching a movie, he observed her. Half-shuttered eyes. Sensual bare shoulders. Her long, dark wavy hair hung freely down her back with a few strands loose in front. The contrast of her dark hair against the creaminess of her skin and the pink of the blanket would delight any portrait painter. He stared for a moment at the swell of her perfect breasts now covered by the blanket, and his body reacted, remembering tweaking and suckling there.

Her hands, elegant with long tapered fingers, smoothed wrinkles from his pants. He wanted her to touch him with the same caress. She folded his pants and then shook out his suit jacket, carefully laying it across the chair.

His body pulsed with need. Her scent ignited his awareness. The warmth of her body lingered. When she had moaned, it was as captivating as her singing. He wanted it all again. Wanted her.

"You have to leave now," she said quietly, not

looking at him. Her gaze appeared focused on her feet. Lovely feet at that.

"Let me stay and take care of you." He wanted the rest of the evening and the entire night with her. A soak in the tub. When had she eaten last? "I'll grab some food from Harbor House Bistro around the corner. You want an oyster po'boy? What do you like to eat?"

"I think it would be best if you leave. If I'm well enough to fornicate, as Kayla pointed out, then I think I'm well enough to work."

Rex shook his head. "I don't think math works that way. You suffered a shock."

"That's an understatement."

"Why do I think that we're not speaking about the same thing?"

Nola lifted her chin. "Would you mind getting dressed?"

"Where are you working?" Rex called as he rose and slipped on his shirt and then glanced around for his briefs.

"Harbor House. I sing from ten until midnight."

"There's no way I can convince you to call out tonight?" He bent and pulled on his pants. "It would be completely understandable after what happened." Even if he couldn't make love to her again, he still wanted to spend the evening with her and then tuck her into bed. He had to get to know her—all about her. Had to understand.

"Rex, please leave." Her voice drooped as much as her shoulders. She retreated into the next room and closed the door.

Unwilling to abandon her after the shock of her attack, and quite possibly the shock of their attraction to each other—it certainly shook him—he went to the fireplace mantel and lifted a frame to get a good look at the photograph. A group shot of a host of people on the front steps of Fleur de Lis. He spotted her right away. Then her sister. There had to be more than twenty people assembled. The smiles on their faces and the way they stood, their body language, revealed this family had a genuine fondness for each other. He and Kayla shared a family similar in numbers, but not even at Mardi Gras did they ever gather together.

As a door opened, Rex turned.

"Oh. I thought you'd gone." Nola was dressed in a deep blue robe. He wondered if he tugged on the belt and it opened if he would find her naked underneath.

Planting himself in the chair, he cocked his head and gazed at her. "I told you I didn't want to leave you alone."

"Singing is healing to me, and I have responsibilities. Not that I owe you an explanation, but since I'm losing one of my jobs imminently, I have to keep this one. I would like to rest for an hour before I have to dress and leave. I'm not your responsibility."

Her words struck him as though he'd been slapped. He wanted to take care of her. He cared for her…probably way too much.

"Nola." He rose and went to stand before her. Moving a strand of hair behind her ears—anything to touch her, to feel her physically and have the energy flow between them—he stroked the side of her face as a chunk of the anxiety he hadn't realized he was holding on to lessened. "I want to explain about the issues at Arceneau's. I have questions that must be answered. If we could take a few minutes to talk…"

"Not now. Not tonight."

"Of course not. It's business. I shouldn't drag it into your personal sanctuary."

"How did you know?"

"Know?"

"That's how I feel about my apartment. It may be tiny, but it's mine. My sanctuary."

He didn't share with anyone about his energetic sensitivities. Never told a soul, not even Kayla. The gift he inherited from his mother was private. But he wanted to explain it to this completely unique woman. He captured her gaze. She looked up at him with questions brimming. He fought the urge to reveal one of the most private things about himself. "Looking"—he pointed around the room—"at things you display, family photos, an ornate cross, embroidered pillows. Handmade items. Feminine. Serene. All this tells me, this is your private hideaway from the world."

Moving away from him, she circled around the couch and sat on the opposite end from where they'd made love. Nola folded her hands in her lap and fixed a stare on them.

Rex dropped into the chair.

"I've never had a man in here," she said quietly.

She'd never made love to a man in here?

All his senses said she spoke the truth. A rush of something close to joy surged through him.

"What is it about you? I feel fluttery and desirable when you look at me. I lose my mind when you touch me."

Whew. I'm not alone in this.

She lifted her chin and locked gazes with him. "But Rex, I don't want what happened here tonight to ever happen again."

Liar!

He straightened, maintaining eye contact with her. Every nerve in his body popped. Why had she lied? Why? She wanted him. Desired him as much as he did her. Their connection ran deeper than physical. Just when he thought they might find an acceptable explanation for the money Papa paid her, when he thought maybe together they could work to find a way to keep her singing at Arceneau's, she lied. He might want her. Crave her touch. But he couldn't trust her. Never trust a liar.

Rising from the chair, he slipped into his shoes. After pulling on his suit coat, he crossed the room and stood before Nola. With a finger, he lifted her chin. Energy pulsed between them. Warm and frenetic. That mere contact made him want her more. Made him want to shove aside all rational thought. From the flicker in her eyes, he understood she felt it, too.

"Nola, darlin', I doubt you're going to get your wish."

He bent and placed a kiss on her lips before leaving quietly, not bothering to close the door behind him.

****

Nola jumped up and slammed the door. With her back against it, she considered walking down to Marquis' apartment to try to explain to Kayla. But explain what? How she had violated her own personal space? How she lost herself completely with Rex? If someone told her the man put a voodoo curse on her—one that would give her a high better than singing when he touched her—she'd have laughed. However, a curse could be reversed. What cure was there for amnesia caused by a man? She'd known from the moment she laid eyes on him at Fleur de Lis and her heart beat the blues, she wanted him. Now her body wanted him, too. Her brain was willing to do battle to resist, though it would lose not only the battle, but the war, since there was no hope of any future with Rex. He was New York, she was New Orleans. That pretty much summed up the chasm of their worlds.

As she turned to open the door, a trumpet blasted out a few notes. Slowly making her way down the open corridor, Nola headed for Marquis' apartment. Peering through the open window, she spied Marquis standing and swaying and playing a few random notes on his trumpet to the jazz music playing on TV. Eyes closed, Kayla swayed to the music. Marquis took in every move Kayla made. Licked his lips. Then he tossed the horn on the couch and reached for Kayla's hand, spinning her around. She leaned back into him as Marquis wrapped his hands around her waist, then slowly moved lower, smoothing over the curves of her hips. The two were locked in their own world.

Unable to intrude any longer on their private moment, Nola stalked back to her apartment. Once inside, she flung herself on her bed. The image of Marquis' hands transformed into images of Rex's and then turned to their lovemaking. She closed her eyes. The warmth of his touch lingered on her body. His breath on her neck. His mouth kissing a trail down her chest to her breast. Her eyes popped open as her pelvis muscles contracted. An ache deep in her core formed. "Oh, God. I want him."

Yes, she'd lied to him, when in fact, she wanted nothing more than to make love to him. Over and over again. A flash of insight startled her. Rex being congratulated by all of her family at Fleur de Lis. She opened her eyes. The image had etched itself in her brain, and she could still see it as plain as powdered sugar on a beignet.

"Bugger. Butter. Bacon!" Frustrated, she made her way to the bathroom and turned on the water. "If a cold shower works for guys…"

She climbed in and shivered when cold wetness splattered against her body. "Sure 'nough. It works." Turning the knob, she moved it until warm water flowed. "*Mary had a little lamb.*" She sang to distract her from the feel of Rex.

After dressing quickly and drying her hair, she slithered into a long black dress and clasped a necklace with red and clear crystals around her neck. The stones captured and reflected light and added a little bit of bling.

The outfit was a bit overdone for Harbor House Bistro, a casual neighborhood place, but the dress suited her mood and the bling served as camouflage to distract from her raw emotions. "Focus, girl." When she got her first big break, a record contract to sing with a famous blues trumpet player, she vowed then, no matter what, she would always give the audience in front of any stage one hundred percent. She'd climbed her way to the top of a short mountain thanks to small club owners giving her a chance.

Nola slid heels into a tote bag, opting to walk to work in flats, and then left the apartment. On her way, she texted Kayla to set up a time for coffee and a chat tomorrow. She didn't want any hard feelings to fester, but she surely wasn't about to knock on Marquis' door and interrupt any kind of private performance. Maybe the good that could come from the awkward confrontation would be a connection between Kayla and Marquis. Nola mused, it would certainly save her time from playing Cupid. Kayla could be one stubborn woman.

The minutes it took to walk the seven blocks to the Bistro cleared Nola's head. Traffic had died down. She kept a close lookout for kids on bicycles. Walking invigorated her mind, though her body complained about the soreness from her fall. As she pulled on the door to the Bistro, the aromas of deep-fried shrimp and the yeastiness of beer triggered hunger pains. Only a dozen customers dotted the place, but the numbers would swell to standing room only by the time ten thirty rolled around.

"Nola, you're early," the bartender said matter-of-factly, without glancing at the clock. "I can usually set my clock by your arrival—fifteen minutes to showtime."

Life had changed suddenly today and directed her along like a tugboat on the river. "I'm starving. Cooper, I'd like a cup of seafood gumbo and a baguette, please."

To the right of the bar, out of view of the front door, she seated herself at a two-top in the corner—the family table where employees took their breaks. Beyond the swinging doors was the kitchen. Yummy aromas drifted from there.

"It'll be right up." Cooper placed a cup of hot tea in front of her on the table.

She smiled up at him. "*Merci.*" Settling into the ambiance, she closed her eyes and pictured herself on stage. In her mind, as she sang, her voice lifted clear and soothing. She hit each of her notes. Emotion carried through her singing touched the audience. Visualization before every performance helped her present her best. It was part of her warm-up ritual.

Laughter caught her attention. She leaned over for a peek toward the bar. The trio who accompanied her, a drummer, pianist, and cellist, stood together sharing a story, and even Cooper chuckled. It would be a good night with easy comradery. As was their custom, the guys had been chilling out in the room behind the stage. Only a select few knew of the secret door in the paneling that opened to the waiting room painted purple and gold.

"Band is here," Cooper said, as he delivered a cup of gumbo. "Take your time eating."

She looked up at him, the bartender who also served as bouncer if needed. "Thank you."

He grinned and nodded. That was Cooper. Always calm with a megawatt smile that appealed to the women who regularly came into the place alone. He was their friend, confidant, and the object of dreams for some. She'd worked with him for nearly a year and knew little about his personal life other than he owned a third of the business, and he made tables from reclaimed items that sold at an artisan's gallery on North Peters Street.

"Hey there, honey," a young man said, approaching the table as Nola lifted a spoonful of gumbo mouth high. He had a mop of curly hair, wore jeans and a black t-shirt. He plucked a card from his back pocket and waved it.

She ate, hoping the man would take a hint and leave her in peace.

"I'm from *Back Beat*. You know, the magazine."

Nodding, she took another bite of her dinner. Not only did she know the local magazine, she'd had the privilege of gracing the cover. But she didn't know this guy. And in the past, reporters usually called in advance for an appointment time for interviews.

He pulled out the chair at the table and sat. She lifted an eyebrow to which he smiled.

"I write the column, 'Breaking the Beat.' It's like breaking news about stuff going on behind the scenes, ya know. Like about how deals get made. I'm Marc Sharp."

She didn't know where the conversation was leading with this guy, but the pinging sensation running up the back of her neck was a warning of something coming—something she wasn't going to like.

"Mr. Sharp—"

"Marc."

"Mr. Sharp, I have a performance that's starting in a little bit. If you'd like to talk with me, why don't we make an appointment for later in the week or even next week?"

"You're Nola Bridgette Dutrey of Fleur de Lis"— she pushed the cup of gumbo away and stared at him— "but professionally you're called Nola Belle."

She didn't acknowledge the information, just continued to stare. Give him enough rope to hang himself. It was only a matter of time before he quoted something as fact, then she would pointedly explain how it was a lie.

"You started a community band for kids— admirable by the way. I understand the performing arts high school is keeping an eye on a couple of your kids."

That news was unsettling. She'd hadn't yet talked

with anyone at the school, though it was part of her master plan—after the band celebrated its one-year mark. No one knew, not a soul, about her plan to showcase the talents of students with the hope of opening doors, creating opportunities for the kids that might otherwise be closed—all because their families couldn't pay for music lessons and quality instruments.

"I see I now have your attention. I know that you work three jobs to support your project—admirable—and I'll bet you're planning a fundraiser…" He tapped a finger at his temple. "If I recall correctly, your birthday, May 1st."

"What do you want, Mr. Sharp?" His knowledge of her business was beginning to unnerve her.

"I want to know if you think sleeping with Emile Broussard is going to make the lease payment on the converted fire station disappear."

"What?" Nola rose, knocking the back of the chair against the wall. Heads turned in her direction, but she didn't care.

Cooper appeared beside the table. "You need to move away from Miss Nola." He looked down his nose at the guy seated at the table.

Marc held up his hands in surrender. "I'm not looking for trouble. I just came to get confirmation of the facts. This is news that people want to know. Music. Politics. Bed partners. Let's face it, this is a sexy story, and I want to be the one to break it."

"Where did you ever get such a ludicrous idea?" But she knew. Emile's signature was all over this move. If she protested she wasn't sleeping with him, how did she prove the truth of her claim? If she worked out any sort of a deal to pay the owed balance on the lease with the real estate owner turned political staffer, then despite the truth, it would still look as though she had been given favoritism—which would cause people to think she was indeed having an intimate relationship with the man she was growing to hate even more.

"Let me show you the door," Cooper said. He pulled the chair out from the table, moving it like it was empty rather than occupied by a man.

Marc rose. "I'll go. But Miss Nola Belle, I've got your scent, and I'll be watching you." He sauntered out saluting to the folks staring at him.

"You okay?" Cooper asked.

Nola nodded. "I'll be fine. I'm going to disappear for a few minutes." She meant hide, but didn't want Cooper to know how Marc Sharp had shaken her.

And if she and Emile met Saturday night at Arceneau's, what conclusions would people come to about their relationship?

Chapter 9

Rex pushed to sitting on the couch in the formal living room, stretched his neck, and turned to check the time on the mantel clock. Six thirty a.m. He'd waited up for Kayla to arrive home, dozing off sometime after two, and now his tailored suit bore the wrinkles of proof of his concern for his younger sister. "Why didn't she answer her phone? Not even a considerate text to say she wasn't coming home."

Kayla was right, he wasn't her parent. But old habits die hard...if they ever passed on at all. Whenever he visited home, he fell into the role of father, mother, brother, and protector. It was about time he defined his role differently, but how? Shoving his fingers through his hair, he rose and trudged up the stairs. He didn't want to pry into her life any more than he wanted her prying into his...but the time had come to crack open the vault of old family secrets, like a crypt in one of the New Orleans cemeteries.

Reaching the second floor, he walked to his room, and his thoughts turned to Nola. There could be worse obsessions. Since he'd heard her sing, her voice echoed in his mind. Last night while waiting for Kayla to arrive, he'd replayed every detail about making love to the songstress. Her bedroom eyes captivated him, her body melted when he touched her, their joining had been dreamlike, yet emotionally intense. He wanted a repeat performance. The same need drove him to create a new dish or play music. Her voice mesmerized him, opening a place in his heart that cried out to be filled with…

Love.

"Love?" He jerked around to find the source of the sound producing the word.

Yes, love.

He flinched. The words came to him on a whisper. He reached for his ear as if he might capture someone's breath there. A whiff of his mother's perfume drifted to him. He quickly scanned the room to see if, just once, he might catch a glimpse of her, even if only a vague hint of an apparition.

"Love?" he said again. "Who's talking about love? Lust, yes. Desire, hell yes. But love? I don't know about that."

Stripping down to his briefs, he did a face-plant onto the bed. Pulling a pillow under his chest, he rested his forehead on his folded arms. He considered rolling over and power napping between the sheets, but images of Nola in his lap, her head tilted back and eyes closed, intruded. The tip of her tongue licking the bow of her upper lip popped into his mind. He hardened. It was as though he could taste her skin, smell her scent, hear her moans, and feel the warmth of her body against his. His breath quickened. The sensations of her made him stiffen more. He wanted to make love to her. To feel all of her. But how? What chance was there for seduction? He didn't have a way to reach her…except at the restaurant. Her employment file resided on the computer there along with all her vital information. Like her phone number.

Now fully awake and unable to deal with the ache for Nola, he showered, dressed quickly, then called for a cab. The first appointment of the day, a rendezvous with an estate attorney. Then meetings with a couple of vendors to source produce for the restaurant. Kayla might not like his involvement in the business, but she craved the freshest ingredients for cooking—he could provide that for her. Then he had to find Marquis. Did he know the name of Nola's tour manager? Maybe with help from friends, Rex could get Nola booked into some clubs in New York City. It would be great to share the summer with her, showing her the sights, feeding her at night at his restaurants, then sharing pleasure together in bed.

Renewed excitement shot through him, a win-win rising from the depths of despair following Papa's death. Nola was his Venus. A goddess of beauty. She energized him, infusing him with hope—not only for a future together, but that he and Kayla could find their way to a new kind of normal in life and maintain their family relationship.

"Thanks," he told the cabdriver as he climbed out at the law office of Talbot Anderson, an old high school classmate. It was time to stop conjuring up scenarios and delve into facts. Talbot had answers. He'd help create a plan, but only after all the facts had been revealed. The attorney who handled the reading of Papa's Last Will and Testament had assured him and Kayla that the olographic will met the requirements of a legal document in Louisiana: entirely handwritten, dated, and signed. But as to the disputable facts, the man had no awareness. Rex had information that could change everything...for Kayla.

****

Nola rolled and slapped at her phone. The ringing continued. "Shh…"

The ringing stopped.

Ding. Ding. Ding.

"Ding. Dang text." She grabbed the phone and stuck it under her pillow. "I'm sleeping," she groaned, wanting her enticing dream to continue.

When the phone rang again, she sat up, pulled it out, and checked to identify the criminal trespassing on her slumber.

"What?" she said hoarsely to Kayla, expecting a lecture about the uncomfortable situation with Rex last night.

"Nola, if our friendship means anything to you, get your ass down here now."

"It's six thirty in the morning."

"Well, I could've pounded on your door at five thirty a.m., but I chose to let you sleep. And not because you might have my brother still in your bed…but I'm going to bust an organ if you don't come."

"Which organ?" She yawned. "A lung wouldn't be bad. You've got a second one. Same thing with a—"

"Get down here. It's important."

"—kidney." Nola punched the pillow and fell backward. "I'm teaching at ten a.m. Then I'm working at Harbor again tonight. Could I come—"

"Fuck you. Come now. Grab a taxi. Hell, I don't give a shit if you come naked. Just come."

"Kayla—" Nola pleaded, wanting to drift back to sleep. No light seeped in around the edges of her curtains. Darkness outside. No time for humans to be roaming around. Besides, in her dream she was just about to make love to Rex again. His lips had been nibbling on her neck and producing waves of desires, not to mention moaning, but Kayla wouldn't appreciate the details. Not after her reaction last night.

"I *need* you." Kayla's voice wavered.

Nola's eyes widened. It was as though a spotlight shined in her cloudy mind. "I'm on my way, girlfriend. And for the record, nothing will happen again with your brother."

"Just get here!"

Nola popped out of bed and headed for the bathroom. Never had she heard a wavering break in Kayla's voice. Never could she even remotely guess that her tough-talking friend shed tears. Ever. She certainly hadn't cried when her father died. Had something gone really wrong? Had Marquis done something? In their limited interactions, the trumpet player always treated her with the utmost respect. She couldn't imagine him being anything other than a perfect gentleman with Kayla...well, a gentleman, if not perfect. Who wanted that?

Rushing through her morning routine, she slathered moisturizer everywhere and combed out her hair. A touch of makeup with sunblock came next. Sliding into yoga pants and a t-shirt, she pulled a hoodie over her outfit.

"Teacher clothes." She went to her closet.

"Shoes? Come here, lickety-split." She knelt down and peeked under the bed for purple, suede ballerina flats. "Come to Momma." She grabbed them and tossed them in a tote bag, slid a notebook inside, a folded purple skirt, then a white blouse on top, and lastly she added the purple blazer, a thrift shop bargain from Christmas. Picking up her purse and grabbing her phone, she was out the door in less than twenty minutes.

Hoofing it over to Elysian Fields, she hailed a cab. "Arceneau's near the corner of Conti and Dauphine."

"I know my city," the driver muttered, pulling away from the curb.

Finally at the restaurant, Nola went around to the back door and knocked. Her heart pounded. What could've happened to bring Kayla to tears? Where was Rex? How would she reach him if Kayla needed his help?

When she banged on the door again, Kayla opened it.

"Finally!" Kayla tugged Nola's hand, pulling her inside. "I don't know what to do."

Kayla clung onto one of her hands as Nola dropped her purse and tote bag in the small office. She allowed her friend to drag her into the heart of the kitchen. Quiet. Eerie. She'd never been there when someone wasn't chopping or some electrical gadget whirred at a hundred and thirty decibels.

"So, what do I do?" Kayla's eyes shown bright. She was like a young puppy eagerly waiting for a treat. Reminded her of her own feelings about a certain man she'd just met.

Nola tried sorting through her muddled thoughts. Her body was present, but part of her mind remained back in her apartment dreaming of Rex. "You can start by giving me coffee." Maybe java would dissolve the cobwebs. Craziness in Kayla's eyes worried her. She didn't want to risk saying the wrong thing. Her thoughts drifted to Rex. Had something happened to him?

Kayla released her hand, turned away, and poured from the decaffeinated coffeepot into a mug. Handing it over, she clasped Nola's fingers around it. "I don't know *what* to do."

"Cream? Stevia?"

"For shit's sake, Nola, this is serious."

"Right. And I'm serious about my coffee." She was stalling to get all of the gears in her brain working in sync.

"I'm in love," Kayla blurted out.

Nola blinked. She put down the mug on the stainless steel work island. "What?"

"I'm so giddy…and scared, all at the same time. I jogged here at five thirty in the morning."

"You were…with Marquis? Until five thirty this morning?"

Kayla beamed and nodded. "We made love all night long."

"All night?" Nola tried to wrap her mind around Kayla's confession.

"It was magical. Exciting. Naughty even." Kayla's smile turned coy.

"Girl, what are you sayin'? You and Marquis…" Kayla never, that she'd ever mentioned, met someone and hooked up, least of all with a virtual stranger.

"Did it about six times."

"A marathon?"

"Don't act so shocked. He triggered a hunger like I've never known. I'm in love."

"Whoa…" Nola shook her head. "Love?" It had to be the music. Marquis was a pied piper, and Kayla blindly followed, seduced by the tones of the trumpet.

"Just thinking about him makes me wet. I wanna run over there now, wake him up, and have him for breakfast. I want to plant myself on him and—"

Nola held up her hands. "Stop. I don't need the naked details." She'd believed Kayla would hit it off with Marquis, but love? Not with a musician. Only pitfalls in a relationship there. Sooner or later, the best horn blowers hit the road and toured. And Marquis was better than good, he was great. Summer festival season was coming. He'd probably be on tour, like he was last year.

"If he were a dessert, he'd be a bananas Foster bread pudding with chocolate sauce." A glow lit Kayla's face. Her eyes widened, her smile softened. It was as though she had drifted off on a dream. "Tempting. Decadent. Warm. Sooo fulfilling."

Nola didn't have the heart to crack the delicate meringue shell of her friend's ideals. "You got it bad." If she were a doctor, she'd diagnose the condition as fatal.

"What do I do next?"

"Next?"

"I haven't felt this way about a man since I lost my virginity in high school to Byron Guidry."

She's comparing a high school boy to a man like Marquis? "What happened with that?"

"Rex beat the shit out of him when I found out Byron was twenty-one, worked at a dealership, and Byron was banging his boss's daughter on the side. He liked fast cars and fast women. I wasn't fast—so he got it where he could."

"Kayla, I don't know what to say. You and your brother are very different." Lordy, Rex was full of surprises. She couldn't imagine him losing his calm demeanor and actually taking someone down. Nola picked up her mug and drank the cooling coffee. Kayla's confession had cleared away the cobwebs, but now a headache threatened.

"Nola! Tell me. What do I do?"

"Wait. This isn't like that time Rex took you shopping for your first bra. I can't measure your boobs and give you a size that fits. What did Marquis say when you left this morning? This is complicated stuff— like doing everything right and praying a soufflé won't fall. No guarantees."

Kayla's brow furrowed. "Say? We didn't talk. Booze started everything. Music brought the ambiance. We made love. Lots of moaning and shouts of ecstasy, but talk? Who wants to ruin the mood with wasted words? We used our hands, tongues—"

"Stop. I got the picture, but when you left this morning, how did you leave things?"

"I don't know what you mean." Kayla shrugged.

"Did you give him your number? Did he give you his? Did he say he wanted to see you again? What did you say to him? Did you have breakfast? What?"

Kayla squinted her eyes closed. "He was asleep. I left him a note."

"What did you write?"

"My full name and cell phone number."

"Oh girl," Nola moaned. "I guess I'm going to take you bra shopping."

"I don't need a frickin' bra. I need that man."

"It was a metaphor. We'll just have to see how it plays out. Love can be a chess game of desire. Who makes the next move? Well, technically, it's his."

A buzzer sounded in the kitchen. "Deliveries." Kayla went to the back door. "Hey, there! How's my produce looking today?"

"Greenhouse fresh." The man placed a wooden crate filled with greens as a doorstop. "I'm going to have a good growing season this year. I can just feel it. I'll unload what I've got. Is Rex here yet?"

"Rex? No. I wasn't expecting him."

Nola focused her attention on the man after hearing Rex's name.

"He had called and asked me to meet him here. Said he wanted to check in the produce with you. Also mentioned something about breakfast. I came early to deliver so breakfast wouldn't put me behind schedule."

"Kayla, I've got to leave. Be at school before my first class at ten." Nola crossed the kitchen to the office to retrieve her tote and purse. "I'm just going to change in here."

Closing the door and the blinds on the small window that looked out over the kitchen, Nola shed her yoga pants and t-shirt, then slipped into the skirt, blouse, and blazer. On Tuesdays and Thursdays, she taught some of the most privileged children in the city at a private school in the Garden District. She also met with select students for private lessons. Parents with money didn't mean her students had talent, but the gig helped pay the bills and her students were always well behaved.

She needed to hurry. She was already losing one job—at Arceneau's—she couldn't afford to be late and give the headmaster a reason not to renew her contract for the fall term. He'd tried to coax her into teaching summer school and was none too happy about being rejected, but the summer tour was planned and would pay nearly four times what the school did for the summer.

"Later, gator." Nola stopped when a woman blocked the door.

"Hey, Kayla! You here?" a woman said. "Rex called me and asked me to help out with prep so you could start on breakfast."

"Did he now?" Kayla chewed the side of her cheek.

The produce guy brought in another crate overflowing with fresh cauliflower. Nola sidestepped to avoid him.

"Nola, wait. What do I do *now*?" Kayla called out.

"Simple. Make breakfast. Be a chef. Bye!"

"Damn it! You know what I mean."

"I'll come by after your lunch rush, and we'll talk about it then. Also, I have to rehearse this afternoon. See ya." As she bolted, just outside the door, a brick wall of a broad chest stopped her. Her breath rushed out. She dropped her tote bag.

Rex caught her around the waist and steadied her. She looked up into his steely blue-gray eyes, her body relaxing from his embrace. Her heart thumped a 12/8 beat. She moistened her lips expectantly. Rex lowered his chin. It was as though he read her mind, felt the desire she had for him racing through her body. Her mental faculties diminished whenever he touched her.

As he stared into her eyes, she recognized what would come next. Her throat turned dry. She closed her eyes and waited with anticipation, impatiently wanting the delight his lips offered.

"Rex!" Kayla shouted from behind her. "A word.

In here. Leave the help alone."

Rex released her suddenly. Nola took a step back. A coolness seeped in and replaced the heat where he'd been holding her. Her heart sank. Disappointed, she shook her head to clear the fog.

"Rex!" Kayla shouted again.

"Got to go." Nola fumbled to grab her tote bag.

"Nola," Rex said softly. "Would you make time to talk with me this afternoon?"

"No. No. Rex. Not a good idea."

"It's important. Decisions that involve you."

"What's up?" She narrowed her eyes, trying to read his mind.

"I understand you're headed out now…a job?"

She nodded.

"I've got some news that might not make Kayla happy. I'm guessing she's going to need a friend. Seems you're filling that position now."

How could one man rain such havoc in other people's lives? First her job, and now Kayla? "I'll be back at two thirty."

Trying to push Rex from her mind, Nola headed for Canal Street to catch the streetcar. When it stopped, she paid and flopped into a seat.

"Man or kids?" an older woman in the seat behind her asked. In other places, purple, green, and gold Mardi Gras beads draped around someone's neck might come off as odd, but in New Orleans, people loved their colors. It was the structured fascinator with the long peacock feather that made the woman stand out.

"Pardon?"

"The only reason a woman sighs that soul achingly deep is cuz of a man or a problem child."

Nola offered a weak grin and shrugged.

"Though there are times," the woman continued, "when a man is a child. Them kind is the worst." She rose as the streetcar pulled to the next stop and then snapped her fingers at Nola. "Search your heart and stand your ground. You hear me?" She continued toward the front of the streetcar to exit.

"It's a man problem," Nola called out.

"I guessed as much, honey. Just remember what I said."

Nola slunk down in the seat. Search her heart? It and her body were speaking a different language from her mind. One beat to the blues, the other sang it—two very different things.

She could turn her back on Rex, deny her heart, deny the physical desire he evoked. Maybe she'd risk the havoc he brought to her life, but for her kids. Teaching taught her to persevere. Kids thought they were invincible. Students pushed against every rule. Sometimes caused her to want to tear her hair out, and then in the next minute, they would do something incredible, like sing a song in perfect pitch or play a piece of music flawlessly. She needed to take cues from them—pool all her inner strength to deal with Rex. Her heart had to be invincible. She could find a way to rein in all her undisciplined emotions about him...

Like imagining what it would be like *if* he stayed in New Orleans.

And what a future with him could hold.

Chapter 10

Rex entered the small kitchen office. He removed his coat and hung it on a hanger behind the door, deliberately taking his time. No need for his sister and others to witness his body's responses to the dark-haired beauty who had just run out. He adjusted his pants and grabbed a clean black apron to hide the obvious.

Nola slamming into him set off a chain reaction, slamming his emotions *and* his brain into hypersensitivity. A moment more was needed to settle his mind. Calm and cool had to be maintained in order to deal with his sister appropriately. No sense in fueling the flames of a fireball. That would be like spitting rum on flaming bananas Foster. Something had set Kayla off.

"Damn it, Rex! What's up with breakfast?"

"Coffee, first." He went to the pot and poured a cup, fortifying himself before entering battle with her. He spied a mug on the work island with a slight smudge of pink lipstick. Nola's. He breathed in, remembering the scent of her. The warmth of her body. The gentleness of her mouth. Damn Kayla for interrupting them. At least Nola had promised to return later. He looked forward to a few private moments with her…to continue where they left off yesterday. With a little coaxing, she would come around. Women like her—

after all, she was a singer—thrived on emotion, and all of hers shouted she wanted him. Just as he wanted her.

"Why is it that no one around here can function without coffee?" Kayla rested her fists on her hips.

"You look like hell warmed over, Kayla," Rex said dryly. "Maybe you could use some. Did you sleep at all last night?" He didn't dare ask where or with whom, at least not now, but soon he'd get answers.

"Rex. Hey, man. Breakfast. We still on?" The produce guy appeared in the kitchen doorway.

"Sure, let me break some eggs. Why don't you have a seat at the bar, and I'll let you know as soon as the food is ready."

Kayla pulled out a slab of bacon and ran it through the slicer. "No grits."

"That's okay, I'll grate some potatoes for hash browns." Hopefully, he'd sidestepped one of her bullets. Unlike his Smith & Wesson locked in the safe, it had only six chambers, whereas at the moment, Kayla was more like an assault weapon than a finely made revolver.

Wham! Kayla slammed two potatoes on the counter. "This what *you* wanted, Chef?"

"Green peppers and mushrooms, please. Would you join us for omelets?"

"Do I need to? I have prep to start for lunch today."

Rex nodded. "I think it would be best. That's why I had kitchen help come early. In fact, why don't you go chat up Mr. Produce and find out why he's charging us so much?"

Kayla scowled and huffed on her way out of the kitchen.

With food on the table, the three of them sat down

in the quiet dining room in front of a window, and Rex unfolded his napkin.

"This is mighty tasty," the produce man said, digging in.

"Good," Rex replied. "Now, let's talk money and produce. My New York business partners and I bought a farm in Pennsylvania. It supplies most of our organic produce for our restaurants in New York."

"Impressive," the man said, taking another bite.

"Now that my father has passed, this business belongs to me and Kayla. I want at least a ten percent reduction in costs of your produce, or I'll find other sources."

His sister eyed him, but thankfully remained quiet.

"But what about Henri—your uncle? I made a deal with him to supply *all* of your produce."

"Uncle Henri? Your agreement wasn't with Papa?" Kayla asked.

"When your daddy couldn't meet his bill...a year ago thereabouts, I carried some balances over to the next month. Your uncle contacted me, told me he'd bought fifty percent of the business. He'd be paying the bills from then on. Never had a late payment after that."

Why would Uncle Henri tell such a lie? Anger igniting in Rex's gut began a slow burn. What did Uncle gain from lying? Rex thought back on their last meeting...and his review of the account books. Was there something he missed in the audit? Had Papa struck other bargains and failed to note them anywhere? No...Uncle Henri, if he truly thought he owned fifty percent of Arceneau's, would've spoken up already.

"Your costs are higher than any other vendor. I've got quotes. I'd like to continue doing business with you, but we want a price break."

"Y'all in financial trouble?"

"No," Kayla said emphatically.

Rex took a sip of coffee, deciding to remain silent and let Kayla step up. Gossip about financial troubles would be a blow to Arceneau's reputation. The money situation hit the dire mark when Papa died. Kayla had to march into reality if the restaurant had any hope of surviving.

"We are as strong as ever. Yes, it's sad that Papa is gone"—Kayla pressed her hand to her heart—"but Arceneau's is still a five-star restaurant."

"And my company supplies the freshest and best produce. We're never late. Surely that's worth something."

Rex bit back a snort. "Well, I can put together a package of investors and buy another farm to supply this restaurant." Rex drummed his fingers on the table beside his plate. "Maybe I need to consider that idea more. There's a lot we could do with a farm in Louisiana. Set up a bed and breakfast. Have harvest days for food banks at the end of each growing season. We could even supply to other restaurants locally. Create a cottage industry."

The man frowned. "My prices are already near rock bottom. I'll be happy to go over my invoices for the last year. I swear, I don't have room to cut ten percent from the bottom line."

Rex's cell phone rang. He rose. "Please excuse me. I need to take this. However, based on our conversation so far, you need to do more to convince us not to find another vendor."

As he walked out of the dining room, he heard

Kayla tell the produce man to take a breath—that she'd have a heart-to-heart talk with her brother and see if something couldn't be worked out. Rex smiled. Kayla was taking a more active interest in the back side of the business. These sorts of conversations weren't always pleasant, but necessary.

Once out of earshot of his sister, he answered the phone, climbing the steps to the office on the third floor. "Hello? Rex Arceneau here."

"Mr. Arceneau, this is Biloxi Dutrey Trahan. We met at Fleur de Lis. You gave me your business card."

Rex smiled. "I recall." *Nice legs, but not Nola.*

"I know this is really last minute, but I need help, and since you know my sister…I thought I would see if you might lend us as hand."

"Nola needs help?"

"*Yes, sir.* More than you know, but that's a longer conversation." She chuckled. "Our problem is next weekend, Saturday after this one. Our parents' thirty-fifth wedding anniversary. Our cook fell and fractured her leg. She's out of commission. My cousin, Camilla, who helps her run Fleur de Lis Café, is pregnant, and as of today, she's on bed rest. We have nearly three-hundred guests coming. I need a caterer, which I hope is Arceneau's."

Thoughts zipped through Rex's mind. This could be the perfect opportunity to grow closer to Nola. Get to know her family.

"Also," she continued, "I was hoping you could recommend someone to fill in until Greta, our cook who runs the café, is back on her feet. Someone who can run a kitchen. Daily. For lunch. Also, we do have a wedding coming up. Your sister is making the cake.

And we have a few other events sprinkled on the weekends for the next two months."

"Well..."

"I'm desperate. Please say yes. Or at least ask me a bunch of questions that make me think you can be persuaded."

"I'll have more questions. Need specifics, if I agree to help you. But first, I need to talk it over with my sister. Though, I'm not sure *your* sister is going to want me anywhere near your parents' party."

"Why?"

"Because we're in a cost-cutting mode, and I can't afford her services any longer."

"I see... Have you told her yet? She'll be devastated."

"I hope to have that conversation with her today."

Devastated?

"Nola is fiercely independent. She'd rather live like a bag woman than ask our family for help. Did you know that every penny she earns from Arceneau's and from Harbor House goes to support her community band? 'Independent cuss' is what our grandmother calls her. Nola's teaching job and summer touring is how she pays for the necessaries for the band. My sister is tight with a penny. She spends more on others each month than herself. I buy her shoes and clothes just so I can be seen with her in public. I can't understand why she prefers thrift shop finds."

At every turn, he discovered something enticing about Nola Belle. She was a giver, not a taker, maybe to a fault. "Mrs. Trahan, would you give me twenty-four hours to get back to you? Since my father's passing—"

"I'm so sorry. I don't mean to create a hardship on

you. I don't want to bother—"

Nola and her sister had a lot in common. They both barged through conversations. "Mrs. Trahan."

"Biloxi, please."

"I'll call you tomorrow. I believe I can help you out, but give me until tomorrow to confirm."

"I'll be waiting, not so patiently."

When Rex returned to the dining room, the produce man had left. All signs of breakfast had been removed, and the table reset for lunch.

"Nice job," Kayla said as he entered the kitchen. "Trying to ruin my supply line. This is blatant sabotage. I instructed him to continue his deliveries. You and I will go over the invoices together."

Rex nodded. He'd been waiting for her to insert herself into the business end of the restaurant. His plan had worked. "Ask him to email the last eighteen months of bills. We'll go over them one by one."

"I admit, I need your help. But I'm not going to let you steal Arceneau's away from me. I know I haven't done the best job since Papa died, but I've done the best I can. I'm willing to listen to all you have to say...but I want you to give me a year."

"Unless things change now, you'll be out of business in three months. You don't have twelve months to turn things around."

"No, you misunderstand. I want *you* for a year. Here. Helping me. Creating new dishes for *our* restaurant. You owe me that."

Rex stared at his sister. He must have heard her wrong. She wanted to share the business with him? Wanted him to move back. For a year? "Kayla...I don't know...but what do you mean I owe you?"

"Time. You left for college and never came back. Now, you've hinted I have to do a yoga pretzel to please you, that it's your way or the highway, to keep the business going. I'm agreeing to your demands, *and* adding something small to the pot."

"I'm listening."

"I couldn't survive the closing of Arceneau's. I want you. If you won't help me—stay and teach me— then I'll call Uncle Henri and offer to sell my forty percent. Then you'll have him for a partner, fifty-fifty. How about that?"

Stunned, Rex grabbed for a stool and sat. Kayla had turned the tables on him. Sell Arceneau's? Maybe. As distasteful as it sounded, it would uncomplicate his life. He could go back to New York. But that would remove him from Nola's world...unless he managed to get her some tour spots there. His mind continued to whirl.

"What do you say, Rex?"

He pondered. Nola in New York. Maybe. She'd already cut one CD. Was a new one with a New York label possible? Could he find a way to entice Nola Belle into his world?

"I *will* sell my share to Uncle Henri, if you don't agree to my plan, big brother. Then, you'll have to deal with that can of shit." She pounded her fist on the countertop. "And one more thing. If I sell to Uncle Henri, I'll be selling my half of the house, too."

Kayla untied the apron from around her waist. "I need air." She turned and stormed from the kitchen, kicking open the back door.

Sighing, Rex massaged his temples hoping to stop the headache from escalating. Nola's influence shone through. Kayla had grown a backbone since the two of them had become friends. Where his sister was concerned, he didn't know whether to hug Nola or strangle her. But for himself, he couldn't wait to kiss her, hold her again. The famous Nola Belle. But shit if she wasn't a harbinger of chaos and delivered on that promise, too. What the hell was he going to do?

****

Nola arrived at Arceneau's a few minutes past two thirty, peered through the window, and waved the hostess over. The young woman rushed to unlock the door, allowing Nola to enter.

"How are things in the kitchen today?" She peered behind a waitress. A four-top lingered after lunch, otherwise the restaurant was empty. Also no Kayla or Rex in sight.

"Strange. Too quiet." The hostess thumbed over her shoulder. "Kayla has barely said a word. Not yelling expletives at anyone."

"Yes, that would be shocking. And where's Rex?"

"Not sure. Haven't seen him since I clocked in."

"Interesting. Well, I'll grab something from the kitchen and say 'hey' to Kayla."

Disappointment oozed with each step as she made her way toward the kitchen. Rex not around? While she didn't want to hear any bad news, the desire to see him again surged through her like an uncontrolled barge barreling down the Mississippi. To be close, to hear his voice, gaze at his marvelous mouth. While the reality of a relationship could never materialize, a girl could dream.

And she would dream big about him.

It was unlike Mister Suit to blow off an

appointment, Mr. Efficient Business that he was. She pushed on the swinging door to enter the kitchen. Maybe he wasn't quite as eager to deliver bad news as she'd thought. That was a point in his favor. But only one.

Inside Kayla's domain, quiet smacked Nola. Dropping her bags in the small office, she paused to take in the scene. The funeral-parlor mood was a shocking departure to the usual frenetic pace in the Arceneau's kitchen. Kayla stood in front of the sink, her hands on either side of it gripping the counter watching water running.

"Hey there! What's for lunch, Chef?"

Kayla turned. Eyes red-rimmed. Blinking. She let go of a shudder. Or was it a sob?

Nola ran to her. "Honey, what's wrong?"

"Marquis hasn't called. I can't do this by myself."

Ushering Kayla into the kitchen office, she sat her in the chair. Nola turned, closed the door and the blinds from prying eyes of the few staff puttering around. It hurt to see her friend so distraught.

"Let's start at the beginning. Marquis." She parked on the top of the desk facing Kayla.

"He hasn't called."

"Oh, sweetie, he works two jobs. He drives all day and performs when he gets gigs at night. There could be a lot of reasons he hasn't called."

"Let's go to your place. Maybe I can just casually drop in?"

Nola chuckled. "It's fine for you to go spend the afternoon at my place, but I have to rehearse. I'm working at Harbor House again tonight. But do you want to be so obvious with the trumpet player?"

"Yes!"

"Is this love or lust?" Nola took her hands. "If it's love, you have to give it time to bloom. It it's lust, then go for it."

"What do you know? You've never had a long-term relationship."

Nola drew back. "True…but I know what one looks like." Relationships had longevity in her family. Just look at her parents. Next weekend, they were celebrating thirty-five years of marriage.

"Call him for me?" The expression of desperation on Kayla's face pinched Nola's heart. Yes, she would reduce herself to high school tactics to help her friend, if she could.

"I don't have his number. Maybe Rex does? Where's your brother? He said he wanted to talk with me this afternoon."

Tears slid down Kayla's cheeks. She shook her head. "I gave Rex an ultimatum and left the restaurant. When I returned to talk with him—yeah, I stomped out pitching a hissy fit—he'd already gone. I don't know where. He hasn't called or answered my text messages. What am I going to do?" She flicked tears away. "I hate crying like a girl."

"Ultimatum? Can you even spell that word?" Could she cajole Kayla into a lighter mood?

"Rex *has* to stay here. Help me with the business. A year. I want a year. Or I'm going to sell my share of Arceneau's to Uncle Henri, *and* I'm going sell my half of the house."

Shock, like a dart, hit Nola in the chest. Did Kayla even know what she was saying? Sleep deprivation created delusions. She couldn't possibly mean it. She would never sell...but maybe she did need Rex to help. Where was he?

Nola slid off the desk and squatted beside Kayla. Wrapping an arm around her, she squeezed her friend's shoulders. "Honey, you haven't had much sleep. You're trying to push through, and instead, you're sucking wind. If you want to nap at my place and try to sneak a peek at Marquis—though I'm thinking he's working—that's fine. But I believe there's another opportunity to be had."

Kayla's expression flipped immediately to hopeful. Nola had to help her friend find a way to get what she wanted.

"Let me find out where's he's playing." Nola smiled encouragingly. "We'll catch his show. But right now, you go upstairs and sleep. Whenever you fly so high, crashing is inevitable."

"Can you even spell that word?" She sniffed.

"Yeah-ya. I can." She rose and motioned for Kayla to follow after she opened the office door. "You've got about two hours until you're on for dinner service at five. Let's get you upstairs for a power nap."

"Nola," Kayla said as she climbed the stairs. "I really don't know what to do. I've never felt like this before."

"I understand, sweetie. But you'll figure it out. I have confidence in you."

Grief had a funny way of twisting the brain and making mush of the heart. Maybe Kayla's overwhelming urges about Marquis would diminish in three months or six. Or not. But she couldn't stand by and watch Kayla do something foolish without trying to protect her.

127

The passing of Chef Arceneau opened a well of vulnerability in her friend Nola hadn't witnessed before. Now she had to be the rational one, the calm voice of reason for Kayla. Hopefully, she could help guide her away from making any terrible decisions. Like selling her share of the restaurant. That kind of major decision needed to be postponed, for a while, if not a year. Nola had experienced life-altering grief after her grandfather died. His passing nearly killed her grandmother. Then both the Old Aunts passed away just weeks before her sister's wedding to Nick. It rocked the lives of everyone in her family. The Old Aunts had been walking, talking reference libraries of history. Their passing hit Biloxi the hardest—maybe because she lived with them before Hurricane Katrina struck.

Could Biloxi help her now with Kayla—offer advice on how best to help her friend? That would please her older sister to no end. Maybe earn her some brownie points—in case she did need a fundraising favor in the future at Fleur de Lis.

"Sometimes one has to swallow pride..." she mumbled as she helped Kayla to the bench seat along the wall.

"I have no pride," Kayla replied. "I just want him so bad."

"I know, sweetie." Her own feelings about Rex were wavering in the same direction.

Nola rolled a couple of tablecloths into a neck pillow and handed it to Kayla. "Girl, I know what it's like when a man consumes all your thoughts. I know what it's like to long for his touch, to ache to feel his kisses."

"You do?"

Nodding, Nola smiled sheepishly. "Yeah-ya, darlin', I do."

"Tell me about him. Who was he? What happened? Did you do the deed last night with Rex to forget him?"

No, darlin'. It's Rex I'm speaking of.

"Just a man."

"Is there"—Kayla sighed—"such a thing as forever love?"

It's what I've been waiting on all my life.

"Shhh. Let me sing you to sleep." Uncomfortable about sharing her feelings about Rex, Nola pulled a chair close to the bench seat and sat facing her friend. Reaching over, she gently placed her hand over Kayla's eyes.

"Sleep." Nola began humming the first few measures of "Killing Me Softly with His Song," then moved into the lyrics. Kayla's eyes fluttered as though she fought to stay awake. Halfway through the song, when her friend's breath evened into small puffs of air and she'd drifted off to a deep sleep, Nola's voice trailed off.

Tiptoeing downstairs, praying the wooden stairs wouldn't squeak, Nola went to the kitchen.

"Is Kayla coming back?" one of the staff asked. "She didn't leave any instructions about who was on what prep for dinner."

"She's asleep in the lounge." She pointed upstairs. "Give her thirty minutes, then wake her up. Otherwise, she might end up in the hospital with a finger missing from that slicing thingy y'all use. Or one of you might end up in the ER with a stab wound."

"When she's quiet, that's when she scares me.

When's she's yelling, I know she's on her best game."

"She'll be just fine. Did Rex show up? Could he provide the direction you need with dinner plans so Kayla can sleep longer?"

"Haven't see him."

"Well, take some initiative and start something. Let Kayla know she can depend on you. The menu is posted on the board, right? Check it out." Picking up her bags, Nola headed out the back door. An unease settled over her. Rex stood for orderly, composed, and dependable. Not showing up for a meeting wasn't like him at all. How worried should she be?

Outside, the height of the buildings hid the warm afternoon sun as Nola crossed under French Quarter balconies and skirted around tourists taking a slow stroll. Not minding the hike, she headed toward the only other suitable rehearsal space—the community center. No one would bother her there. As she approached Elysian Fields, she spied a kid on a bike. Stopping, she scooted close to the wall of the nearest building for protection, then reached for her phone. Just in case. Was the kid one of the ones who'd tried to mug her? Her heartbeat quickened. Her palms began to sweat. But she had to find a way to get past the fear if Leon joined the band.

As the bicycle rider moved closer, Nola's breath hitched.

Then she recognized him. Sighing deeply, she waved back. The guy was in training for a fifty-mile ride for a charity. She'd met him at a coffee shop and promised to sponsor him a dollar a mile.

Crossing the busy intersection, Nola waited until she had made it safely across the street to check for a missed call. "Biloxi?" She only called during the day if there was a problem. Usually they talked once a week unless they were both at Fleur de Lis, and then the girl talk was unlimited.

"You did the ringy-dingy thingy?" Nola said after her sister answered the call.

"There's trouble in River City."

"Do tell." Nola chuckled. Her sister, the Chicken Little of the family, always thought the sky was falling. But her attention to detail was part of what had made Fleur de Lis more successful over the last ten years.

"It's serious. Greta fell and fractured her leg. She's home with it elevated. There's some jabber about possible surgery, but the swelling has to go down first."

"For the love of seafood and a *good* Bloody Mary, what did she do?"

"Fell off a stool."

"What?" Nola walked a few steps to a house and sat on the front steps.

"She was trying to get that five-gallon pot from a top cabinet. The step stool wobbled one way. She wobbled the other. Her foot tangled in a rung of the steps. The pot landed on top of her. And as bad as that is, it's not the worst of the situation."

"Is she going to be okay?" Greta was invincible. The news was too shocking to believe. She'd have to call her. Send flowers. Do something to help.

"Don't know yet. Maybe. Maybe not. But we've got a bigger problem."

"We?" With the phone pinched between her shoulder and chin, Nola imploringly lifted her palms heaven bound and looked up. Was there a message written in the sky she'd missed? A carrier pigeon hadn't yet arrived with a note outlining her responsibilities.

"Okay, not we. Just me. Camilla's on bed rest. She can't work until after the baby is born."

"Crap on a stick. What about the café? The party? What are you going to do?"

"What am *I* going to do? I'm not alone in putting on this party. There's me, and you, and Linc. But I've taken the first steps in getting this boat to float again."

"You're good in a crisis. What can I do to help?"

"You can convince Rex Arceneau to take the catering job for Momma and Daddy's anniversary party."

Oh no she didn't!

"Hello?" Nola shouted. "Hello?" Her pulsed raced.

"Yes?" Biloxi snapped.

"I don't think I heard you correctly. You want me to do what?"

Anything but ask a favor of Rex.

"I met him at the Bridal Extravaganza," Biloxi said. "He gave me his card. Anyway, I know Kayla is a cake artist, but full-on catering? So I called him today to ask, beg really, if he would cater the party."

"No. You. Didn't. Say you didn't do that without asking me." Anxiety roiled in her gut.

"My bad for not consulting my magic Nola ball first. I'm not in the habit."

"Sarcasm isn't helping." Nola snorted.

"Look, sister. If there's a problem, I'm the Keeper. I fix problems. I could give the business to someone else, but I know how close you've become to Kayla…so it seemed a logical fit. And I got a vibe from him—he likes you. Remember I told you, I'm married, so I can look, but you're single—you can touch. Please convince him to cater the party."

"What are you? My pimp? Frick and frack. I'm not doing it."

"Please?"

Nola rose and stalked down the street toward the community center. "He's going to fire me from Arceneau's. I'm not asking him for anything."

"It's not for you. It's for all of us. It's for Momma and Daddy."

Nola sighed. Rolled her eyes and shook her head. "Fine. I'll do it."

"Today."

"Maybe."

"*Today*!"

"If I can find him. He stood me up already."

"Stood you up?"

"I've got to go. I've got a rehearsal." Nola arrived at the community center and rooted around in her purse for the key to the padlock on the metal screen.

"I'll call you tomorrow if I don't hear from you by noon."

"Whatever. Bye." Nola scrunched her face and ended the call. "Just cuz you call doesn't mean I have to answer the phone." Opening the door, she wondered why Rex had bailed on their appointment.

Plopping into a metal folding chair, she hit Kayla's number.

"Hello? I'm up," Kayla said.

"Hey... All's gonna be fine. But listen, I need to talk to Rex. Will you give me his phone number?" Nola grabbed a pen and wrote on her hand as Kayla rattled off the number.

"Thanks! Got it."

"I want you to help me find a way to make him stay," Kayla said quietly.

"I didn't quite hear you." She shook her head as though clearing away a fog.

"*I* want *you* to help me find a way to make him stay."

She had heard her correctly. Anxiety churned in Nola's gut. "Sweetie, I love you, but you're going to have to stand in line. It seems several people want me to convince Rex of something. We'll talk about it later. Got to go."

And meanwhile, the rest of the story… My heart is trying to convince my brain that Rex staying could link us to a future together. How?

She shook her head. "Girl, only in fairytale land."

Chapter 11

"Damn her!" Rex charged out of the kitchen right after Kayla had stormed out of the building. Shoving on the door to the dining room, he didn't care if the damn thing slammed off its hinges.

"She's not stupid. I *am* trying to help her. Teach her something. But I can't stay here for a year."

Stomping upstairs to the third-floor office, he gathered the collection of photos and framed articles about his father and the restaurant from the wall, stacking them in his arms as he went.

"Why did she do this to me?" He clenched his jaw. "Mother! I hope you feel every prick of my pain tenfold."

Rex dropped the armload on the desk. They clattered. Wood and glass banged together. He never drank at work, but this wasn't his legitimate place of business despite what the will and other legal documents said. The only DNA he shared with Papa came through Papa's brother, Uncle Henri. Rex's stomach lurched, and he swallowed hard. Henri was the last man he wanted for a father. Always scheming. Papa put his brother to shame... Now all the family's dirty laundry had to be aired. No matter what, he wouldn't allow Kayla, under any circumstances, to sell the restaurant to Henri, and leave him to deal with his bio sperm donor.

"Damn it! How could she ask me to give up my life? To move back to New Orleans to work for her?"

His mind's eye flashed, and he was ten years old again, walking to the side of his mother's big bed in their Garden District home. She reached for his hand. When he offered his, she clung to it, exacting a promise that had haunted him all these years later—to always look after his little sister, Kayla.

And now little sister was asking for his help.

But a whole year?

Grabbing the cognac bottle from the shelf, he plunked it on the table in front of the window. A small flowerpot with miniature roses crashed to the floor. The petals of a spent bloom scattered. Rex flicked them aside, stepping on a crimson one, crushing it beneath his shoe.

"Never. Never, you hear me, Kayla." Rex banged his fist on the wall.

Life was crashing down on all sides. Papa died believing a lie. He never knew the boy he thought was his son had been sired by another. Never knowing his wife betrayed him thirty-four years ago. Momma had dropped her secret guilt into the lap of an innocent ten-year-old when she died. Twenty-plus years he'd carried what had been entrusted to him gingerly, as though it were a vial of poison, which if unleashed would destroy his family. It didn't matter that over the years he could barely face Papa and Kayla. The last ten years were especially bad with the lie eating away at him. But he'd promised Momma to never tell Papa the truth about his parentage.

What compelled her to make him keep that secret? Did she do it to keep him from the clutches of Henri who treated his children indifferently, only good when he could put them to work? A son was a cheap dishwasher. But she never made him promise not to tell Kayla.

Instead, his job required he protect her, look after her well-being.

Rex reached to the shelf behind the desk and grabbed a cut crystal tumbler. He splashed deep amber liquid into a highball glass, drank, and slammed it on the desk.

"What happened between my parents? *Why* Uncle Henri? *How* did he and Momma hook up?" A shudder ran through Rex. No kid, no matter how old, liked to picture a parent in the throes of passion, especially one that resulted in birth. "Henri might have made a sperm donation. However, the title of father will never cross my lips when referring to him."

After he finally learned to separate his emotions from those of a hurt ten-year-old boy carrying a secret, he saw things in a different light. But even still, he maintained a guarded distance from his family.

"I should've asked Papa about more private family stuff." He had little knowledge about his parents' married life before he was born. They'd each supplied regaling stories of their individual childhoods on the one night a week when they gathered to eat as a family. Momma and Papa were disgustingly sweet as they spoke of how they met—he was an executive chef at a local award-winning restaurant, and she applied to be a pastry chef there. Claude gave her the job. She was fresh from culinary school and fifteen years younger than the famous Chef Arceneau. Papa said they had an idyllic three-month courtship and married. Momma had said they went on a two-week honeymoon backpacking around Europe and returned to settle into life in New Orleans. Festivals and parties. Life in the Crescent City always revolved around food and music.

"The same stories over and over again," Rex muttered, pouring more cognac and downing it in one long gulp. "Haaa." The liquor with its cinnamon, orange, and hazelnut flavors warmed him. He poured again and sipped.

Dropping into the chair and closing one eye, Rex stared at the framed photo on top of the stack on the desk. Papa had stood proud and smiled wide when he received the prestigious James Beard Award. Rex turned thirteen that year. He wondered if Papa managed to win the award because Momma died. Papa had poured all his time, love, and attention into Arceneau's after she passed away.

Pushing the photo aside, he read a framed article from that same year announcing Arceneau's had received restaurant of the year from the local restaurateurs association. A proud moment for Papa and the family. It was the first and only time he witnessed Papa drunk...and in a compromising position with some woman he'd never seen before or since.

Her legs. Papa's hands. The memory burned in his brain. Rex turned over the frame to avoid looking at the photo in the article, but the memory couldn't be avoided. While a party played on into the night at the restaurant, he'd gotten tired and searched for a place to escape the noise and to sleep. Kayla hadn't been allowed to attend the party. She was home tucked in her bed by a sitter.

Rex climbed the stairs to the office. Giggles drifted

to him. Curiosity drew him closer to the office. Silently, he peered through the narrow opening of the mostly closed door, then quickly drew back. But on the verge of puberty, Rex couldn't *not* look and took a second peek that turned into a long stare.

A woman was bent over the desk, the same one he sat at now, her dress flipped up over her back. Papa's pants puddled around his ankles. His hands held her rounded hips. He thrust against the woman over and over. She moaned. The pitch of her voice rose. "Oh," came out in little breathless bursts.

Transfixed, Rex couldn't turn away. Tingles of excitement ran through him. He gripped at the crotch of his jeans. His body stiffened. He wanted to thrust, too.

Then Papa roared.

Shocked, Rex stepped backward and fell, hitting a small table in the hall, the same one now in the office. A vase wobbled before crashing to the floor.

Papa jerked the door open. His pants were zipped.

From the floor, Rex peered up at him.

"Rex," Papa shouted. "Get out of here."

He'd stumbled his way down the stairs and hid in the dark in the small office in the kitchen. He wanted to cry but didn't know why. Maybe Papa didn't want him.

Hours later, just as the sun came up, Papa found him curled up on top of the desk, asleep.

"Son," Papa said softy. "Let's go home."

"Papa? What were you doing with that woman?"

"Did you see anything?"

Afraid to lie, Rex nodded.

"Well…if you have any questions, you ask. What you saw was between a man and a woman. Don't be thinking boys go around doing it."

He'd nodded, scared to utter a word.

"I'm sorry you saw that. It was a private moment."

He wanted to ask, "But what about Momma?" but chose silence instead.

Never again had he caught Papa in a compromising position with another woman. During his college years, he tried to broach the memory of that night and suggested that Papa having a relationship with a woman friend or "keeping company" was understandable. Papa had waved him away. "Fathers don't discuss such private matters with their children."

There had been other women, but not one was ever introduced to him and his sister. Maybe he and Kayla had other siblings out in the world somewhere. It was the stuff of reality TV these days.

Continuing through the stack of frames, he touched on a memory for each, including the time Papa set up a buffet line and fed people after Hurricane Katrina. Pride swelled in Rex's chest. Childhood had produced some tough moments, but held good memories, too. He swiveled in the chair and scanned the bookcase. When he found what he sought, he pulled it out.

"Memories." He flipped open the picture album and took a long draw on the remaining cognac in the glass.

"Christ, she was cute as a doll on a cake." He smiled and touched the photo of Kayla when she was six, right after Momma died. Because Momma had made a photo album for him of all the important moments in his life, until she couldn't anymore, he had wanted the same for Kayla. He carried on where Momma left off.

Rex poured another two fingers of amber liquid

into the tumbler. "Ahhh…Rémy Martin. You're an excellent friend. *Tchin-tchin* to Papa and Kayla." Lifting the glass, he drained it. Maybe the smoothness of Rémy would smooth out the fist-size lumps of confusion his thoughts kept bumping over.

"Shit. What am I going to do?" He rubbed his temples, leaned back in the office chair, and propped his feet up on the desk. His experiment with Kayla had worked, but the results backfired. She now understood the business needed his help, his guidance. The plan was to spend three months to move the bottom line into the black, then leave her to follow her own fate. But once again, fate played him. He had his own businesses to attend to in New York. Splitting his time between two cities wasn't much of a life. How could he make this work? How could he keep his promise to Momma and also answer Kayla's plea for help?

Rex yawned. The alcohol had seduced him. He still had some time to figure out the best plan of action. After all, strategizing was a skill that took his cooking career to the top. A few minutes of shut-eye wouldn't hurt anything. He closed his eyes and sighed. "Momma, you got me into this. Now, I need you to help me out."

After he woke, he dropped his feet to the floor. Sounds drifted up from the lounge below. He paused to focus. Listening closely, he recognized the voices. Kayla. Nola.

Unconcerned, he leaned back in the chair again, intent on continuing his nap, but the conversation took a shift. Quietly, Rex removed his shoes, moved to the office door, and opened it enough to hear more clearly. He owed Nola an apology, but now wasn't the right time, and he didn't want Kayla running out again.

"Girl, I know what it's like when a man consumes all your thoughts. I know what it's like to long for his touch, to ache to feel his kisses."

Rex blinked. His heartbeat quickened. Nola's words sparked within him, lighting him up like a Mardi Gras parade. Could he hope that the man she spoke of was him? If not, who did she ache for? He recognized longing in her voice. A wave of jealousy washed over him.

Nola had melted in his arms. He craved that again. Yes, sexual desire was a hard-driving boss, but he wanted more.

A realization hit.

He sucked in a breath.

For Nola Dutrey, Miss Nola Belle, he wanted to be a better man. But how?

Chapter 12

Thoughts of Rex flowed from one to another in her mind as Nola walked home from rehearsal. Every love song she had practiced reminded her of him. It was as though her body had memorized the firmness of his jaw, the tenderness of his kisses, and the warmth of his touch. The feel of him hard. So satisfyingly male. She understood exactly what Kayla was feeling, down to the wetness in her most feminine spot. Then worry flitted into her thoughts.

Why didn't he show up?

As she approached the last block from her apartment, a shout broke through Nola's thoughts.

"Hey! I'm watching you."

Looking in the direction of the voice, she stopped. Leon on a bicycle. She clutched her purse and backpack, then picked up her pace. Adrenaline surged. A fourteen-year-old boy caused this reaction in her? No. He might be a thief and mugger, but he wasn't a murderer. Living in fear was not an acceptable way to live.

She slowed her pace, calming herself with deep breaths, and continued toward her apartment.

"Teacher. You best worry. No one makes a fool out of Leon."

In order to convince the kid, in order to help him, she couldn't be afraid. But what plan could bring him into the fold of the community band? So far, all efforts turned up zero.

As she opened the gate, he rode past her. "Bitch be scared."

"Leon," she called out. "Music is the answer." Quickly, she closed the gate. Anger bubbled up. At herself for ever fearing he would want to hurt her and anger that no one had loved this kid enough to teach him a better way. He might be her biggest challenge yet, but she was up for it.

She turned and caught Marquis' wave from the landing outside her apartment. "I've been waiting for you to return."

Nola climbed the stairs.

As long as he doesn't want to talk about what happened the other night...all is good.

"I'm here. What's up?" Something good could still come out of this day if she could find out where he was playing next and then haul Kayla there...unless Marquis planned to call her friend sooner without any cajoling. Nola chuckled. High school all over again.

Marquis rubbed his hand across his jaw. "I feel kinda awkward. But I need to talk to you for a minute."

After pulling her keys from her purse, Nola unlocked the door to her apartment. "Come on in. I've a few minutes before I need to get ready. I'm at Harbor House tonight. Where might you be playing?" Proud of herself for slipping the question in nonchalantly, she dropped the keys on the table for two in the kitchen, then walked through the living room to open the drapes.

On a table near the window, the ivy plant her mother had given her drooped from continued lack of sunlight. She made a mental note to water it and put it on the kitchen table in front of the window. Maybe there was hope for its revival. Maybe.

"I'm not." Marquis leaned against the doorjamb. "Driving the stretch around town tonight. A band of Japanese businessmen want to see the sights. I'm thinking about taking them to the burlesque show. It'll keep me from having to scrub out the limo tomorrow."

Nola kicked off her shoes and motioned for Marquis to have a seat in the chair as she plopped onto the couch.

He came and stood in front of her.

Surprised, she drew in a short breath.

He held out his hand.

Curiosity plucked at her. She placed her hands in his, marveling at the smoothness of his palm. He helped her rise. She'd never been face to face with him like this before. Uncertainty pinged in her chest. Marquis had strong broad shoulders, but Rex did too, and he was definitely taller.

"I want to apologize for my behavior last night. The things I said." His thumb brushed over her fingers.

Tilting her head to one side, she scanned her memory, trying to remember exactly all that had taken place in her apartment. Her thoughts went to Rex and making love.

"I was out of line." Marquis raised his eyebrows, his forehead wrinkling.

While she waited for him to continue, her mind landed on an image of him with Kayla. She stifled a smile. "You're going to have to be more specific. I'm not very good at guessing games."

"See. That ought to tell me something right there. After all these months that we've been neighbors, I haven't made a good enough impression on you. You don't remember what I said last night?"

She sensed his distress. Her breath caught again. What to do? Her hand still rested in his. Should she pull away? Step back? Put more space between them? All of this was new territory with him. He was Magnificent Marquis. Eye candy. Ear candy. And the man her best friend was trippin' out about. She just couldn't blurt out how Kayla wanted him badly.

"I have to do this." He grinned sheepishly. The tone of his voice held a warning. She gazed up at him, inhaling another quick short breath as Marquis' gaze searched her face. The tenderness in his eyes captivated her. His hands moved and cupped her neck. He lowered his chin until his lips touched hers, and he closed his eyes. When the tip of his tongue outlined her lips, she froze.

"Ahhh," he whispered, stepping closer to her, then added pressure to the kiss.

Stunned, Nola remain rooted to the floor. Tiny bubbles of uncertainty pinged through her body. His hands were warm, but everything else…just wrong. She squinted. Stood perfectly still. Waiting for him to stop.

Marquis broke the kiss abruptly. His hands moved to her shoulders and gave a light squeeze. "Nothing, huh?"

Nola glanced from side to side, unable to make eye contact with him. "Not sure what you mean." It was a lie, but only a little one. It wasn't his tongue or lips or hands she wanted to feel on her. It was Rex's. Damn that man!

Marquis stepped back and sank into the chair. "I've had this fantasy ever since I heard you sing. You have the voice of a siren. It calls to me."

Bewildered by his words and weak-kneed, Nola lowered herself to the couch. She primly folded her hands together, not knowing what to say.

"Nola, I had this idea that we could tour together someday. Like *really* together." He winked. "You catch my drift?"

She nodded.

"I was waiting for the right time to...entice you. I thought when I returned from my gig in New York, you could see I'm a good measure of man. Then, maybe next summer..."

"I've always thought you were a good man—by every measure."

"But there's no..."

"Sparks?" she asked.

"Yeah. For me, between your voice and your"—his hands moved to create the outline of curves—"I'd been having dreams about you for a while."

A flood of heat rose in her cheeks. What could she say without hurting his feelings? "Oh?" Her hand went to her chest.

"Oh, but don't you worry none. I had to take the kiss because I had to know."

"Dare I ask what?" She was still flustered by the direction of the conversation.

"Chances. You and me. A fantasy in the head isn't as great as a live one in the bed. The vibes of that blonde, your friend Kayla"—he reached into his pocket and pulled out a piece of paper—"turned a spotlight on inside me. Hot. And bright."

Nola raised her eyebrows, uncertain whether or not she wanted Marquis to share more.

"Anyway, before I call Kayla, I had to know about you."

Another flush heated her neck and rose to her cheeks. "Ahh, I guess I should thank you." Since the man had a definitely craveable body, any woman would look twice at him…okay, three times at least. If she'd held any far-off fantasies about him, Rex crushed them last night.

"I'm thinking you better make use of that phone number, dude." She winked.

"I will. But, we're good, you and I, yeah? No problems, neighbor."

"It's all good."

He grinned wide. "Ya know, Kayla, she's golden in so many ways…and places."

"Enough." Nola rose. She pointed to the door. "I have to get ready for work. Take your tour group by Arceneau's. But call Kayla first. I'm certain she'll give you the VIP treatment." Nola smiled. He had no idea just how well her friend would take care of him, like privately in the office while his gaggle of Japanese businessmen sampled Arceneau's award-winning food.

With Marquis out of the apartment, Nola fanned herself. "It's like a hurricane of hormones has blown into New Orleans."

Heading for her bedroom, Nola flipped on the light. Scanning the room, she wondered how Rex would enjoy the ultra-feminine décor. She'd never brought a man into her bed in this apartment before. It was sanctuary, her own personal retreat when the demands of the world weighed her down. Yes, she loved her bedroom at Fleur de Lis, but it was classic and filled with nearly priceless antiques. Sometimes, she had to escape from family and all the trappings that accompanied them. In the entire world, this apartment was her own private domain.

She flipped on music and danced to her closet, opening the double doors. "What to wear?" Moving several dresses aside, she pulled out a black crepe and fluttered it before her. "He can't resist me in this." As the words escaped her lips, she recognized how much she wanted him. Wanted? Desired? Needed? Her knees weakened. She sat on the corner of her bed. Rex was what she'd been waiting for. He could quite possibly be the one.

"No...really?" she said aloud. "Well...maybe. For just one whole night. To get him out of my system. That's all it would take. After that, Rex Arceneau will be banished from my mind."

Liar! He makes you hear the blues.

Nola swallowed. She scrunched her eyes tightly as a single note rang in her ears. "This just can't be. Like, yes. Lust, definitely. But love?"

She wanted to shake off the sensations shooting through her and lighting her up like an old-fashioned pinball machine. Huffing out a breath, she flexed her shoulders to relax and continued to slip into the dress. She zipped it on the side, then adjusted her breasts within the structured fitted bodice that plunged to a "v," stopping halfway between her breasts and her navel. It was the most revealing dress she owned. The hem hit halfway between her hips and knees. Every time she'd worn it, some man acted like an animal loose from a cage and had to be bounced from the club. Would Rex respond the same? She smiled. Would she have that effect on him?

149

Maybe after tonight's last show, she'd find him at Arceneau's and see just how tempted he could be. Adding dangling rhinestone earrings to catch the spotlight and sparkle while she was on stage, she surveyed herself in the mirror. Puckering her lips, she blew a kiss. This was what Rex would see if fate conspired for her...hopefully later tonight.

Nola pulled on a long coat to protect her from prying eyes on her walk to the bistro on the cool spring evening. Opening her backpack, she tucked her wallet and her stilettos inside. After she locked the front door, she remembered to text Kayla.

Let me know when M contacts you.

A rush of warmth washed through her. Tonight held promise. Optimism. It gifted her with feminine confidence, which in turn, brought out her sexy side— the side of her that loved to be on stage. She planned to rock the Harbor House tonight, no matter the size of the crowd.

"Ohhh...Prissy is working the bar tonight. I'll have her video the song I want Rex to hear. I can replay it for him. To help him get in the mood. Just in case this dress doesn't hit the mark."

Afterward, he goes back to New York. I go on tour. Life will return to a happy equilibrium.

Then reality smacked her. "He's going to fire me. I need every penny for the band. Life won't be the same with him gone. And talk about crap hitting the fan, I've got to deal with Mr. Unsavory, the one and only Emile Broussard."

She trudged in sneakers to Harbor House, mentally making a list of the clubs where she could audition, in case Harbor House wouldn't offer her more nights. A half block away from her destination, she spied Mr. Unsavory exiting from a taxi. He glanced around as though looking for something before entering the bistro.

"Frick. Frack. And burnt French fries. Is this karmic payback for a past-life sin?" She slipped in through the back door to the waiting room. Emile presented a problem she hoped to avoid…at least until Saturday night.

Chapter 13

Rex slowed his stride, arriving at Harbor House. Jerking on the door, he entered the enclosed foyer. Dark wood. Small, white hexagon floor tiles. Classic bistro décor—vintage and intimate. Beyond the next set of doors leading inside to the main room, the din of the bar crowd droned. Another drink would help him maintain the perfect buzz he had going on and help him forget anyone else around him.

Except Nola.

He spotted a large framed poster on the foyer wall and pursed his lips. A captivating black and white image. He crossed the small space and stood directly across from it to take it all in. A spotlight shone downward as Nola Belle looked up, her lashes casting dramatic shadows on her face. Her full red lips puckered for a kiss. The sequined dress she wore reflected light in tiny stars, magic made by an accomplished photographer. No mistaking Nola's star quality. The camera enhanced her alluring mystique. As uncomfortable as it was, his heart and body tugged him in her direction regardless of the resistance from his brain.

"Stunning," he murmured. Yet as splendid as the photo portrayed her, Nola's voice had more depth and richness than any image could capture. It soothed his blighted soul. He could spend the rest of his life falling asleep to the sound of her voice, then waking to the sweetness of her lips.

Making a fist, Rex released it. His heartbeat quickened. A quick slice of fear shot through him. Was he falling in love? Had the woman with her sultry bedroom eyes and sexy voice snared his heart?

He laughed, shaking off the idea. "I barely know her. Lust, that's what it is. A big amount of curiosity. A large dose of attraction. Can't be love."

He turned as the bistro's outside doors opened. A large group of chattering people piled into the foyer. Rex held the inside door to allow them to continue farther without stopping, leaving him alone with his thoughts of Nola. Wrapped in a modicum of quiet, he took a last look at the poster of the lovely Nola Belle. A swelling of possessiveness filled him.

Damn her.

Once inside Harbor House, he sidestepped and maneuvered through the crowd in order to reach the bartender. Leaning against the polished antique bar, he tapped his fingers twice on the counter to get the barkeep's attention.

"Hey! You're Kayla's brother," the bartender said over the din. "I'm Cooper."

"Nice to meet you." Rex shook Cooper's hand. The last thing he wanted to discuss was his sister. "Do you have distilled or spring water?"

Cooper smiled. "Ahh, a man who likes his whisky the right way."

"I need a top-shelf single bourbon with a splash of water, please. But only with the proper H2O."

"Got it covered." Cooper moved away and reached for a whisky bottle from the shelf.

Rex gazed around the standing-room-only bistro. Waitresses weaved and ran an obstacle course to deliver food and drinks to tables. Clearly, the entertainment tonight drew a good crowd. On a weeknight. That was good for business.

"Whisky with a splash." Cooper set a drink in front of Rex and slid it close.

"So you know my sister?" Rex lifted the glass in salute to the barkeep before taking a sip.

"Met her at a fundraising event more than a year ago. She introduced me to Nola. Best thing that ever happened."

Rex lifted an eyebrow. "How so?" A pang of something close to jealousy speared him.

"See this?" Cooper waved his hand with a flourish over the noisy bar patrons. "My sales receipts have steadily climbed every Monday and Tuesday night since Nola started singing here."

"She draws a crowd."

"Worth her weight in fine whisky." Cooper winked. "But then I guess you know that since your place hosts her on prime party nights—Friday and Saturday."

Uncertain how to answer given the predicament he faced with the imbalance of the business accounts, he lifted his glass again, nodded, and sipped.

"Man, what would it take for me to pry her away from you for one of those nights? Even if only once a month. There's got to be a way we can do some cross-promotion. You know, businesses helping each other out."

"Does she know you want to book her for the weekends?" The whisky went down smooth as Rex sipped.

"I haven't mentioned it to her yet. I'm working on my third and fourth quarter projections, but I know she's off for the summer touring, which will seriously impact my third quarter bottom line."

"The whole summer?" The news took him by surprise. Kayla hadn't mentioned it. Nola hadn't either, but it wasn't like they were actually engaging in a lot of verbal exchanges. Most of their interaction would be classified as the physical kind.

Before Cooper could answer, a voice shouted behind Rex. "Arceneau! Rex Arceneau! How the hell are you?" Emile Broussard was making his way toward the bar. Rex stood straighter and lifted his chin in acknowledgment.

"Cooper, my man, you know Rex?" Emile started to slap Rex on the back. Rex drew up his hand and blocked the gesture, then reached out and shook Emile's hand to make the interaction less awkward. His high school friend had done well for himself. Gone were the t-shirts and backward-facing caps of a rebellious teenager with a chip on his shoulder. College had schooled Emile in more things than political science. Word was he bought up a lot of property after Katrina for dirt cheap. From the looks of the cut of his charcoal gray suit and the shine on his black shoes, he'd invested well in his political image.

"We're just getting acquainted." Rex looked from one man to the other, sensing a strain between them.

"Didn't know you were back in town." Emile elbowed for more room at the bar. "Sazerac." Cooper nodded and then stepped away.

"Sorry I didn't make it to your dad's funeral."

Emile unbuttoned his suit jacket and leaned against the bar on his forearm. "Heard it was a fine send-off, Second Line and all."

"You know it." Papa had been an optimist and made a name for himself. He deserved the grand wake to celebrate his life and a proper, old-timey New Orleans funeral.

"Saw the pictures in the paper."

Rex mused about the man before him. An opportunist. It was surprising Emile hadn't shown up, for no other reason than to get his name and photograph in the paper. After all, Papa's funeral was well attended. But maybe Emile feared being upstaged by the presence of the mayor.

Cooper placed a drink in front of Emile, who nodded, dismissing the bartender, then turned back to Rex. "What brings you here?"

"Family business."

"At Harbor House?"

Rex paused. He'd thought Emile was remarking on his presence in New Orleans again. In truth, the issues of Nola Dutrey were blended with his family's business. However, his presence at Harbor House tonight was purely personal. "I've not seen Miss Nola Belle perform before. Seemed like a good time to take this opportunity."

A slow grin spread across Emile's face. He lifted an eyebrow. "No need to look twice at that piece." He leaned in close to Rex. "She's legit."

Legit? Hell yes! A dart of possessiveness stuck him again.

"I'm going to wine and dine her, then collect on my investment. I set a trap for the mouse, and now we're going to play."

Rex fought the urge to plant his fist in Emile's lecherous smile. How well were he and Nola acquainted? As anger zipped through him, Rex calmly sipped his drink. It was unreasonable to think Nola wouldn't have had relationships, but that idea tangled a knot in his gut. And she'd said she never had one with Emile.

"How is it she works at your place, and you haven't heard her sing?"

Rex ran his finger around the rim of his glass. "Timing. It's everything, ya know. But I'm here tonight."

"Checking in on your investment? You're going to lose it soon."

Rex schooled his expression to remain neutral. "You don't say." He picked up his drink and downed the remaining contents. Lifting the glass, he signaled to Cooper. "Another, please."

"Me, too," Emile hollered. "Like old times! Let's party."

Rex smiled tightly. "We've been out of college a long time."

The last time he'd been out partying with his friend, they were about to graduate from college, and he had to haul him off Bourbon Street after the police cleared the French Quarter on horseback. A near miss kept them from charges of public drunkenness and disorderly. He practically carried Emile to Arceneau's where he slept off the binge upstairs in the lounge. Papa had been more understanding than he had. The thought of a New Orleans jail cell always deterred him from making a public drunken ass of himself. After that night, their friendship became strictly professional.

"All the more reason to cut loose. I've got a deal in the making. A *big* deal. I'm celebrating," Emile shouted.

"Deal?" Rex reached for the new glass Cooper placed in front of him and sipped.

"Ever have someone backed into a corner? So backed they've got no way out but to bend to your will? I'm going to collect big time. You wait, I'll make the society page with this one."

Tipping his head to one side, Rex eyed his old school friend. "You know what they say...about counting your chickens before they hatch?"

"This is a *sure* thing."

"Tell me more."

"If I get my way, and I usually do, she won't be singing for you much longer."

Emile's testosterone-infused confidence irritated him. He contemplated his answer before responding.

Nothing worse than a salacious politician.

His old high school classmate had honestly earned the moniker of Most Likely to Screw You.

A grin spread across Emile's face. "In time it will be the old 'bought her a ring to make her my wife' story. What can I say? I'm crazy over this woman."

Nola and Emile? No. And no.

As the band began to play softly, Rex turned to his left, facing away from the man, thankful to be saved from further conversation. A voice boomed through the bistro speakers planted around the room. "All y'all having a good time so far?"

The crowd cheered. Some patrons pounded on the tables. Cooper clinked longneck beer bottles together.

As the raucousness grew, Rex held his breath waiting for Nola to appear. He was as eager to see her as he'd been to experience his first outdoor jazz festival.

"Well, your good time is now gonna be a grrreat time! Welcome, Nola Belle!"

The cheers reached a feverous pitch, which quickly settled when Nola entered on stage, appearing from behind a panel that had opened in the wall. Rex swallowed hard. Anticipation had a stranglehold on him as the sound of the music swelled.

Nola whispered out the first line of "If You Really Love Me." Waving, she said, "Hello, New Orleans."

The crowd whistled and clapped. Nola continued the song.

Rex stared. She might have been stunning in the dress in the poster, but this one set his heart pounding. He swallowed to be sure his mouth wasn't hanging open. Gazing at her, his eyes focused on the v-opening of the dress at her navel, then traveled upward, taking in the swell of her breasts, the creaminess of her skin, and the beauty of her delicate bare neck. His gaze lingered on her full red lips.

People snapped their fingers and swayed to the beat. A few stood up and danced. The brightness of the music belied the undertone of the lyrics Stevie Wonder had made famous.

For a brief second, Rex caught Nola's gaze. Her eyes widened slightly, but she continued singing, feeding the audience with her voice and seductive presence.

The lyrics captivated him. He understood them in a completely new light.

When she got to the line about playing around,

Emile thumped him on the back.

"Remember that line. I'll tell you something confidential later."

The negative energy stirring with Emile's words had Rex draining his glass and refocusing his attention to the beauty on stage.

Nola performed like the pro he expected. Her star quality was more alluring than he'd realized. Maybe that's why Papa paid her double. If the restaurant didn't have the customer draw created by Nola on the weekends, maybe weekend receipts would have plunged the bottom line deeper into the red.

Had Nola had any sort of intimate relationship with his father? Any which way he tried to conjure an image of her with Papa nothing came. Whatever the reason for the overpayment to Nola, it couldn't have had anything to do with a sordid affair. Could it? There had to be a reasonable explanation. But to learn it, he needed to talk to her. Now wasn't the right time. Her in that dress, singing that song to him—she had sung it to him, right?—made him want to strut backstage and tell her he loved...making love to her. He imagined taking her home with him and seducing her there. Maybe he should call Marquis to pick them up—they'd use the privacy partition in the limo and begin foreplay while crossing the city.

Flexing his hands, Rex ached to touch her.

After several songs, Nola took a break. Rex called Cooper over. "I'd like to send a drink back to Miss Nola. What's her cocktail of choice?"

"Tea."

"No, I said, cocktail."

"She doesn't drink alcohol during work. Won't.

Too bad. I'd make a fortune if she accepted a beverage from every person who wanted to buy her one."

"Then, will you send her tea with my compliments?"

"Already got it covered. Part of her contract."

"Any chance I can get backstage to see her?" Rex considered sliding a big tip across the counter at Cooper.

"Naw." He shook his head. "She doesn't see anyone during her sets. She'll be around afterward. We keep copies of her CDs. She'll autograph one if you buy it."

Rex nodded. "Got it."

Unable to resist the pull of Nola, Rex patted Emile on the back. "I'll be back in a few." Heading toward the men's room, he made a detour to peek inside the kitchen. Aromas of oysters in the deep fryer and gumbo on the stove stirred his senses, though food was the last thing on his mind. Based on his calculations, to reach the room behind the stage where Nola was relaxing, he had to make it across to the other side of the kitchen.

"Can I help you?" An approaching busboy toting a garbage can and entering through the back door brought in a rush of night air.

"Heyyyy. Back door to waiting lounge?" Swaying slightly, Rex palmed the kid twenty bucks and blinked back a haze—a gift from fine whisky starting to kick in.

"Sure. Go through here." The kid pointed to the door from which he'd just entered. "Go left. The double doors on the side lead to the room you want."

"Good." Rex grinned.

The kid laughed and stuffed the bill in his pocket.

Rex made his way back to the bar, dodging servers

with trays of drinks. Emile stood near a table chatting up a group of women who looked to be on a girls' night out. Maybe they would keep him occupied. When Emile touched the arm of one woman, she giggled and fluttered her eyes. Rex hoped his friend would grab a seat with the group and leave him in peace.

With a whisky buzz humming perfectly through his body, Rex checked his watch. Nola had another hour-long set, however, he intended to be waiting for her when she walked backstage. A few fans might be disappointed, but no autographs from Nola Belle. He planned to whisk her away for a night he hoped she'd never forget.

Smiling, he flagged Cooper down. "One more."

The band started their intro for the second set, and Emile returned to the bar. Rex hoped the music would dissuade further conversation.

Soon Nola sang. Sexy. Sultry. Singing to him. Her set list was a walk-through of the top love songs of all time. Was she telling him something? Could she have real feelings for him? Why else would she choose those songs on this night?

"Thank you for the fun," Nola said, as the end of the hour neared. "This is my last song."

"No!" was the resounding cry from the crowd.

She held up a finger and began to sing. "I Will Always Love You" quieted the crowd.

Rex turned when Emile slapped him on the back. The half-closed eyes and staggering stance clued him in to his old friend's condition. "You're drunk."

"Not yet. But headed there. Confidentially." Emile slurred his words. "I got her dangling by a string."

"Her?" He pointed to Nola working the crowd.

"You heard me."

Narrowing his eyes, he fixed his stare on Emile. If the man thought for one second he was getting anywhere near Nola with his catfish lips and octopus hands, then he was misinformed. Rex smiled. He'd be delighted to educate Emile.

Cooper arrived a second later. Rex handed him money. "Thanks. I'm done for the night. We'll talk later about your cross-promotion ideas."

"Don't take hissss money. Put it on myyy tab," Emile ordered the bartender.

Cooper rolled his eyes and walked away without responding.

"Not necessary," Rex said. Then he pulled out his phone and texted Marquis with instructions on what time and where to pick him up.

Emile faced the bar, both of his hands wrapped around the glass in front of him. He bumped Rex with his elbow, and Rex cut his glance back to the man. "*I* knowwww what you think of me. But you don't know shit. I'm tellin' you, I *got* it going on." Emil slid his hand to his groin and cupped himself. "She can't resist me. I'm balls deep. I got the right mix to seduce that little singing bee. And timing is right on Saturday night."

Fury hit Rex. At least on Saturday night, Nola would be at Arceneau's, and he could protect her. Emile didn't know it yet, but he'd already crossed the threshold at the restaurant for the very last time. The man was barred from returning ever again.

"Hey, Cooper! Sorry, man," Rex said. He reached for a bar towel, folded it, then grabbed Emile's glass and turned it upside down on the towel. "You've had enough to drink. Sober up."

"Hey!" Emile turned and swung at him.

Rex blocked the punch and slammed his fist into Emile's gut. "Stay away from Nola. Or I will rain a pile of shit on your head. You heard me, yeah?"

The crowd applauded as Nola took her final bow. Rex clapped, too. Apparently, no one took notice of his exchange with Emile at the bar, though Nola's gaze widened when she cut her eyes in his direction.

With Emile bent over and clutching the bar to stay upright, Rex stalked to the back door, shoved it open, and walked to the double doors on the side. As Nola entered the waiting room behind the stage, Rex walked in.

"You're not supposed to be back here," she said.

To be so close and not touch her was impossible. He closed the distance between them and pulled her into his embrace. "Your chariot awaits. I'm taking you home with me," he whispered, running his hands down her arms. He tried to link fingers with her, but she pulled away.

"You're drunk?" Nola frowned.

"No. I've had a few. Miss Nola Belle, I promise you I'm in complete control of my faculties." There was no offering the same promise about other parts of his anatomy. She in that dress ignited a fire that had been smoldering all evening. His fingers itched to slide beneath the fabric of her top and cup her firm breasts while he kissed her breathless.

Ding.

"I'll bet that's our ride." Rex checked his phone. "Limo waiting out front now. Let's go."

"I can't—"

Rex gently rubbed a strand of her long hair between his fingers. "I want to touch you in so many places...but not here."

He searched her face. It was as though she were part of a hazy dream. He took another step closer. Lifting her chin, he pressed his lips to hers again and wrapped one arm around her back closing the space between them. Breast to chest. He slid his hand lower to the small of her back. Ground against her. It took every ounce of control to not drop his pants and lift her dress to satisfy himself like a lust-filled high schooler. Maybe he was no better than Emile after all.

Nola wrapped her arms around his neck. "You're a dangerous man, Rex Arceneau." Her breath caressed his ear. She rocked her pelvis against his hardness. "Let's get that limo."

He tugged on her hand, leading her beyond the doors of the bistro and to the waiting car.

Marquis climbed out.

"You said it was an emergency, so I came. But you gotta ride up front. Got a contingent of Japanese businessmen in the back."

Nola stepped away from him and whispered something to Marquis. Then he ushered them around the car, helping Nola into the front passenger seat. Rex slid in next to her to the cheers from Marquis' other passengers. Obviously, they'd consumed plenty to drink. They were singing in a language he could only assume was Japanese.

Nola pushed a button, and the partition window between the front seat and the back rolled up.

"I had imagined doing just that," Rex grumbled. Reality marred his dream.

"I have customers and fans to see. Marquis is going to take you home now." Nola slid out of the limo on the driver's side, and Marquis slid in, blocking Rex from reaching for her.

Before he could shake off the haze clouding his mind, Marquis pulled away from the curb. "Buckle up, man. You're in for a bumpy ride."

"What?" Rex fumbled with his seatbelt. "Wait. Nola."

"I'm going to restate the obvious. You've got problems ahead."

"What the hell are you talking about?"

"What you want…you don't have a clue how to get. She's a conundrum, that one. And you're in for a two-pronged attack."

"I know you think you're speaking English, but it's sure coming out like Japanese. Straight up, what?"

"She's going back inside to make nice to Emile for what you did."

"Turn around. Right now!"

"Sorry, man. I can't let you ruin things for her. She's got a deal in the making with Emile that's critically important to what she's doing with her band. You screw it up for her, she'd cut your heart out— figuratively speaking, of course."

"What you're saying is that any which way I turn, I'm screwed?"

"You do understand." Marquis chuckled.

"Pull over," Rex shouted.

"You're drunk. I'm taking you home."

"Unless you got a clean pair of pants in here somewhere, I'm telling you—pull over. I'm going to be sick."

A little while later, Marquis pulled up in front of the Garden District house.

"You can bring your Japanese friends in to see a historic New Orleans home and party. I'm sure the bar is stocked. The tour is free."

"Nope. We're going to the burlesque show on Chartres, then back to their hotel. But I'll see you after that."

"Don't bother. I don't need a babysitter." Rex opened the door and climbed out. The dark house loomed before him more like a crypt than a home. In his mind's eye, he imagined Nola waiting at the door to welcome him home to warm and inviting surroundings. He pictured an entire life with her. They'd be the toast of the town. Together, they'd open up a club where she could sing as the headliner, and they'd also showcase new talent. The movie playing in his head went so far as to show them riding on a Mardi Gras float with two children. Theirs. But the only way that dream could come true meant he had to discover the right path to Nola's heart.

"Man, you okay? Like I said, I got a date with your sister tonight, and then in the morning, she's promised to make me breakfast." The trumpet player turned limo driver smiled showing all his pearly whites.

"Fuck you, Marquis."

"No, man. I think it's you that's fucked." Marquis laughed and drove away.

Rex unlatched the gate, trudged up the steps to the front gallery, and sat in a chair, leaning his head back. He resisted entering the house. Inside, he sensed the energy of his mother, but more importantly, the absence of Nola Dutrey in his life.

Chapter 14

After sending Rex off with Marquis, Nola snuck around back to the entrance of the kitchen and waved a dishwasher over. "Buddy, will you grab Cooper and tell him I need to talk with him?"

The kid left.

Cooper returned. "Make it quick. We need two people on the bar right now."

"Is Emile Broussard still out there?"

"Yeah. But I just called him a cab. I don't know what happened. He doubled over in pain. Says he's fine now, but maybe I should call an ambulance for him."

Nola shook her head. "Please, just get him out of here. Otherwise, I can't go out there. I'm certain he wants to talk with me...but I'm not yet prepared for that conversation." She couldn't admit to Cooper that she'd witnessed the assault. Something about Rex's movement had caught her eye. When he landed the punch, she had an unobstructed line of sight.

"What's going on? What do you know?"

Nola hoped her poker face worked. "He wants to talk to me about...a charity fundraiser."

Cooper, a very principled businessman, would insist on calling the police if he knew Rex threw the first punch. He maintained a strict image for Harbor House and even the most well-dressed and moneyed patrons were expected to behave. She had to remain silent to protect Rex despite the fact that in their personal lives they were circling around and around like a tropical storm forming in the Gulf. Emile couldn't use her as a witness if he pressed charges. Besides, he had to have instigated the problem. In all likelihood, he deserved what he got. If not for something he said to Rex, then for karmic restitution for trying to box her into a corner.

Cooper lifted an eyebrow. "I'd say talking isn't on his mind. I overheard his conversation with Rex, you know, Kayla's brother."

"Yes. I'm acquainted with him." Nola folded her hands together. She didn't dare say more. On top of everything else, she need not drag her problems with Emile and Rex into Harbor House and risk getting fired.

"Seems Emile's interest goes beyond business, more like he's enamored with you."

She pursed her lips and shook her head. "Enamored is a polite word for what he wants."

"I don't know about that... He talks big, but I've known him a while. He's kind of old-fashioned at heart."

Nola bit back a laugh. Emile was old-fashioned in the same way prostitution was an old profession. "Really?"

"Are you in any trouble?" Cooper eyed her.

"No." Maybe teetering on the edge of a cliff, but if she kept on the straight and narrow, everything had to work out. Had to.

"You'd ask for help if you were?"

She smiled brightly. "After Emile's gone, please send someone to the waiting room to let me know. I'll come out and mingle with the customers after that."

"I'm here for you." Cooper reached out and touched her arm, giving it a light tap. "Just ask." He turned to leave.

"Watch out!" someone in the kitchen hollered.

Nola stiffened and flattened herself against the wall. At the same time, a waitress carrying a tray of dirty dishes hoisted above her head tripped trying to avoid Cooper. The tray tilted. Several half-full glasses slid. Spilled over the edge. The cold contents splashed over Nola.

"Oh!" she squealed as liquid slid down her hair, face, and exposed skin of the plunging neckline of her dress. Her toes curled in her shoes.

"Sorry!" the waitress called, recovering her footing. Expertly, the woman swirled the tray from overhead to around in front of her.

Nola glanced at the contents in the dishes and smiled grimly. "Could've been worse. Gumbo would've ruined my dress."

"Let me get you a chef's coat." Cooper darted away.

One of the male kitchen staff handed Nola a clean dry towel. "I'll be happy to blot for you." He grinned wide.

She yanked it from his hand. "Thanks. I got this." Dabbing wetness, she attempted to clean up.

"Back to work, everyone." Cooper tugged on her hand, guided her into the hall, and then handed over a clean white coat. "You need to go home, but not in the same cab with Emile. It arrived. He's headed out now."

Sighing heavily, Nola said, "I'll be thankful to get home." She slid her arms through the sleeves of the coat. Cooper startled her when he stepped close and began to button it up. Silently, she watched his hands.

He pulled her into an embrace and whispered, "It's not only Emile who's been watching you from afar." He tilted her chin and placed a kiss on her forehead. "I called you a cab. If I had another bartender handy, I'd take you home." His tone held a promise of what he might do if he got her there.

Stunned, she smiled and moved away. He wasn't Rex. No 12/8 beat. No heat swirling inside her. But had the universe tilted? What triggered all this unwanted attention? Had Momma paid a voodoo woman to put a love spell around her? What other explanation could there be? She certainly hadn't changed her perfume.

"My bag and coat are in the waiting room. I'll grab them and wait for the taxi out front. Thanks for your help, Cooper."

A few minutes later, after settling in the backseat of the cab, Nola began counting. "One, two, three, four…" She forced herself to focus on the numbers in their correct order to stop her thoughts from slipping to Emile, Cooper, and most of all, Rex.

"Five. Six. Seven. If Rex hadn't been drunk…" She would've been so tempted to join him for the night. The longing in his eyes. The tenderness of his touch. The warmth of his hands on her… Her body craved what he offered. If her heart were a book, pages would be filled with anticipation about him. But her brain held up a large red octagon with bold white letters spelling STOP.

"Shake it off. Eight. Nine. Ten. Eleven. Twelve."

Finally, she was inside her apartment. She slid out of her dress and stepped into the shower. What would it be like if Rex joined her, sliding soapy hands over her body? Would he wrap her in a clean pink robe and whisk her off to bed? Make love tenderly. Exploring each other's bodies.

With the blues playing softly in the background, her heart thumped to the 12/8 rhythm whenever her thoughts turned to Rex. Longing filled her.

"Words might lie. Music never does. But like all good songs, they come to an end. What's the ending with Rex?"

****

Rex opened one eye. His head pounded. The aromas of bacon and coffee floated to him. He flinched when a giggle came next. Glancing toward the windows, he found no light seeping in around the edges of the drapes in his bedroom. The clock illuminated the time. Five thirty a.m.

Another giggle reached his ears. Then a bang of a pan.

"Shit," he groaned. "If they're having sex in the kitchen…"

Pulling on sweatpants, he padded downstairs. "Hey," he called out to announce his presence before the kitchen came into view and hoped they heard. Given the pounding in his head, he didn't dare yell. "Everyone better be decent in there."

Following the scents and sounds, he rounded the corner to the kitchen. Marquis sat at the large island counter on a barstool with his bare back to Rex. Kayla, dressed in a tank top and an apron, appeared to be wearing nothing else. She stood on the other side of the island, facing Marquis, running a pan across the gas cooktop.

"Good morning, Rex. Did we wake you?" He'd

never seen his sister chipper and glowing in the morning. She gave off a shine that was too damn bright for sunless five thirty a.m. Especially given the alcohol haze still clinging to his brain.

Marquis swiveled on the stool. Rex started to avert his eyes. Thankfully, his friend wore basketball shorts.

"Breakfast?" Marquis asked.

"Coffee," muttered Rex. He raked his fingers through his hair. "Can't you keep it down? And no sex on the countertops. I would never be able to get that image out of my mind."

Marquis' chuckle rumbled deep. "At least give us credit. We stayed in the pool house last night."

"In fact, we haven't been to bed yet. I'm off to work as soon as I finish here." Kayla beamed.

Rex nodded. "Yeah. Yeah." They had shown some consideration. Given the cacophony Kayla created making breakfast, if they'd been rockin' out last night, even with Kayla's room on the other side of the house, he would've heard them. Sound traveled easily through the mansion.

"Want to join us?" Kayla slid a mug of hot coffee his way. "I'll cook your eggs next."

"No, I'm going back to bed. Don't wake me."

As he walked away, he heard a drawer open, the sliding of metal against metal, and the drawer closed with a quick snap.

"Ohhh," Kayla giggled. "I *like* that."

Rex flinched at the *whack*.

"Like that?" Marquis asked.

Rex turned back. Kayla was slightly bent over the counter. Marquis raised a spatula and quickly brought it down, but it barely tapped its target—Kayla's ass.

173

"Hey, have some respect," Rex called out. "Wait until I'm asleep again. Or better yet, go back to the pool house."

He sipped the hot brew before climbing the stairs. Focusing so as not to spill the coffee, he ascended and went to his room, then set the mug on the nightstand. For good measure, he slammed his bedroom door, hopefully shutting out any further noises his sister and Marquis might make.

Who knew they'd hook up?

After the encounter the other night at Nola's, he thought Marquis still had his eye on her. He couldn't blame the guy for being interested in the enticing singer, but at the same time, he couldn't have the trumpet player being a player with his sister.

Maybe it was time for a man-to-man talk to clear the air. Set the tone.

He would always try to protect Kayla, despite her disdain for his interference.

Rex rolled over and closed his eyes, drifting back to sleep.

A little while later, an annoying shove woke Rex.

Kayla whispered, "You awake?"

Beside him, he felt the bed move where she sat down.

"Am now." Groggy, he didn't open his eyes. "What's the time?"

"Two thirty."

"In the morning?"

"No. It's Wednesday afternoon. I was worried. You okay? You've slept for a long time. Didn't answer my calls."

Rex swallowed as he pushed to sitting. Nola taught

band on Wednesday afternoons after school. If he put it in gear, he could make it there in time.

"Phone was turned off. Whatcha need?" His headache was down to a minor throb.

Kayla rose and went to the windows, opening the drapes. "I need to talk to you about something important. I want your decision about staying. For a year. I know I talked about buying that condo and moving. But I could be persuaded to change my mind."

"About which part?"

"I want you to stay so I can learn from you. I don't want to sell the house after all."

"Oh?"

"I want Nola and Marquis to move in here. As you said, we have plenty of room."

Rex blinked. Was he actually talking to his sister, or was this an alcohol hallucination? He and Nola under the same roof?

"You want what?"

Kayla crossed her arms over her chest. Her lips drew into a thin line. "This is my house as much as it is yours. Just like the business. If I don't have cash from my portion of the sale of the house, then I can't support Nola's band. I'm in love with Marquis. I want to live with him—but not in that cracker-box apartment of his. Seems your suggestion was a good one. Let's fill up these rooms."

"Are you crazy? What will the neighbors think?" They couldn't run a boarding house, the neighborhood wasn't zoned for that. But…on second thought, it would be perfect to have Nola living under the same roof. It would create the intimacy they needed to really connect. "Wait. Marquis? He's going to be in New

York all summer."

"Well…" Kayla sashayed back to the side of the bed and sat. "That big brother"—she poked him in the chest—"is where I want you to help, too."

"Clear up the confusion. My brain isn't functioning yet."

"I want to work in one of your New York restaurants while you work here. For the summer. So I can spend time with Marquis. Besides, how else are you going to make all the changes needed here? It'll take more than texts, emails, and phone calls."

"Kayla. You're crazy. No. No. No."

"No?"

"First"—he raised one finger—"*I* want the house. I'll buy out your share. You can buy the condo, or whatever you want. Make it a commune for all I care. Then you can help Nola. Second, I don't want a house full of roommates. Haven't had one since college. I don't care how much lust you have for the trumpet player, he isn't moving in here." He shook his head. "And third, I am not about to turn you loose in New York. If you want to learn from me, sister, it's gotta be here. Right now, though, my plan is still to return to New York."

"I can see you're hung over. I'll give you more time to think about it. I'm open to compromise. But only if you agree to not fire Nola. On Monday when the restaurant's closed, we'll have a sit-down and iron out all the details."

"Oh shit. I need to call Biloxi Trahan back."

"Why?"

"She wants us to cater her parents' anniversary party."

"Us? Oh, that's rich." Kayla laughed. "Nola's gonna love that." Chuckling, his sister left the room.

Rex hopped out of bed, reached for the mug, and sipped. "Yuck." He hated cold coffee, regardless of the current trend.

Pulling on jeans, he finished dressing. He had to make it to Nola's band practice. She was going to talk to him, damn it! He could only solve one problem at a time. Starting with the excessive payments she was receiving.

Grabbing for his phone, he looked at the list of recent calls, then pushed a button.

"Mrs. Trahan? This is Rex Arceneau."

"You have good news? Tell me you have good news. Nola talked with you, right?"

"Whoa," he laughed. "No, in fact, your sister seems to be on a mission to avoid talking to me. However, Arceneau's will be your caterer. We need to talk menu. Is now a good time?"

"My sister didn't convince you to take this job? No matter. Thank you! I already have a menu and a food list. What if I email them to you now? You could look at them, and then give me your recommendations."

"That will work. Let's talk tomorrow."

"Perfect."

"And if you don't mind, I'm headed over to see your sister now. I would like to break this good news to her."

Biloxi chuckled. "Good luck, sir. If you've got any ancient armor laying around, like a shield and a broadsword, I suggest you take them with you."

"Good to know." Rex smiled. He had the element of surprise on his side. He would disarm her if she had any objections to him catering her parents' party, with the one thing that she couldn't resist—music.

Chapter 15

Nola scooted her chair closer to the small table in her kitchen. "I'm not going to think about him. I'm not going to think about him." She bit into half of a warm croissant filled with ham and Gruyère cheese. Before taking the next bite, she slathered the top of the pastry with strawberry jam and lifted it to her mouth. A spot of jam dripped onto her blue caftan before she could catch it. Scooping it with her finger, she wiped the fruity blob on a napkin resting beside the cheese plate holding the other half of her breakfast.

In her mind, she heard Great-Grandmother Grace's admonishment over her poor table manners.

"I know, G.G. Grace, if I'd used the napkin properly, I wouldn't have a spot on my clothes." She pulled the napkin onto her lap to prevent a repeat of the mess. Too bad she couldn't do the same with Rex Arceneau. No napkin could stop the next thought of him from spilling into her brain. The man doggedly refused to leave her thoughts.

"Focus. Music. Trumpet? Marquis? Curious…" She glanced at the time displayed on the stove. No horn woke her this morning. Her reliable neighbor hadn't practiced. His first notes were usually her alarm clock during the week whenever he was in town, religious as he was about his practice time. Either he had an early call to drive…or he hadn't come home last night, but she'd wait a while before worrying too much.

Finishing her breakfast and café au lait, she headed poolside to dip her toes into the water and make use of a lounge chair in clear view of the gate—until it was time to get ready for band practice. The minute she spied Marquis, she intended to have pointed Q & A with him about Kayla. As for her friend, why had she suddenly taken to not returning phone calls?

Wednesdays were the one day of the week she had a handful of hours to relax alone. It was the only time she listened to music without picking apart a composition. Instead, she allowed her mood to guide her musical selection and enjoyed it flowing through her like gentle waves of healing water. Settling into a chaise by the pool, she adjusted her earbuds and waited for music to carry her away as though she were on a raft floating with the current down the Mississippi River.

After the first few chords, an image of Kayla popped into her mind. She held a broom. Her stern expression let everyone know she didn't barter in her kitchen—a woman in control. So very different from the lovesick woman of yesterday. Did the image have some meaning she needed to decipher?

"No. Not now. Deep breath." She practiced her yoga breathing to lessen the tension building in her neck. With each breath in and then out, torment slapped her around. Kayla, her very gifted friend, was pitiful outside the kitchen. Marquis' trumpet silent and nowhere to be found. Plus, her sister in her professional capacity as Keeper of Fleur de Lis insisted she convince Rex to cater the family party. And what about Leon? How could she convince him to join the band? His chosen path promised a definite future in and out of jail.

How could she help him? Maybe a chat with his mother? The police were a last resort. But above all, the looming payment of the lease sat at the top of the heap of her problems waving like a flag.

"Stop it. Focus on the music." Whenever she let go and the music vibrated within her, then the answers to life's problems revealed themselves. After another deep breath, she cleared her mind and pictured musical notes floating around her in the air. The warmth of the morning sun caressed her skin.

The ring of her cell phone brought her out of her bliss.

"Uhhh," she groaned, pulling her cellphone from the pocket of her dress. Emile Broussard.

"Nope. Not talking to you until *I'm* ready."

Days were counting down to the due date of the six-month lease payment. Could she put together a fundraiser in a week or two that would net enough to stop the wolf from destroying the musical house she was trying to build?

"Not a worry for today. You'll find a way. You always do. Just focus on the music." Resettling into the chair, she adjusted a small pillow behind her back, hiked the hem of the caftan to just above her knees, adjusted her sunglasses on her nose, and closed her eyes. If Marquis lifted the latch on the gate, it would wake her—if she managed to drift into a nap.

"Da. Ta. Daa." A small breath with each count to the music drained tension away. Her shoulders sagged. She started to drift off to sleep.

"We are family."

Startled by the phone ringing, Nola jerked awake.

If she didn't answer, Biloxi would keep calling or

start texting until she did.

"Yes, sister, dearest." She used her sweetest tone, hoping to defuse any bomb her sister might deliver.

"Good morning, my beautiful, talented, and oh so helpful little sister. Have you talked to Rex yet?"

Something was definitely up. Biloxi only complimented her this early in the day if she wanted something or she had bad news to deliver. Her sister practiced the "three good things for each bad" strategy of management. "About catering Momma and Daddy's party?"

"Well, that or anything else?" Biloxi's voice lilted on the *anything else* part.

Nola frowned. Something was up. "What? Just say it. What do you know?" She steeled herself for bad news.

"Why are you accusing me of something?" Her sister sounded hurt. She imagined Biloxi fluttering a hand to her chest as though to cover the wound her words had just created.

"There are problems here in Crescent City. The Big Easy is anything but. So, please get to the point." Nola sighed.

"Rex has agreed to cater the party. Be nice to him." Her sister's tone switched to authoritative—the one she used whenever projecting her role as Keeper of Fleur de Lis. "Look, I called the only other two caterers I would even consider allowing to cater here, and they're booked—no surprise. We need Rex. We, as in you and I, can't do without him for this event. It's the largest we've ever hosted at Fleur de Lis. Smooth the way with Rex, and I'll do something for you."

Nola squirmed. Why was it whenever her sister

played the "you scratch my back and I'll scratch yours" card that she was the one who ended up with claw marks?

Squeezing her eyes tight, Nola sucked on her bottom lip. She opened one eye and then the other. "What gift is it you want to bestow upon me?"

"I'll give you the money for the uniforms you need in exchange for you bringing the band to Fleur de Lis to play for the 4th of July party."

"There might not be a band by then." The words just slipped out. Her mouth was channeling thoughts before her brain was truly in proper gear. Inwardly, she groaned.

"Nola. Bridgette. Dutrey."

"Forget what I said. I'll figure it out. Talking with Rex is the least of my problems, even though I know he's going to fire me."

"Oh? So you do know about that?"

"You know?" Nola sat up, pulling on the arms of the chaise and moving the back of the chair upright. Crossing her legs into a lotus position, she gave her sister her full attention.

"He mentioned he was going to speak with you...about his need to cut back on expenses. It's not personal. But I told him you'd be devastated."

Fury burned in her chest. "He told you before he told me? And why are you sharing personal information with my boss? Telling him I'd be devastated? Why?"

"In the corporate world, what he's doing would be a restructuring of the company. You can't possibly expect him to close Arceneau's without trying to save it. What would Kayla do? Besides, you will be devastated. I know how much that job means to you."

The words echoed in her mind. *What would Kayla do?*

"Nola, you know the old saying, 'pride cometh before the fall.' Put yours aside. And I'll help you. Now, tell me, there's more to this story than uniforms. Why might there not be a band by July?"

Nola's shoulders slumped. "Because I signed a contract with a fine-print clause. Now I have to raise a year's worth of rent. I need five-thousand dollars in thirty days to pay on the community center lease, or Emile Broussard is going to lease to someone else."

"The same Emile Broussard?"

"Yes."

"Oh, my."

"And he's made it clear, that he's willing to negotiate the price."

"He didn't!"

"Are there ABBA songs in *Momma Mia! The Musical*?"

"Will you let me help you?"

"No. I'll figure it out. I have to do this on my own. Besides, if I let you help me, before long, you'll own my soul."

"Nola…"

Her sister meant well. Had been a guiding force in her life growing up, but in the last ten years, it was as though Biloxi needed to be needed. She had the rest of the family, three kids and a husband who depended on her. The more needed she felt, the better she liked it. Nola refused to burden her sister with problems.

When the latch to the gate clicked, Nola looked up. "Biloxi, don't lecture me. I need to go. I have other business to attend to."

"Wait. What's more important than your band? Let's think of something. Two brains are better than one."

Marquis danced through the gate opening and tossed a bowler hat around like he was Bob Fosse. "This business isn't more important, just equally important. Talk with you later." She ended the call, then shouted to capture the trumpet player's attention. "Hey there, Mister Horn Man, what's got you dancin' a number this morning?"

A wide smile spread across his face. He tossed the hat into the air, did a side step and slide, then caught the hat, flipping it onto his head. "A woman, of course. Got to go. Have to get ready for work. I'm already late."

Nola's stomach dropped. Kayla had the worst case of the wants over a man that she'd ever seen. How would she take the news that Marquis had another woman in his life? Could the day get any worse?

Her phone beeped. A new voicemail message. She listened.

"Nola. Emile here. Meet me for dinner *tonight*. Arceneau's. Seven thirty. You know what this is about."

Her stomach clenched. Mr. Unsavory was pulling all the strings. His "or-else" threat rang loud and clear.

****

Dressed in jeans and a chambray shirt, hopefully appearing casual, relaxed, and...the opposite of the "suit" she'd accused him of being, Rex exited the streetcar and walked toward the community center. He smiled and nodded at the few who passed, mostly kids on their way home from school.

His heart pumped with anticipation. Would she be

pleasantly surprised, or throw him out?

A half block ahead, he spied a kid on the bike. Looked to be the bigger of the two who tried to mug Nola. The kid moved closer toward him. He was the one. Their gazes locked. The boy, defiant in his stare, narrowed his eyes. Rex gave a little nod. "Hey," he called out. "Stop for a minute. Let's talk."

The kid rode closer, then past him, staring him down the whole time.

"Wait," he shouted. "I want to talk with you about a job." He turned around to determine if his comment sparked any interest.

The boy came back in his direction. "What, man? You say somethin' to me?"

Rex put down his trumpet case and reached for his wallet. The boy stopped about ten feet away, one foot on a pedal, poised to take off again.

"How old are you?"

"None of your biz."

"Here. My business card. If you're fourteen and want a paying job at my restaurant, you have to join Miss Nola's band. And you must apologize to her. You could've hurt her."

"This a trap?" The boy leaned on the handlebars and looked up. Wariness in his eyes. "I didn't try to mug nobody."

"Yeah, sure. Tell that lie to your priest or your preacher." He pointed to the boy and then to himself. "You and I know differently. Anyway, those are your options."

"Man, I don't have to do anything I don't wanna."

"And I don't have to contact the police, but I will."

The kid scowled. "You can't tell the cops squat.

You don't know it was me."

Rex smiled. "I do. And Miss Nola does, too. She kept me from calling the police to begin with. She sees something in your scrawny ass. If she sees it, it must be there. What have you got to lose? A job that pays money, friends in the band, and no time in juvie."

Rex shoved the card at the boy again. "Take it. You have until Friday. Show up for band practice, then at the restaurant."

Twisting his mouth to one side, the boy yanked the card from Rex and stuck it in his back pocket. "I'll think on it."

"You do that, Leon."

Surprise widened the boy's eyes. A glimmer of understanding appeared to take hold—Leon was no longer a nameless face in the crowd.

"I'll find you. The cops will find you. So do yourself a favor. Make a smart decision." Rex picked up his trumpet case, turned, and continued in the direction of his destination—the community center and Nola's band.

Arriving about fifteen minutes into the start time for rehearsals, he lingered near the door. The group belted out the notes for "Big Chief."

"Okay. It's getting better. How about we try it again?" He overheard Nola pause, and he took that moment to enter.

The metal door creaked as he opened it. Smiling wide, he crossed the threshold, his palms starting to sweat.

At least thirty pairs of eyes turned to him. He stopped. Nola turned slowly. Her hair hung loose in big waves. She licked her lips as her brow furrowed. A soft blue sweater and black skirt added to her feminine appeal. He imagined dancing with her, dipping her back, and then carrying her off to bed. Their gazes met. His heart skipped a beat. "Wondered if I could audition? I brought my trumpet."

Nola's eyes widened. Her mouth opened, then closed.

Say "yes," Nola. Say "yes."

He willed his thoughts to her. Her eyes widened a bit more. Had she heard him? Or had she read the will of his energy and understood his desire?

"Whatcha got, dude?" one of the students called out, breaking the intensity of the silence.

Rex crossed to the middle of the room, stood next to Nola, and bowed to her. Frowning, she crossed her arms over her chest and then stepped out of the way, her lips in a pout. Fully aware he'd captured everyone's attention, he opened his case, pulled out his trumpet, and lifted it over his head. "Horn, dude."

"No, man"—the kid shook his head—"I mean what kinda chops you got?"

"Show us," a few students taunted. "Show, not tell."

Rex glanced at the woman he wanted to impress. Nola remained rooted a step away. It was as if dock lines secured her ankles in place. She looked him over as though she weren't certain what she was seeing. He wondered which surprised her more—his casual appearance or his instrument.

Cocking his head to one side, he waited for approval.

"Let's hear him, Miss Nola," a drummer insisted, his voice full of doubt.

His eyes focused on Nola. He waited. He wasn't there to hijack her practice, but showing up was the only way to ensure she'd talk with him. And if he started the dialogue off with music, a language they both loved, he might be able to segue into the issues needing clarifying—her job at Arceneau's and unignorably, the relationship budding between them.

After a moment more, she forced a half smile. Her head moved slightly. She lifted her hands, palms up, gesturing that he had command of the group.

Rex took a deep breath and blew it out, then began to play "The Look of Love."

By the fourth note, she sank into the nearest chair, nearly collapsing. Closing her eyes, her head swayed to the flow of his clean, clear sounds. She lifted her hands upward as though in praise. The serene beauty of her face transfixed him—the music utterly captured her, and she allowed it to carry her away. Her full lips parted slightly. She breathed in deeply, as though breathing in the notes. He wanted to continue playing the song just to watch the changing expressions of her lovely face. But more than that, he wanted a private moment alone to kiss those lips and feel her body move against his.

Rex finished the last note and lowered his trumpet. Nola opened her eyes. For a brief moment, he witnessed love…for the song or his playing? Would she ever look at him with that same dreamy expression? A definite look of love.

"Miss Nola. He's the one!"

"What?" She pushed up from the chair, but held on to the back for support as if her legs were wobbly.

"He's the one!" another student echoed.

Rex scanned the faces, looking for hints of familiar ones.

"Remember? We told you about the guy who tucked paper into my hand? The one that gave us a hundred dollars when we played on the street corner, you know, on Saturday night."

Nola directed her stare at Rex.

"You were the one who paid them to play in the French Quarter?"

He shrugged. "Guilty."

"Oh, goodness!" She ran to him and planted a kiss on his lips. "They donated the entire amount to the band fund. You made a big impression on them."

"It takes courage to play on the street. People pass by. Half of them don't bother to stop. Two-thirds of those that do, don't tip. I wanted to encourage them to keep up the hard work."

Nola's eyes widened, lit with a blaze. Her excitement was palpable. He wanted to reach out and harness a bit for himself, like reaching into a candy jar and grabbing a coveted piece of chocolate. Mesmerized, he swayed, taking a half step closer to her.

A coy smile spread across her face. She pushed on his chest. "Rex Arceneau, I have a deal for you. And you can't say 'no.' Your love of music won't let you."

Rex nodded, not certain what he was agreeing to, other than falling more in love with her.

Chapter 16

"You, mister, grab a chair and take a seat over there." Nola pointed to the brass section of the band. "Keep up. We'll give you a try for today, but it doesn't mean you're in the band."

"Fair enough." Rex bowed slightly and sat.

"We'll talk later. Right now, focus on the music. Practice and discipline are what will make you great." Nola lifted the baton. "Again, 'Big Chief,' please."

Too frequently, she cut her gaze to him. Did the students notice? Did he? Her foot, tapping to the beat, wanted to take a step closer. Heck, her feet wanted to carry her across the room to him. He'd set her heart pumping. She could barely stand still. Her lips wanted to taste his. A fluttering deep in her core spread a warmth over her. Her arms wanted to wrap around his neck. Her body wanted to—

"Miss Nola?" One of the girls waved her hand frantically.

Shaking her head to clear her meandering thoughts, she smiled and lowered her baton. "Yes?"

"Leon's here." The girl pointed to the door. "He just poked his head inside. I can still see him through the crack. He left the door open."

Nola went to the door and opened it. Looking around, she saw only adults on the sidewalk. No kid. No bicycle. Definitely no Leon. "Guess he's gone. I sure hope one of y'all can convince him to join us."

The drummer in the back smacked his fist into his palm. "I can convince him. But Miss Nola, *why* do you want him? He's big, but really a turd-muffin."

A few of the students sucked in a gasping breath. Name-calling and foul language were verboten in the band.

Drawing in a long breath, she pondered, wanting to choose her words carefully. Whatever she said could find its way back to Leon, and also, end up as dinner conversation at any one of her students' homes tonight. If her intentions were misinterpreted, rumors could fly. The last thing she wanted was a barrage of concerned-parent phone calls. Leon wasn't especially liked in the neighborhood. Blamed for many things, most of which she was certain were of his making, but probably some blame heaped on him wasn't his to claim.

"Miss Nola believes in all of you." Rex stood and scanned the room. "Music is part of our heritage, for everyone in New Orleans. The more instruments in the band, the bigger the sound, right?"

"Yes!" most of the students cheered.

"Music is a path that can open up many opportunities. Miss Nola hopes Leon will hop on the bandwagon."

Nola laughed. "Oh, that's a bad pun, but still true." How sweet that Rex would jump in and help. But she didn't need it. "Leon is a member of our community, and as such, he has every right to be a part of the band."

"But he can't play."

"How do you know?" Nola asked.

"Cuz he tried when he was five. He's my cousin. It sounded awful!"

"Well...let's be honest"—Nola raise a finger—"many of you weren't so great when we started, but with decent instruments and lots of practice, y'all are sounding really good. It can be the same for him. And the bigger the band the better sound we'll have come time to parade. I have several instruments available in storage that could still use a student's love."

A few of the kids grumbled. A change of subject was needed. She wanted everyone to leave practice on a high note. "How about we jam? Lead drummer, give us a beat."

The boy on the drums *tat tat tatted* with his drumsticks.

"Now all y'all find your groove and let those notes fly."

The cacophony was deafening, but her students loved the free rein. Some stood and rocked out. A few swayed to the left and right while they played. The freedom sparked something magical in them, like demanding they color outside the lines.

As notes swirled, ideas twirled in Nola's mind. She tried to focus on the music as the band played, but worry about the looming monetary problems blazed like a red flashing Open-All-Night sign. A benefit concert to raise money? Then no need to ask her sister for help with a fundraiser. Nola smiled. If she could book the Reunion Shelter at City Park, it could hold a thousand guests, and she could have a jam session. Kayla could do the hors d'oeuvres. Marquis and Rex could be dueling trumpets. The band could show off the three tunes...and a few of the individual students had repertoires she could draw upon. She could convince some local musicians to come and jam—and she'd be there to collect donations.

Excitement bounced through her, sending waves of tingling anticipation. All she needed was a venue. If not City Park, there had to be a place. The musicians were a given. A few calls to the local radio stations, and maybe she could get one of the TV stations interested in covering the event. Also, flyers in the windows of every shop that would post them to spread the word.

I can do this!

Hope surged, blooming into heady confidence. With a little help from her friends, she could make it work.

As the jam session came to a close with a few errant notes from a trumpet and trombone, the drummer beat on the cymbals signaling the end.

"Okay. Okay." She laughed. "That's all for today. See all y'all on Friday." She stood at the door and hugged or patted each kid as they left. Smiles on their faces recharged her as though she were a storage battery and they electricity.

After the last child departed, she closed the door, locked it, and flicked off the main overhead lights. Only the spotlight over the big drum set shone. Rex had his back to her, his trumpet case open, and he was tucking his instrument into place.

"Ah, Mr. Trumpet Man…"

He clicked the case closed and turned to her. "Yes, Teacher."

She took a step toward him. He stepped closer to her. Together they closed the distance between them. He reached for her hand and kissed it, then placed it on his shoulder, swaying as though music played. She wondered if he could hear her heart pounding and the music her heart danced to whenever she laid eyes on him. Lacing his fingers with hers, he captured her other hand and began to hum "The Look of Love."

Her knees weakened. She nearly melted. But he held her secure within his arms. Then he angled his head and brought his lips close to hers. She rose on her toes. The urgent need to kiss him took over. Rex tenderly cupped her face. Dizzy, she blinked. It was as though he were spinning her around, like they danced a waltz, yet they stood still.

"You smell so good. You taste even better." Rex rested his forehead against hers.

Wanting to connect deeper, she wrapped her arms around him. The warmth from his body seeped into hers. Hungrily, she captured his mouth again. His hands floated down her arms, and she wanted his touch on all her skin. The connection with this man didn't disappoint. Sliding his hands under her sweater, he caressed her back.

"Hmmm," she murmured. "Let me show you my stash of instruments."

His wicked grin set her pulse skittering.

She led him to a short hallway at the back of the room that led to the door of a storage closet. A long narrow room, barely wide enough for one person, with shelves on one side holding the last few instruments, and a bare light bulb on the ceiling. Pulling the door mostly closed, open enough only to allow a bit of light to filter in, she faced him in the constrained quarters.

"Come here." His voice was low and gravelly. He tugged her closer until they were touching.

The deepest, most feminine part of her core contracted with want. Heated desire brought a flush to her cheeks. An ache bloomed. She wanted him. Craved him. She waited for a sign from him that he wanted her, too.

Cupping her jaw with both his hands, he claimed her lips once more with the hunger of a starving man. Urgently, she reached for his shirt and pulled the tail from his pants. Stroked her hands over his chest. The magnetic current running between them made her daring. Hugging Rex, she pressed her chest to him and slid her hands down his sides feeling the muscles of his torso.

"Fair play," he murmured. His hand slid beneath her sweater. Reaching behind her, he unhooked her bra and repeated the tender touches she'd given him. Gently, he massaged her breasts, then cupped them, rubbing his thumbs across puckering nubs. Her skin tingled. Her heart was giddy with want. He lifted her sweater and captured her breast in his mouth. She nearly crumpled. He caught her and backed her two steps against the wall. It kept her from puddling onto the floor.

"Fair play," she whispered in his ear, then licked there, as she reached for the button on his jeans.

He peppered her face with kisses, then sucked on her bottom lip. "Woman," he growled. "I want you."

Her breath hitched. Nodding, she lowered his pants. Then rising, she grasped his hardness and stroked, marveling at the beauty of his erect maleness. His expression went slack, his lips parted. He arched back slightly and moaned. A tone so sensually arousing she couldn't tug off her panties fast enough.

On her tiptoes, she melted against him, her arms circling his neck. Warm hands cupped her butt and hoisted her upward. With a tiny adjustment, he fitted her slowly and expertly on his hardness. Impatient, she wiggled a bit to allow for his full entry and contracted around his erection, He groaned. She contracted again.

In the confined space, she leaned backward, her upper back resting against the wall. Rex held her securely. He braced against the shelving for support. The space between them allowed her to catch his every expression. He slightly bent his knees. Thrust forward. She licked her lips, waiting for his next move.

"Fair play," he murmured, his gaze fixed on hers. He tweaked her breast, and she arched. Wetness seeped as she contracted around him again, relishing in the pleasure that gave him. He thrust his pelvis again. Then again. When she closed her eyes and moaned a sigh, Rex continued with a steady rhythm. Her aching desire skyrocketed. Pleasure enveloped her as she undulated her pelvis against him.

As though sensing her need, he increased the pace of his movements in and out. Quicker. Harder. The tension in her core twisted and spread throughout her body with luscious exhilaration. She wanted to reach for him, but that would break his pace. Instead, she braced her arms against the wall. To alter the thrill of the ride would be criminal.

The sound of rushing blood filled her ears. Her breath quickened. The first fissure of bliss appeared. She swallowed hard. Shivers of pleasure cascaded.

"You win!" She closed her eyes and watched heaven burst into sparkling lights with shooting stars. It was as though the essence of her being shot upward and rapture claimed her. Her breath came in short pants. She savored the thrill washing through her body.

A fuzziness filled her brain. She was barely aware of Rex holding her hips, her butt resting on top of his thighs. His thrusts slowed, but grew more powerful. With each movement he made, she gripped him tighter with her inner muscles, holding on to him and the euphoria he produced within her.

She floated as though on the wings of a bird, then descended gently. Lifting her chin, she gazed at Rex, relaxing into a love-induced haze.

****

Rex thrust deep inside her again as the power of his orgasm hit him. Shot him upward. Mountaintop high. His body stiffened. He held her securely in place.

"Ohhh…" The sound of his voice broke through the trance of lovemaking with Nola. Elation drenched him. Slowly he smiled and gazed at her through heavy-lidded eyes. No woman every looked so lovely with her long hair spilling around her, sweater askew, and skirt bunched above the swell of her gorgeous hips.

She wrapped her legs around his waist, and he bounced her for a last couple of short thrusts. Never had a woman consumed him the way she did. Shit. They were in a closet pounding away at each other like high school kids. But he wouldn't change it for the world. As traditional as she appeared on the outside, she possessed a naughty side. He wanted to explore it with her. She was like praline whipped cream on top of sweet potato pecan pie making a luscious dessert extraordinarily tasty. He would never order pie again and not think of her.

As Nola loosened her legs from around him, Rex set her on her feet. They hadn't exchanged many words, but something much deeper than words bound them together. She looked up at him with her eyes wide and glowing. Cheeks still flushed. Reaching for him, she cupped his jaw and planted a delicate kiss on his lips. "And I thought I wanted to play cowgirl with you. I think I liked the teacher-thing even better." Her mouth curved into a coy grin.

Her touch. Her lips. Her words. His heart quickened again. "If you liked that, Madame, I've got some other ideas in mind." He winked.

Turning her head bashfully and shrugging her shoulders, she said, "Trumpet man, you take my breath away."

With his heart thudding in his chest, he swelled with a new possessiveness. He wanted more than games to stimulate their erotic side and satisfy their lust. Whether his brain liked it or not, his heart was involved for the long haul. A satisfying realization took hold. He truly loved her. All of her.

He pulled up his pants and straightened his clothes.

"Here, let me." He hooked her bra back in place. She smoothed her skirt, adjusted her sweater, and plucked her panties from the shelf behind him. She folded them and slid them into her skirt pocket. He schooled his expression to nonchalance. He might not have Superman's x-ray vision, but his imagination was keen.

"Nola." He stroked her cheek with the back of his fingers, reveling in the sensations of the connection they shared. He pulled her into a hug and whispered, "There isn't another man in your life who means something serious to you, is there?"

She chuckled. "I'm not *that* kind of girl, Mr. Arceneau."

"What kind is that?"

"To be committed to one and have sex with another."

Her words made his heart thud quicker. Then the question swirling in his mind spilled out. "Why is there no one special in your life? To love you. To cherish you. To share the wonders of lovemaking with you."

She sighed. "My family says I'm too picky. Part of me is rather old-fashioned. I don't do this with just anyone you know." She raised her eyebrows. "Sex isn't a recreational hobby or a workout to me."

Pride swelled in his chest. Nola Belle had picked him! A flood of thoughts washed over the joy thrumming through his body. He wanted her in New York with him. A record deal. That could ensure she'd be there for a while. Once he got everything set up, he'd create a romantic evening and share the good news with her.

She took his hand. "Mr. Arceneau, do you have plans for dinner? I know a place nearby—in walking distance—with a table for two."

"I'm hungry, Miss Dutrey, but I need more than food to satiate my cravings."

"Well…" She chuckled. "I think the place I have in mind will be able to accommodate *all* of your appetites."

"Hmm," he growled, sniffing at her. "Yes, I think you're right. Let's go." He tugged her from the room.

****

Giddy, she looked down at her feet to make sure they were touching the ground as she walked with her fingers laced with Rex's. He carried his trumpet case in his other hand. She imagined him standing on the landing outside her apartment with Marquis in the moonlight serenading her and Kayla while they lounged with drinks by the pool. Watching an accomplished musician use his instrument expertly ranked high, maybe only a notch below love, honor, and family. She giggled. Rex had proved to be an expert with his manly instrument, too. Her insides clenched in anticipation of the appetizer she planned for him when she got him in her bed.

Together they raced up the stairs. Rex took her keys from her trembling hand and opened the door.

"Welcome to my home. Again." She pulled him across the threshold. "There's the table for two. I'll call the butler and have him bring dinner round—he works part-time at The House of Peking because I can't afford him but once a week." She moved the plant off the table, but left the curtains open to capture the last rays of the day. The pre-dusk light cast a beautiful golden glow in her apartment.

Rex placed his trumpet case behind the chair, out of the way, in the living room, and stood beside it.

Breathless, she scrutinized him from nearly ten feet away. A fluttering began in her belly. She was no better than a crazed kid in a candy store on a mission to grab a sugar high—posthaste.

"Is something wrong?" Rex asked.

"Oh, no. I assure you *nothing* is wrong." She backed and kicked the front door closed. Putting her finger to her bottom lip, she surveyed him from top to bottom, almost wishing he'd worn a suit. Disrobing him, article by article of clothing, created a tantalizing image in her mind.

This was her turf, and she intended to take control.

From the moment she'd laid eyes on him and heard that fateful bluesy 12/8 beat, her resistance to him had been futile. The best course of action was to go with the flow. Lordy, Rex Arceneau gave her hedonistic fantasies.

She reached for the remote and turned on a CD. Chris Botti played "The Look of Love." With half-hooded eyes, she gazed at Rex and swayed to the music.

When she kicked off the first shoe, it landed five feet away in the efficiency kitchen, hitting the refrigerator with a thud.

Rex raised an eyebrow as though concerned.

"Oops." She giggled. The second shoe followed the first.

On her tiptoes, rocking her hips in a figure eight like she'd been taught in a long-ago hula class, panty-less, she reached for the bottom of her sweater. Continuing her dance, she lifted the garment over her head and tossed it at Rex.

He caught it. This time, he raised both eyebrows.

With only her bra and skirt on, she stepped and thrust her hips, dancing in a circle in place. He licked his lips. She motioned with her finger for him to come closer. She held up her hand after he crossed the room to stand before her. They remained an arm's distance apart.

She leaned and whispered, "I want to ask you a favor."

"You name it. You got it." His eyes widened.

"Don't be too hasty. You don't know what I desire."

"Well, short of it involving blood, I'll do anything

for you right now."

The music continued and Nola danced, undulating her hips to the sounds floating around them. His manly arousal made her smile.

"You promise you won't disappoint me?"

"Not if it's within my control." His words came out in a rush.

"Take your jeans off."

Quickly, he disposed of them.

She pulled on his shirt, then began to unbutton it. When it hung open, she pressed herself to him. He wrapped his arms and the loose ends of his shirt around her.

"Gorgeous, name what you want. After that, I'm taking control. You're my fantasy."

She undid her skirt and let it fall to the floor, then kicked it out of the way. His mouth gaped. His eyes widened.

Wiggling, bent forward, her hands on the edge of the table for support, her butt pressed against his straining erection.

"You fantasize about this?"

A guttural groan sounded behind her. He bumped her from behind. She giggled. "Well, Mr. Arceneau. I want you to do a fundraiser with me. Dueling trumpets with Marquis and a jam session with local musicians. All to raise money for my band."

"Yes!" He ground himself against her butt.

Tat. Tat. "Well, hello!" a voice sounded from outside the window. Nola looked up into Emile Broussard's eyes. His wide grin nearly hid the rest of his face. She gasped. Squeezing her eyes shut, she opened them. He leered back.

"Shit," Rex growled.

Nola turned quickly to face Rex, who moved her aside and closed the curtains.

"Knock. Knock." Emile Broussard pounded on her door.

Nola froze. Rex removed his shirt and tossed it at her. She caught it. He grabbed for his jeans and slid into them.

"Hello! Hello!" Shouts continued from the other side of her door.

Still in shock, Nola remained rooted. Rex crossed the room, opened the front door, and leaned in the opening, blocking Emile from entering. Nola caught a peek of him. He appeared like a jack-in-the-box trying to dodge the barrier of Rex's torso and catch a peek inside her apartment.

"I was certainly misinformed," Emile snarled. "Nola, you're going to want to talk with me! We can make this a public scene or conduct business professionally and quietly inside."

"Professionally? You want professional?" Rex asked. "Then make an appointment, and she'll come to your office for a meeting. We're otherwise engaged right now."

"Fuck you. Arceneau. Take your ass back to New York. I'm here to talk with Miss Dutrey. You're the one impeding her business concerns."

Nola ran to her bedroom and pulled on a robe. Once at the front door, she tapped Rex's shoulder. "Please let him in and let me deal with this once and for all." She hadn't returned Emile's call about dinner— this was payback for that?

Rex raised one eyebrow. Clearly, he was disgusted.

How funny a twitch of the same eye could convey such different meanings in a short span of time. She almost laughed about the contrasts of his reaction, but he stepped aside to allow Emile to enter.

"I went by the community center, but you'd already gone," Emile snapped.

Thank goodness he hadn't discovered us there. Rex makes me lose my mind. Act irresponsibly.

"You following her?" Rex asked, taking a seat on the arm of the couch.

"I happen to have a copy of her schedule. It's required for use of the property."

"How may I help you?" Nola pulled the robe tighter and held the lapels closed over her chest.

Emile's eyes narrowed. "You can't now. You had your chance." He pointed to Rex. "His career has reached its pinnacle. I'm on the way up. We'd make a perfect pair. In time, I could give you all you need, all you want. The community center was just the beginning. I own several properties and was willing to have you utilize one of them to avoid any look of political impropriety."

Confusion swirled as Nola tried to make sense of his implications.

"I wanted you. *You.* By my side. We both want to do great things for this city. We have a common mission. A friendship. That's the first step toward a binding relationship...love even."

"Oh, Emile."

He can't be serious.

"Save it. I thought I might be in love with you, but seeing you bending your ass over for him! I didn't love you. It was just lust." Emile grabbed his crotch. "I wanted to fuck you. And I'm going to. Now."

Rex stood. In a flash, moved between her and Emile. He shook his head. "No."

"Oh, don't worry, Arceneau," Emile spat. "I wouldn't touch that piece of ass now for anything. I'm going to screw her in a way that hurts her hard and for a long time to come."

Nola trembled. What was he ranting about? Hurt her? How? Her palms began to sweat. Her muscles tensed. She stepped to Rex's side. He put an arm out, blocking her from moving any closer to Emile.

"Miss Nola Dutrey." Emile waved a set of papers in front of her. "This was the new agreement for the use of the space. Lease free."

He ripped the papers in half.

"No. Wait!"

He leered. "There's a clause in the original agreement that I'm exercising. The building is needed for a cause that will be of greater benefit to the community. You have thirty days to get your shit out." He continued to tear the paper into smaller and smaller pieces.

"Stop. Please. Let's talk about this." Nola's heart plunged.

"This is me fucking you."

"What do you want from me?"

He ignored her. "And ya know, it feels really good." He dropped the pieces to the floor. "Ahhh." He grinned, then nodded his head. "Yeah, feels good."

Her stomach clenched. She shook her head slowly, trying to clear away a haze that had to be from a bad dream. She tried to push past Rex and reach for Emile. There had to be a way to make him see reason.

A guttural growl emanated from Rex. He lunged with an uppercut punch that landed on Emile's lower jaw, whipping his head backward. Emile stumbled. He hit his head on the door. Rex landed a second punch in the man's gut before Emile sank to the floor. Grabbing him by the suit jacket, Rex jerked him up, opened the door, and shoved him out, locking the door as soon as he closed it.

"I'll have you arrested for assault, Arceneau!"

Nola crumpled. Her vision blurred with tears. "Nooo," she wailed.

Rex scooped her up and sat on the couch with her in his lap. "I'm sorry. Sweetheart, I'm sorry."

She buried her head in his chest and sobbed while he tried to soothe her.

"It's bad enough he's throwing my kids out of the center," she cried. "But what will we do when he presses charges against you?"

"We'll cross that river with a barge."

"How can you be so calm? Neither of us needs a scandal to hit the papers. The parents of my kids will see it as a broken trust. They won't allow their kids to play in the band anymore."

"Shhhush. Baby, it will all work out. It's not the first tussle Emile and I have had."

Nola wiped her eyes with the sleeve of her robe. "But Rex, I don't have money to pay the lease. How will I ever make bail for you?" Her chin quivered.

What a mess she'd made of things.

Chapter 17

Buzz. Buzz.

Rex woke slowly. Vibrations in unison with a buzzing nudged him from sleep. His phone, annoying thing, continued to pull him to reality. He moved. His neck ached from the uncomfortable couch pillow. His right leg tingled with near paralysis. A weight on his body prevented him from moving as he tried to stretch. He looked down. Nola lay with her head on his bare chest, her torso nestled beside him. He grinned, recalling their night together. They'd shared their life stories from beginning to end. There wasn't anything about her that he didn't enjoy.

Easing off the couch, he rolled onto the floor. His pants were wrinkled, but she remained mostly undisturbed by his movement and looking so cute in his shirt. Grabbing a pillow, he gently placed it under Nola's head. Her nose twitched, but she remained asleep.

"Note to self. No more bourbon."

Slowly pushing to standing, he headed outside to the landing to avoid waking Nola while he answered the phone.

"Rex here. Uncle Henri, what can I can do for you?"

"I need a decision, son."

Rex rubbed the back of his neck. His uncle had to

punch his buttons before even saying hello. The muscle in Rex's jaw ticked. If he could blink and go back in time, he wouldn't start the day by answering the call. "Ever think that silence might mean my answer is no?"

Henri laughed. "You're too decisive for that. You're direct. Say what you mean. Don't leave loose ends. Like me. What is your decision?"

"When I'm ready to give you one, I'll let you know."

"I'll be by the restaurant at two thirty to finish this conversation. There are things you need to know. Don't disappoint me by being late." Henri ended the call.

Staring at the phone, he noticed the time. It plucked his consciousness into recognition.

"Nola," he called, running back into her apartment. "Sweetheart, you need to get up. You're teaching at ten, yeah?"

Eyes closed, she lifted her head from the pillow. "Stop screaming, please," she whispered, pulling her hands over her ears. "What time is it?" She looked pitifully hungover. It would be a sunglasses day for her.

"Nine."

Groaning, she flopped on her back. "Let me sleep for five more minutes. Coffee. Make coffee. Please."

He opened the curtains in the living room. Sunlight filtered in. The glow of soft spring light caressed her face making her look angelic. "I'll make you a cup, but you need to get in the shower to wake up." He stood over her waiting for her to make a move that suggested she intended to rise.

She shook her head. He scooped her up and carried her through her bedroom and into the small adjoining bathroom. "This is me helping you."

He leaned her against the wall. She winced. Pushing the curtain aside, he turned on the water. "Nola. Sweetie, let's get you ready for work."

"Coffffeeeeee," she groaned, her voice raspy with sleep. "Kayla knows how I like mine."

"Sorry, babe. She's not here. You're gonna get it like I make it. But first, do you want my help to undress?"

A slow smile appeared and widened on her face. From the floor, she looked up at him. "You just want to see me naked."

"Absolutely. Right now." He felt the warmth of the water. Just right. "But I think it would be in your best interest if you got ready for work."

Crawling on her hands and knees, wearing his shirt and her bra from last night, Nola entered the shower. As water pelted her back, she squealed and stood up. "I'm awake! Coffee. Now."

Rex shook his head and wandered to the kitchen. It wasn't any larger in size than her tiny bathroom. Why did she live in a place not much bigger than a phone booth? The memory of a prior conversation popped into his brain.

She helps others.

Her coffeemaker was simple, and the filters and coffee were jammed into a plastic container on the counter. He made quick work of his task. Opening the refrigerator, he found skim milk. Not hard to spot it in a mostly bare fridge. She had the basics. Hot sauce. Ketchup. Cajun mustard. Mayonnaise. A wilted leftover salad. And a plastic takeout container with gumbo.

Leaning against the wall next to the shower with a towel in one hand and a cup of coffee with milk and sweetener in the other, Rex waited for her to pull back the shower curtain. Yes, she was right, he wanted to see her gloriously naked, which hadn't happened either time they'd made love. Last night, though it was on his mind to seduce her—sex wouldn't have consoled her— he held her instead, talked with her, kissed her, and when she drifted off to sleep, he dreamt of her though his eyes were open and staring at the ceiling until nearly three in the morning.

At some point during the evening—maybe when the need to protect her from Emile punched him as hard as he'd hit his old friend—the tide had changed and pushed him off balance. Like at the beach when he scrunched his toes and flexed his knees to stay upright against strong incoming waves, Nola changed the landscape of the world beneath his feet.

He loved everything about her, down to and including the little mewling sounds she made when she slept fitfully. His heart swelled with love, with pride. She owned it. Yep. Nola Dutrey spun like a vortex and her whirring had sucked him into her universe. Hell, he even liked her sister and respected her family roots.

"Towel and coffee waiting, Madame."

Her hand reached out from the shower. He draped the towel over her wrist.

"This is ironic, don't ya think?" Her voice was sing-songy.

"How's that?" He sipped her coffee, then turned up his nose against the sweetness.

"You're rushing me off to one job while you wait in the wings to fire me from another."

Rex sighed. "We do need to have an official boss-to-employee chat, but not now. I don't want to fire you per se. I want to reduce the expense outgo to get the business expenses in line. Otherwise, Kayla won't make it another six months."

"Things are that bad?"

"The short answer is yes. But could we discuss this later, like this afternoon? I want you to actually see on paper the documented issues I'm up against."

The shower curtain flung open. Nola stepped out. "Thanks for the coffee." She plucked the mug from his hand and crossed the room to her closet. She pivoted on her toes and turned. "Oh. My. God."

The changing expressions on her face captivated him, then signaled an alarm. "What's wrong?"

Nola's eyes were wild and overly bright. "If there are any headlines over what happened last night...I could get fired from the school, as well. A proper private school can't have a teacher casting a shadow over its reputation."

He shrugged to release the tension in his shoulders. He had known about Emile's attraction to her. Could've handled things differently. But under no circumstances was another man going to put hands on his woman. "Look at me." With two fingers, he pointed at her, then back at himself. "Focus on one thing at a time. Go teach. Meet me at Arceneau's later today. You can't do anything about Emile shooting his mouth off to the press... Besides, he might not be as eager to do that as you might think. After all, we ended up sleeping through the night—no cops showed up to haul me off to jail."

"You're right. You're right." She opened the closet door and picked through its offerings.

"I'm going to make myself a cup of coffee now

and let you dress in peace. But I'll stay and ogle you properly, if that would help." Trying to make light of the possible fate looming, he hoped to be a calm voice of reason for her. And he'd risk hurting his body and reputation to protect Nola.

A few minutes later, standing in her doorway, he watched as she braided her still damp hair. He cocked his head as she leaned closer to the mirror and smoothed lipstick on her lips, then puckered as though preparing for a kiss.

"You can practice on me." He chuckled.

"Be sure of it." She crossed the short span of the room to him. "Later." She ran a finger down his chest. "I want to have dinner at eight at Arceneau's. It's this place in the French Quarter. Have you heard of it? Maybe I can convince one of the owners to let me use his office." Her raised eyebrow signified her suggestion.

"We'll see. I think a more...traditional setting would be better for coupling number three."

Her eyes widened. "Wow. So romantic. Old fashioned even. And yet so clinical at the same time. Be still my heart."

She reached for her purse and searched for her keys. "Will you lock up when you leave, and I'll pick up my keys when I see you this afternoon? Once and for all, I can't wait to see the proof for the reason you have to fire me."

"You're a hardheaded woman."

But I love you for it. Your determination knows no bounds.

"We'll debate the merits of your pronouncement later. Oh, and downstairs, you'll find a room with a washer and dryer. Wouldn't be dignified for you to wander around in a wet shirt."

The minute she was out the door, Rex searched his contact list. "Gerald, my man! You played with Nola Belle on her CD. I need your help. I want to get her an audition in New York with your people."

Rex looked around for a piece of paper and a pen. He found what he sought in the drawer of the end table. "You agree, she's good enough for a shot at another record contract?"

"Hell, yes. But she won't come to New York. Good luck getting her here. Look, I'll make a few calls and let you know. I can't just give out numbers. You understand."

"Yeah, I get it. Thanks for the help. Let me know when you hear something. I'd like to surprise her."

After a few more phone conversations and a few messages left for contacts who might help him with Nola's career, Rex headed downstairs to search for the laundry room.

"Well, look who's sneaking around half naked like a jaybird."

"Marquis." Rex nodded. "I need a dryer."

"Follow me."

Marquis led him to a door at the far end of the building and punched in a code. The door opened to the laundry room.

"Listen, your uncle called Kayla this morning and said he was meeting you at two thirty at the restaurant. He wants Kayla there, too. She says he got weird. Something about the real truth, and she's got you to thank if she hopes to have a job in the future. My girl's upset. What's going on? I'm going to be there, just so ya know."

Rex tossed the shirt into the dryer and dropped in change to make it start. "You know as much as I do…well, almost. He's crazy like a fox. Who knows what shit he might say. But be there. I'm fine with that."

Marquis nodded and left.

"The produce receipts better be in my inbox," Rex muttered, pulling on his shirt. He shuddered involuntarily against a chill moving between his skin and the shirt just warmed from the dryer. Could he figure out what Henri was up to before his uncle stepped over the line? Could he find a way to keep Nola employed? Would she go to New York? At the very least, she could move in with Kayla at the house. That would save her money. And give him comfort that he was helping her, too.

****

The banging in her head had finally subsided as she walked to the streetcar stop. Teaching had a way of reviving her, though she purposely stayed out of the crosshairs of the headmaster today. A couple of her students had snickered about the shades over her eyes, but she ignored them. Thankfully, her familiarity of the arrangements eliminated her need to try to read sheet music while she taught.

Waiting at the designated stop, Nola pushed up on the sunglasses sliding down the bridge of her nose and lifted her face to the warm spring sunlight. Through earbuds and the help of the playlist on her phone, Chopin's "Prelude No. 15 in D-flat Major" musically massaged the tension in her body, melting it away. "Positivity," she whispered and then repeated the mantra several times.

After drawing in a long breath, she let it go. The rest of the day would be wonderful. Calm and peacefulness strengthened her resolve. All the loose dangling ends—Biloxi and the catering, space for the band and uniforms, her developing relationship with Rex—could be braided together for a positive outcome. Emile might have shoved a barricade in front of her, but perseverance and some karmic luck would create a new opportunity. No need to panic yet. Yes, it was challenging, but Dutreys never gave up. If the women in her family cowered in the face of adversity, there would be no Fleur de Lis. Her sister wouldn't be married to Nick because of a silly old family feud. And she never would've left the comfortable nest of home.

Determination and optimism flowed through her. She felt it the same way she felt sunlight warming her face. Besides, Rex would help her out. The music-jam fundraiser would work. Responsible Rex, she could count on him. Look at all he'd done for Kayla.

"Home. Springtime." She opened her arms and spun around. If possible, she'd wrap her arms around the whole city of New Orleans, the place where she was born. Why her mother decided to name her children based upon the city of their birth had never mattered; however, of the three kids in her family, she got the best name. It was as though the pulse of New Orleans thrummed in her blood. Touring had taken her many places, but no place was better than home, well, except for Fleur de Lis.

With a glance, she took in the sight of the dogwoods blooming white along the street. They spotted the landscape along with the towering oak trees in spring green. Azaleas, finishing their blooming season, still offered last pops of color—all shades of fuchsia. City Park was beautifully dressed in florals this time of year, and she promised herself a trip there very soon to soak up the ambiance. Someone like Monet could put paint to canvas and do this landscape justice.

Her stomach rumbled.

Checking her phone, she had plenty of time to get to the restaurant before they closed after lunch, but sooner would save her from reaching that hangry place—where hungry makes her angry—and where others needed to fear crossing paths with her. With only a protein bar and a bottle of water after all the bourbon last night, she looked forward to Kayla's tasty delights.

"Hmm. Maybe I can get Rex to cook for me."

Her mouth watered. Crawfish jambalaya. A salad with strips of fried chicken. Her stomach rumbled louder again. "I'm going to feed you ASAP." She rubbed her belly.

Nola checked her ringing phone. Pushing the button, she answered it. "Jason? Hello. What's up?"

"You tell me." His immediate irritation was puzzling.

"I just got off the phone with a producer," he snapped. "You said you didn't want my management. You just wanted to do the summer festival circuit."

"Wait. It's not personal. I explained. I need to be home more. It's not about you."

"Then why are you looking to set up auditions and looking for a record deal? In. New. York. City."

Nola smiled at an approaching woman and nodded. "Nice day."

"It was until this!"

217

"Shh. I didn't mean you. I'm waiting for my ride. I know I'm still a bit hungover from last night, but I have no memory of contacting anyone about anything in New York City. If I had wanted all that you're talking about, I'd have called you."

"As your manager—"

"Tour manager only," she corrected. Her blood pressure started to rise.

"As your manager, I don't like you trying to cut deals behind my back. You want an audition? You want another record deal? You talk to me."

"Deep breath," she insisted. "Redirect that anger someplace else. *I'm* not the source of your anxiety." Okay, her hangry was pivoting on hostile. She took her own advice, breathing deeply in and out.

"You are infuriating, Nola. I hate being caught off guard. Don't like to be made a fool by someone I trusted."

"Whoa. Back up the accusations. No one thinks you're a fool."

Sometimes, maybe a donkey's butt. Like now.

"I helped make you who you are. Don't think you can torpedo me."

"Be careful." She lowered her voice. "Let's not say anything we'll regret."

Locking her jaw, she intended to take her own advice, though she hadn't fully put her last New York experience behind her. Jason had made promises that he hadn't kept. Two summers he continued adding more appearances to her already tight schedule—all in the name of "the contract says." As a result, she'd ended up sick with bronchitis and couldn't sing for months when she returned home.

A rumbling reached Nola, and she turned as it grew louder. The iconic green of the St. Charles Line streetcar moved toward her. "I've got to go. Don't be mad at me about a misunderstanding. Find out the source of this and have a dressing down with them. You know the band is my focus most of this year. By this time next year, it will be running, and moving forward on its own. Then we can discuss my next career move. I'm getting on the streetcar now. Hanging up. Call me after you know what's *really* going on."

"Nola!"

"Bye, Jason."

What the frick frack. After this tour, she needed a new manager. "Deep breath, Nola, dear," she muttered, hoping to recapture her calm.

Sinking into a seat, she faced forward as the houses along St. Charles whipped by outside the window. The odd lady she'd met before with the funky hat sat across the aisle from her.

"You got more man troubles?" The strands of purple, gold, and green Mardi Gras beads had tripled since their last encounter.

Letting go of a deep sigh, Nola nodded.

Emile. Rex. And now Jason.

"The only reason a woman sighs that soul achingly deep is cuz of a man or a problem child."

The words echoed with *déjà vu*. Nola smiled.

"Though there are times," the woman continued, "when a man is no better than a child. Them kind is the worst." She made crazy figure eights in the air with her fingers as though conjuring up some sort of magic and pointed at Nola.

Nola flinched. It was like a bolt of energy hit her in

the chest.

"Girl, search your heart and stand your ground. You hear me?"

"Yes, ma'am." Slipping the strap of the backpack over one shoulder, Nola exited the streetcar, ready to be away from the odd woman. She rubbed near her collarbones to sooth an unfamiliar pain.

"Maybe Momma paid a voodoo priestess, and this woman was her messenger."

Shaking off the lingering unease, she started toward Arceneau's. Light-headed from hunger, she trudged the few blocks to her destination.

"Hey there, Nola." A waitress unlocked the door after she knocked. "I was asked to be on the lookout for you. Rex is upstairs. He said to let you know. Kayla's in the kitchen."

"I'm going to check out Kayla's lunch leftovers, in case Rex asks."

Entering through the swinging door, she spied Marquis leaning over one of the islands, propped on his elbows. Kayla lifted a large spoon to his mouth. He closed his eyes while he sipped the offering.

"Hmmm. That's great."

"You really like it?"

"Absolutely, Sugar." Marquis opened his eyes and licked his lips.

"Ah…permission to enter Chef." Nola squared her shoulders and saluted to prevent the moment turning more awkward.

"Nola, come taste. It's my seafood stew. Oysters. Shrimp. Crawfish. I'm going to julienne strips of fried catfish as a garnish on top for texture. Add some thinly sliced scallions for added flavor."

Crossing the kitchen, Nola tossed her backpack in the small office and leaned on the island next to Marquis. She opened her mouth just as he'd done.

Kayla laughed. "I feel like a mother bird feeding her chicks." She spooned it up for Nola.

The flavors burst on her tongue. "More. Need more. I'm starving."

"Here." Kayla slid the rest of the bowl in front of her. "Marquis, will you grab her a baguette?"

"Thanks." Nola took the offered bread. She tore a small chunk, dipped it in the savory liquid, and popped it in her mouth. "Lady, you can cook for me anytime, day or night."

"Exactly what I said," Marquis chimed in. Nola caught his wink at Kayla and then her friend's pinking blush. Kayla looked radiant. Nola mused, she should've tried to set the two of them up months ago.

Grabbing another chunk of bread, Nola dunked again.

"Slow down, girl," Kayla said.

"Only had a protein bar and water today. Didn't have dinner last night. Too much bourbon."

"Curious." Kayla eyed her.

"What?" Nola took another spoonful of the stew and chased it with more bread.

"Now I know where my brother spent the night."

Nola stopped, spoon midair. She cut a glance to Kayla and then to Marquis. The pair wore smiles as wide as circus clowns.

"So...what's up?" Kayla asked.

Nola tilted her head slightly. Echoes of that same question she'd asked Jason earlier rang in her ears. "You tell me. Did you get a phone call of some sort?"

"Phone call?" Kayla laughed. "Hell no. My brother presented himself during the height of our lunch rush. Perky. Happy. Said he has some very interesting news. I'm guessing it's about the two of you."

A flush heated Nola's cheeks. How much should she share about her feelings for Rex?

A buzz on the intercom interrupted her thoughts.

Kayla walked to the wall and pushed a button.

"Kayla, has Nola arrived?" Rex's voice rang through the kitchen.

"Yes, she's here."

"I need all of you up here. Has Henri arrived?"

"No."

"That's fine. I have news I want to explain before he gets here. March upstairs. Now."

Kayla rolled her eyes. Nola stifled a laugh.

"Yes, sir." Kayla saluted.

"Excellent. And I'm making this a public announcement. I love Nola Dutrey."

Nola's eyes widened. Rex loved her? A wave of tingling caressed her skin. Her cheeks heated. Her heart fluttered, and she pressed a hand to her chest to calm the breathlessness.

Kayla scrunched her nose, smiling, and shivered as though with excitement. "I see a plethora of wonderful positive possibilities."

Nola never thought her words of encouragement to Kayla would return to her in quite this way.

"Well, well," Marquis said. "This is a happy day for all of us."

"I think I'll float upstairs now." Nola turned toward the door. "I can't imagine what other news Rex Arceneau has to share."

Chapter 18

Waiting for his sister and Nola to reach the third floor, Rex answered an incoming phone call. "Hello, Phillip."

"We've got a problem." Anger, tight and hot, reached Rex. All his senses flipped to high alert.

"What?"

"Arson."

"Where?"

"The farm and at 29N & 90W."

"Our flagship restaurant?" Rex pounded his fist on the desk. "What are you telling me?"

"The restaurant burned. The dining room. Kitchen spared. The small barn at the farm burned to the ground. Contents a total loss."

"When?"

"During the early morning hours. I'll give you details when you get here. Text me your arrival information. I'll have a car pick you up at the airport."

Rex raked his fingers through his hair. His brain stuttered with disbelief. Fractured images of the farm and restaurant flipped through his mind. All he'd helped build. And buying the farm had been his idea, requiring a mountain of coaxing to get his two business partners to agree.

"When can you be here? We need you. This has to take top priority—over that. There's so much at stake for all of us."

The insinuation that Arceneau's wasn't as important rankled Rex. The New York operation had all the necessary insurance to handle the fire loss. His sister, on the other hand, was family and had no safety net. The only asset she had beyond the restaurant was the Garden District house. If Arceneau's didn't move the bottom line into the black, Kayla would lose her legacy and her dignity. What good would the house be to her if she didn't have a job here?

And Nola. She lived here. His chest tightened, then constricted more. His heartbeat rang in his ears. The last thing he wanted was to leave her. With him in New York and her in New Orleans, what chance did their love have to survive? Never before had he framed his life with a woman to share it. After all, as much as he loved his mother, she'd not been an honorable wife, then she died. Had that impacted his life decisions more than he realized?

But honor and integrity required that he fulfill his primary duty to his business partners. Someone had to deal with the details of the insurance and rebuilding. If he ranked the needs of those counting on him rather than their wants, Kayla and Nola would manage without him.

"Give me a few minutes, Phillip. I'll get this figured out. I'll call you back." Rex ended the call.

"Hello?" Nola waited in the doorway, brow furrowed. Behind her stood Kayla and Marquis. "Is everything okay, Rex?"

Footsteps sounded behind them.

"Hello. Nice to see all." Henri smiled wide. He tapped Kayla on the shoulder, then pulled her into a hug. "How's my favorite niece?"

Delight lit Kayla's face, annoying Rex. Henri didn't deserve the affection and devotion his sister gave freely to the old man. "Uncle Henri. You've been absent lately. What's this mystery meeting about?"

"I'm Henri Arceneau," he said, releasing Kayla and reaching out his hand to Marquis. The cuff on his shirt revealed gold cuff links. Rex wanted to yank them away from Henri. But everything in right time, he assured himself.

"Uncle Henri, that's Marquis, and that's Nola."

"Ah, yes. We've met." Henri stiffened and barely glanced in Nola's direction, whereas she smiled up at him.

A curling of unease tightened in Rex's gut. His bio sperm donor had proven what he'd intuitively always known about him—he was a manipulating scumbag.

"Before we get down to business, Kayla, honey, why don't you make us some coffee?" Henri asked.

She nodded.

"No," Rex interrupted. Henri would not treat his sister as though she were a kitchen lackey or there to do his bidding. Above all others, Arceneau's belonged to her. She was the true heir of Claude Arceneau's estate. "I'll call down to the kitchen and have someone bring some up, if you must have coffee."

"I can wait. Business it is." Henri stepped between Kayla and Marquis and took a seat in one of the chairs inside the office.

Rex stood and motioned for the others to enter. "Kayla, I'd like you to sit there." He pointed to the office chair. It was her rightful place. He perched on the two-drawer cabinet off to the side of the desk, strategically wanting to be on the same side of the desk as Kayla and opposite Henri. Their positioning in the room was intended to send a subtle message of solidarity between himself and his sister, even if Henri didn't pick up on it.

"Well," Henri began. "Being the elder of the family, I will begin."

Rex raised an eyebrow but let him continue.

"Kayla, you're a fine pastry chef. One of the best in the city. You're a good sous chef, but...honey, the truth is, you're not executive chef material. I think you know that."

"Uncle Henri—" Kayla started, but Rex put a hand on her arm and stopped her. Henri deserved an opportunity to say all he needed. Yet Rex could barely contain the urge to blurt out the sins of the man he'd called "Uncle" all his life.

"Continue, Henri."

"The business is failing. Expenses are too high. You have no way to infuse capital to turn things around. Rex won't take over as executive chef. So...I want to buy you out. Rex and I will take over the restaurant. You will stay on as the pastry chef. This way, we can ensure the continued success of Arceneau's, which will mean you will always be gainfully employed."

Kayla's mouth gaped. Her knuckles whitened as she gripped the arms of the chair.

Rex couldn't quite read Marquis' expression, but he had one hand wrapped around the other that was curled into a fist. Nola's eyes widened, and she cast her gaze to her lap where she laced and unlaced her fingers.

"Is that all?" Rex asked.

Henri shrugged. "I'm willing to unburden you of the big house. I'll buy it from the two of you. Rex, you're rarely here. I would expect your visits to New Orleans and your dealings with the restaurant to remain about the same. The house is too big for Kayla. You don't want to manage the upkeep, do you darlin'?"

Kayla blinked as though she hadn't quite heard all that had been said.

"Kayla mentioned she wanted to sell the house. Wanted to buy a condo in that converted warehouse facing the river."

"Is there anything else, Uncle?" Rex asked.

"No. Short and sweet. This is about business, though I am trying to look out for the interests of my favorite niece and nephew."

"What the fuck," Kayla snapped. "I'm your only damn niece. He's your only nephew. It's like blinders have been ripped from my eyes. You want to steal Arceneau's from me."

Rex squeezed Kayla's shoulder, wanting to offer support.

She swatted his hand away. "Are you in on this? You want to take Arceneau's from me? How could you?"

Rex squeezed her shoulder again. "Henri, is there anything else you'd like to say?"

"I took the liberty of getting an appraisal on the house. Here it is." He pulled an envelope from his back pocket. "I'm willing to pay the appraised price."

"I want to be sure I've given you every opportunity to make your positions clear—about the restaurant, the house, and our family. Is there *anything* else you have to say?"

Henri chuckled. "Always so serious, Rex. Practical-minded. Taking care of business. So like me. Yes, one last thing. I brought champagne. It's cooling downstairs. I had all the necessary paperwork drawn up. If you're ready, we can conclude the transactions today." He leaned forward, resting his forearms on the edge of the desk. "Kayla, honey, this is a great solution for you. You get the condo you want, the job you love, and the security you need."

Rex glued his gaze on her, wondering what she might say.

"Part of your offer is tempting," Kayla began. "I don't have the same attachment to the house that Rex does. I don't object to selling. However, I won't give up my stake in Arceneau's. Discussion over."

She started to rise. Once again, Rex placed a hand on her shoulder. "Actually, it's not. Not yet. I do have some say in this, too."

"I won't be guilted into doing something I don't want to do. You want the house, then buy me out. Or sell to Uncle Henri. Doesn't matter to me. But you"— she thumped him in the chest—"nor you"—she pointed to Henri—"will force me to give up what I love. I'm not selling my share of the restaurant."

Henri leaned back in his chair. Lacing his fingers together, he reached behind his head. His smile widened. "Kayla, honey, together, Rex and I can force you out. Together we own the controlling interest in the business, right, son?"

Nola cleared her throat. "Maybe I should leave. I don't think…"

"Stay." Rex and Kayla spoke at the same time.

Rex stood and paced to the door and back. "Right,

Henri, right. It's true, Kayla. Uncle Henri and I could join forces. With his ten percent and my fifty, we would have controlling interest. I think Uncle Henri, if he's running the kitchen, could make your life a living hell. Like he's done for me all of my life."

Henri bolted up in the chair, scowling. "What?"

Marquis stood, scraping chair legs against the wooden floor. Shock flashed on Nola's face. Kayla slowly turned. Rex locked gazes with her.

"Kayla, we are brother and sister...but only half."

Kayla shook her head as though confused.

Rex sighed deeply. "Henri is my biological father. You and I share the same mother."

Henri's expression shuttered, as though a magic spell had changed him to a robot. He rose.

"Sit," Rex snapped. "You started this. I'm going to finish it. Kayla, open the right bottom drawer of the desk."

"Rex?"

"Please do as I ask."

Once the drawer was open, she looked up at him.

"Please pull out the folder and open it."

As he instructed, his sister complied.

"I still don't understand. Your birth certificate?"

"Look at the information under father."

"Claude Arceneau."

"Keep reading, Kayla. Birthdate."

"It's wrong. That's Papa's name, but not his birthday."

Henri, gaze cast downward, exhaled deeply. "It's mine."

"Rex?" Kayla whipped her head to stare at him. Her eyes were wild with disbelief.

"I don't know the details, but I'm sure Henri will fill us in, won't you? It seems that my sperm donor is Papa's older brother. I've known since I was ten. Since before Momma died. I also learned our house originally was titled to her, never to her and Papa. She left it in trust to be passed to the two of us. He put the house in our names. We've always owned it since we were children."

Kayla shook her head. "I'm not able to navigate this river of crap. You knew? You didn't tell me?"

Was she not getting the crux of the truth? He was the one betrayed by his own father. *Her* father loved her. She'd always known who he was and enjoyed his love. But not him.

"Henri is my father. Claude Arceneau never had a son. I doubt he died knowing the truth."

"He did," Henri insisted. "We had an arrangement. He paid me not to tell you."

Rex's heart seized. Papa knew? "You lie."

A vortex of thought nearly made Rex sick. His palms turned sweaty. He wouldn't give Henri the satisfaction of witnessing his discomfort.

"You're lying," Kayla spat.

Rex raised an eyebrow. "The extra payment to Nola Dutrey every other month?"

"What?" Nola asked.

"Oh yeah, he was using you, too, but you didn't know it. Before you, it was the combo who played in the lounge. And before that. Then there are those produce bills…"

"What about them?" Kayla narrowed her eyes.

"I finished going through the receipts the produce guy sent over. Checking the books against the information, it proved Henri marked them up an extra ten percent. Each and every one of them."

"That was payment for the money I gave your father to bail him out a few years ago. There's nothing illegal about what I've done."

"Illegal? Illegal?" Rex shouted. He stood in front of Henri. "You immoral son of a bloodsucker. You robbed Claude Arceneau, *my father*, of his dignity."

"No. I. Did. Not." Henri stood. He poked Rex in the chest with his finger. "Claude knew when he married your mother that she was pregnant. He loved her. He didn't care. He just didn't know I was the father. He didn't want to know. Forbade her from ever telling him about the father. She tried."

"If he didn't know, why was he paying you to keep silent? And what about the house?" Kayla demanded.

"The house belonged to your momma's grandparents. No one in her family could afford to buy it when the old people got sick and needed money for healthcare and nursing homes. So I bought it. I gave it to your mother. Claude thought she inherited it. It was my wedding present to them. To make up…"

"Make up for what?" Kayla pushed.

"What?" Rex demanded.

"A single error in judgment."

"In English." Kayla looked ready to skewer him and roast him on a spit.

"You kids don't really want to know this."

"Now!" Kayla ordered.

"It was a party. We were all there together. Another man paid attention to your mother. Your father left, rejecting her, saying she was too young for him. The party went on. We got drunk and ended up together. She never loved me, always loved your father." Henri hung his head.

"And him paying you?" Rex demanded.

"When your momma died, I wanted to claim you. You are *my* son. My firstborn. But Claude threatened me. And he gave me ten percent of the business...so I could look after you."

"You douchebag! You think the two of you can rip the business away from me? I'm Papa's heir. I'm his only child. You can't have the restaurant, Rex. It's mine."

"Kayla, hold on. There's more to the story."

"Fuck you. I'm out of here. You have anything else to say to me, talk to my attorney. I'm hiring one right now. You're my brother. Even if you're only half, but you won't steal what's mine from me." Shoving him aside, she stormed from the room. Marquis followed on her heels.

Nola stood. "Mr. Arceneau, I'm deeply disappointed to learn that I've been used. Rex, please call me later. I'm going to try to calm Kayla down. We can't leave things like this...though I can understand her sense of betrayal."

The sound of Nola's footsteps faded as Rex stared at Henri.

"It didn't have to go like this," Henri said, sinking into the chair.

Rex snorted. "You talk about knowing me. About I'm practical and responsible. How good I am at business. But what you have failed to understand about me is that I'm loyal, too. And I believe in the truth, whereas you have no loyalty to anyone but yourself. As for the truth, you're willing to cover it up as long as you get paid."

"I wanted to claim you."

"Only when Momma died. What about the ten years before that?"

Henri's shoulders sagged.

"You prick. Don't you think my cousin and I ever talked about the fact that we were born only a few months apart? You were married with a kid on the way, and you banged my mother."

"Don't call it that. It wasn't like that. I loved her. *Loved* her."

"And what about my aunt, your wife?"

"I loved her, too."

"Not enough to make the marriage work."

"Now, Rex." Henri straightened in the chair. "You know that having a restaurant isn't always good for a family life. You date beautiful women, but you haven't married. You're too dedicated, *loyal*, to your business. That's what feeds your soul."

Henri was right about not being married, but not for the reason he put forth. The ten-year-old boy who learned the truth of his parentage, learned his momma had lied to him all his life, left him with a secret to carry alone, had walled off his heart to true love, never fully trusting a woman...until Nola, and even she lied about her feelings. Kayla was the only woman he believed would always tell him the truth.

"Henri, the house isn't for sale. The restaurant, well, Kayla and I will figure it out, but count on getting an offer to buy out your ten percent from the two of us."

"Be reasonable, Rex. You're going back to New York imminently. Don't make any rash decision now. I promise, together we can take Arceneau's to the next level, and Kayla will always have a job."

"Why do you think I'd return to New York now? I need to work things out with Kayla first."

"Ah. Well." He licked his lips and cut his gaze toward the door. "Listen. You do what you need to do." He stood and took several steps. "Let me know what you and Kayla decide. I'm going to go now."

"Not before you hand over the cuff links that belong to my father. I don't know when you stole them, but I gave them to Papa for his sixtieth birthday. Custom-made."

"No. Prove it."

As Henri started down the stairs, Rex shouted, "I'm wondering if the D.A. would have any interest in this case I'm building against you." Could he bring charges for fraud or embezzlement? Maybe not, but it wouldn't hurt to ask. But in the meantime, he had to make Kayla see the big picture, make her understand, and make the best decision for her future.

But what about Nola? Disappointing her cut just as deeply. He couldn't possibly help cater her parents' anniversary party, and in all likelihood, wouldn't be around for the fundraiser she planned. How could he make her understand? He had to go to New York.

"*Now.*" Echoes of Henri's words swirled around him. Momentarily dizzy, Rex held on to the side of the desk for support. Something wasn't right.

Chapter 19

Nola made her way to the kitchen. "Kayla?"

She'd never seen her friend so angry as when she'd stormed red-faced from the office. A nagging worry filled Nola. Good-natured Kayla always saw the brighter side of things. She was snarky at times, true, but always optimistic. Always willing to lend a hand, like with the community band. Kayla made people feel comfortable with more than just sumptuous food. Could she offer the same thing to her friend now that she needed it the most?

"She left. Flew out of here like rockets were strapped to her feet. Marquis went after her." One of the waitresses thumbed in the direction of the kitchen's back door.

Walking outside and into the shadows cast by buildings in the late afternoon sun, Nola ventured to the corner. A young man jogged toward her. "Miss Nola Belle. A word, please?"

Nola recognized Marc Sharp, the sleazy news reporter from *Back Beat*. She turned in the opposite direction, hoping to avoid him.

"Wait. I need confirmation of a story."

Nola kept walking, picking up her pace. Behind her, his steps pounded the sidewalk. He could only mean bad news. Panicked, she turned into a daiquiri bar. Headed for the ladies' room. The place was half-full with tourists, not a good place to hide. But in her current state of agitation, the newshound was the last person she wanted to talk with. She'd hide any place she could find.

Bang. Bang.

"You'll have to come out sometime," he shouted. "I'm going to print the story I have, but I do want to give you a chance to add your slant. Document the facts. Give me a quote."

No purse. No phone. She couldn't call and ask the manager at the bar to distract the menace chasing her. Glancing up, she noticed a frosted window. She'd never fit through the tiny space even if she managed to pry the bars off.

"Get it together," she muttered, then washed her hands. After patting her face with damp hands, she dried them.

Squaring her shoulders, she pushed on the door, nearly smacking him as it opened.

"Miss Nola. Thanks for talking with me." His palms were pressed together as though offering gratitude for her time.

"Mr. Sharp. I have nothing to say."

He grinned. "You might once you hear what I've learned."

Glowering at him, she pursed her lips.

"Is it true that you had a little tickle and slap with Emile Broussard at the Carousel?"

"What did you say?" She couldn't have heard him correctly. Tickle and slap?

"After which, he gave you the key to his hotel room. And *after that*, he gave you the lease for your community band. Over other charitable organizations

236

bidding on the same lease."

So far, what Marc had said, was mostly true, though very misconstrued. She slapped Emile when he tried to tickle her while they were at the Carousel. He did slide his key to her, but she'd left it on the bar in front of him before walking out. And after that, she had received the contract in question, but nothing sordid or untoward had ever happened between her and Emile Broussard. That day. But years ago, they'd had one date—he was a charismatic college boy and she a senior in high school. At a Mardi Gras party, he humiliated her when he dumped a bucket of Hurricanes—rum and passion fruit syrup—on her and demanded she participate in the wet t-shirt contest. Now if she confirmed the facts Marc Sharp offered, people would have the wrong impression of her...worst still, of her relationship with Emile. On the other hand, what did it matter? Emile had reneged on renewing the lease and was kicking her out of the community center. But the parents of her band kids and the headmaster at school would take a dim view of things if Mr. Sharp splashed the allegations as front-page news.

"I'll take a 'no comment' if you'd like. That's certainly printable." He grinned. She wanted to wipe the smile off his face. But dare she even utter a word? It would end up in print for perpetuity. People would think the worst. Her parents would be outraged—hopefully at him and not her. Still, her family would be shamed. But none of what he'd said, if examined beyond the shallow meanings, was true. Well, except that if he printed her 'no comment' that would be a direct quote.

"Mr. Sharp, do you want a full story? A real story

that has merit?"

"Sure, that's what I'm after."

"Then prove to me you're a serious journalist and meet me tomorrow at the community center at three p.m. I'll give you 'the rest of the story' and you'll be able to quote me on everything. But…"

"But what?"

"I want the local councilwoman there, too. If you can't get her there—then, I'll be happy to give you an interview in her office."

Marc's grin grew wide. "This suddenly got very interesting. Okay, I'll see what I can do. How do I reach you?"

"I'll check in with you." Nola nodded and saluted. This was her chance to grab an audience with the councilwoman and bypass Emile. She didn't want to destroy his reputation or career, but just get him out of her way. She wouldn't allow a single error in judgment to haunt her for the rest of her life. Besides, cowering wasn't her style.

Turning her thoughts back to Kayla, she had to find her. She needed her phone, but it was at the restaurant. Heading back, she couldn't wait to call Kayla. Also, while there, she could talk with Rex. He had to be upset. Kayla didn't own all the rights to anguish from bad news.

She entered the kitchen at Arceneau's. Rex stood writing the dinner specials on a whiteboard. The kitchen was beginning to bustle as staff readied things for the dinner service.

"Did Kayla come back?" she asked, finding her backpack and phone.

"She called and said she was taking the night off."

Rex continued writing.

"Where is she?"

"Marquis said he took her home. She says she's going to swim in the pool."

"That's just crazy." Why wasn't he upset? The world was rotating off its axis and Rex was working on a menu? The rope of anxiety twisting her in knots made her want to fly to Kayla's to make sure she was okay, then talk some sense into her.

Rex set a marker on the tray and turned to her. "Can you encourage her to talk to me? I don't want to take the business away from her. I came back to help her get it on track, to teach her how to run it on her own. That was my plan, then head back to New York. I've accomplished my mission. It's time for me to go."

"Go?" Her heart sank. She shook her head. She'd predicted it from the beginning, but now that he'd spoken the words, all doors slammed shut. There could be no hope for them.

"My plane leaves tomorrow morning. Kayla needs to get her ass in here to work. Help me help her make sense of this. I'll even consider swapping out my share of the business for her share of the house. She'll own ninety percent of Arceneau's."

"You're leaving tomorrow?" Her aching heart bounced against the ground. She bit down on her bottom lip to stop the tears welling in her eyes. Her chest tightened in the spot where her heart used to beat. "I won't get involved in your financial negotiations, but I'll certainly talk with her and see if I can get her to talk to you. I need time. You can't leave."

"She's being irresponsible. If she wants this place so much, why isn't she here"—he motioned with a flourish—"to toss me out of the kitchen like she's done in the past? Now that we know Henri was siphoning money, *and it's stopped,* I believe she can do this—all on her own."

In her vision, Rex blurred.

You can't leave. You can't. I love you.

Nola went to him. Slipping her arm around him, she led him to the small office and closed the door. "Don't you see, she doesn't want to do this without you. You're her big brother, not just her business partner. She still looks up to you. Counts on you. She surely doesn't want to be in business with Henri."

"Well, legally, he does own ten percent."

"I'll bet he'll sell," she prompted.

Just don't leave.

Wrapping her arms around his waist, she leaned into him. "I have ulterior motives for wanting you to stay." She rested her head against his chest. Her heart skittered as he hugged her in return. "You're catering my parents' anniversary party, and you promised to help with the fundraiser for my band."

Stepping back, he put space between them. His hands gripped her arms. "I have to go. There was a fire at my flagship restaurant."

She drew a sharp breath as her hand flew to her mouth.

"The small barn at the farm burned, too."

Her eyes widened. "Rex, I'm so sorry. I didn't know."

He leaned back against the desk, putting more space between them. "That was the call you overheard before Henri arrived."

"You do have to go." Her heart ripped a jagged

tear. Problems came at her rapid fire. Sharp's interview. The anniversary party. The band. Her job at Arceneau's in limbo. Kayla grieving. Rex leaving. Her knees weakened. Rex moved quickly and pulled out a chair. She sat. Biting her bottom lip, she fought telling him she loved him. He might take that as emotional blackmail—her forcing him to choose her over all he had up north. She couldn't do that. And she couldn't leave New Orleans.

Rex knelt on one knee next to her. "Come to New York. I'm pretty sure I can get you an audition. There's lots of work there for you. It will give us chance."

"Audition?" She eyed him warily.

"I made some calls, yeah? Talked to some people. I'm pretty sure I can get it lined up for you. We can be together."

How could he go behind her back, not tell her, that he was trying to engineer her career? Jason accused her of backstabbing him, only she hadn't, but now understood where he got that idea. Rex was used to fixing things. Mr. Responsible. But she didn't need fixing. She needed to make her own decisions. Make her own mistakes. Had Rex been one of them?

"No." She folded her arms over her chest. She couldn't live anywhere else but New Orleans. Not even Fleur de Lis offered the lifeblood she needed to live. The energy of the city was the essence of who she was and all she hoped to be.

"Nola?"

She swallowed past the lump forming in her throat. "You need to go. You. Need. To. Go. I'll talk with Kayla and tell her your offer about the swap. In fact, I'll go now. I'll be back to sing at ten, just like my contract says. But, I won't work for you, Rex Arceneau."

"I don't understand."

"It doesn't matter. My contract was with your father. Not you. Not Kayla. I'll come back because my fans, your regular customers, expect me to be here. I won't disappoint them."

Like you disappointed me.

Her heart breaking and with only anger to shore her up, she rose, grabbed her belongings, and left without looking back...not even to see her broken heart dragging the ground.

Blindly walking toward Canal Street, Nola flicked away tears. She stepped off the curb and onto the brick-paved street to avoid a crowd on the corner being entertained by a mime.

"I should've known. All the signs were there." The minute she'd laid eye on him, she'd experienced a connection. It surpassed time and place. But intuition gave rise to all of her fears. Just what she had surmised would happen came to fruition. She might love Rex Arceneau forever...a pain she would be forced to endure. But never would she remain in a relationship with a man who tried to manipulate her.

"As my granddaddy used to say, 'you bet on people like you bet on horses—by past performances.' Sage advice."

Rex...she recalled the limo and his first appearance at Fleur de Lis. How her heart had beat in 12/8 time. How his captivating smile nearly pulled her from her second-floor bedroom window. The yin and yang of attraction battled. Desire won out in the end.

What to do now? Her list loomed large. She'd counted on Rex's help. But he had more pressing matters. Business responsibilities. They came first. Managing obligations, she understood that fact of life. However, she couldn't disappoint the kids in her band. Kayla could cater her parents' anniversary party. By comparison, all easy fixes.

But how did she go about replacing her heart?

Chapter 20

"Do a last check of the dining room. Light candles on the tables," Rex told the headwaiter. Back inside the kitchen, Rex gave final orders to the kitchen staff. Everyone scurried to carry out his commands. Everything was ready to begin dinner service. The doors would open promptly at five p.m. He'd manage tonight without Kayla, but what about all the tomorrows? Would he have to break down and ask Uncle Henri for help just to keep the doors open? He shuddered at the thought. But his brain had produced no further options.

At five minutes to five, Kayla sauntered through the back door in black slacks and white chef's coat. She grabbed a white apron from the cupboard and tied it around her, looking the part of a professional chef.

She didn't acknowledge him, and he crossed the kitchen to stand beside her. "Kayla, can we talk? Did you talk to Nola?"

She walked to the sink and washed her hands, then dried them with paper towel. Grabbing a clean cotton towel, she tucked it into the waist of her apron.

"This is silly. We need to talk. We can work this out. I'm still your brother."

"Half," she snapped.

"Papa recognized me as his legal heir in his will. I own half of the house with you. I'm still your business partner."

Kayla clapped. "Attention. Thank all y'all for pulling together today, and all the days since my papa died. One quick announcement. *I* am the executive chef of Arceneau's. Regardless of any gossip leaking through the walls, those rumors are as thin as broth. The meat of the matter—*I'm* running Arceneau's. Not Chef Henri. Not Chef Rex."

"Yes, Chef," came a chorus of responses.

Rex jerked his apron from around his waist and tossed it into the hamper with the rest that needed washing. She didn't need his help? Fine. He'd hang out and watch, make notes of things that needed to be corrected, improved, or just eliminated from the workflow of the kitchen. He wanted her to run things. Wanted her to believe in herself. Wanted her to step up. And he wanted to be there to lend a hand, if and only if, she needed it. Intruding was never part of his plan. She was Papa's true heir. The house...that held special meaning...the house they would have to share. Or he would buy her out, but he'd never allow it to be sold. It had to remain in the family.

An hour into service, Rex left the kitchen. Kayla had everything running masterfully. Climbing the stairs to the office, he adjusted any photos and framed awards that hung askew. The restaurant held so many memories. Could he truly walk away?

He opened the office door and sat at the desk, then glanced over to the small side table in front of the window. He missed the little plant that used to sit there. Regret tugged at him. Once he was back in New York, he'd call a florist and have a plant delivered to Kayla to replace the one he'd killed.

Tidying the office, he pulled the folder with his birth certificate from the drawer. He planned to put it in the safe at home. There were other loose ends to finalize, and he jotted down a menu for the Dutreys' anniversary party. Made a few notes in the margins—tips for Kayla, in case she needed them. She'd never catered an event the size of this one, but he had faith she'd manage it just fine. Biloxi Trahan wanted Arceneau's for the party. The restaurant would deliver as promised—only he wouldn't be involved, but he still needed to offer her a referral of a cook for Fleur de Lis Café.

Taking another small notepad from the desk drawer, he drew lines that merged into a trumpet. Who could he call to replace him in a trumpet battle with Marquis? Best person to ask would be the trumpet man himself. He put a star by Marquis' name. Pulling out his phone, he texted him:

—I need a ride to the airport tomorrow. 8 a.m. Will you? Also, fundraiser for Nola. Dueling trumpets. You and who?—

Below the drawing, he began a list of musicians he'd grown up with, and if called, they wouldn't be kept away from any fundraising event to help kids. Especially if Arceneau's catered the food. He'd donate the funds for the spread, but he'd ask Kayla not to mention it to Nola, just make the offer from the business.

Kayla. She had to talk to him. Had to deal with him. He had every right—as her brother, Papa's heir, and business partner—to come to some consensus with her about the future of the restaurant. In a week or two, she'd come around. He could wait her out.

But what about Nola? The connection wasn't just magnetic. He would carry her in his heart forever.

"I have no right to expect her to stand with me." Dejected, he shook his head.

After reflecting on her heated words about the audition, he could understand the reason she was angry. But he didn't have time to offer her the perfect apology. Her anger would keep them apart. For now, that was probably for the best.

Why couldn't they try to make it work? She had only a couple of months until the summer. Until then, she had teaching and band and performing. Once he got things running in New York, he could visit her in New Orleans during the week... Could he persuade her to move into the house? His heart lifted at the thought of opening the door to the Garden District home and finding her there, waiting for him.

If she agreed to move in, it would help him out as much as her. She could give up her apartment and save that money, or put it toward the band. Kayla wouldn't be alone. The idea had merit. Maybe he could make her see the benefits...maybe. He clung to that sliver of hope.

They could work a schedule to see each other while she toured during the summer months. After all, a few of the great festivals where she was performing weren't far from New York City. The community band...how could he help her with that? Donate uniforms? Find her a new space to hold band practice? What would she *allow* him to do? Her independent streak required she be in control.

What about next year, once Mardi Gras came and went? Could she cut back on her involvement with the band? Would she allow someone to take over for her? She could be the spokesperson and the fundraiser, yet give up the day-to-day work, turning it over to someone else.

"Of course she couldn't. It's who she is." Rex shook his head. The hope that had surged a moment ago now twisted into a rope of pain.

There had to be a way. He didn't want to live without her. But there was nothing keeping him here now. Other than the magnetic pull of his heart to hers and the surging connection between them. She felt it. How could she ignore the specialness of what they shared?

But all of his business pursuits were up north. His daydream of a restaurant and club where they worked together had been a pipe dream to nowhere. Something pleasant to dream about, but waking reality cast a harsh spotlight on the truth of his existence. They couldn't hope to build a lasting bridge between New York and New Orleans with love and expect it to withstand the rigors of daily life.

****

"Thanks, Marquis." Nola climbed into the front seat of the limo. "I appreciate the ride to work." After he dropped Kayla at the restaurant, he'd driven her home for a short nap and to change. Now he was her chariot driver taking her to work.

"It's on my way. But tonight, you take care of my girl."

"Kayla isn't a fragile flower. She'll be fine."

He scowled.

"Fine. I promise to watch out for her."

The short drive lasted only moments. The digital

clock on the dash flipped to nine p.m. She blew Marquis a kiss as he pulled away from the curb, then she entered the restaurant through the front door, as was her usual way. Waving to customers, she pointed upstairs, a little reminder of where they could find her after they finished their dinner.

Lifting the skirt of the simple ankle-length navy dress, she climbed the stairs. Her black patent leather, peep-toe shoes showed off her bright red toenails. Reaching the second floor, she stood tall, adjusted the dress and the three-strand pearl necklace dangling around her neck. She nodded to the employee filling up a water pitcher for her behind the small bar in the lounge. The trio playing for her tonight wasn't due to arrive for another few minutes. She noticed their instruments were already set up. Clearly, they'd been there and gone at some point. Or maybe they were in the kitchen scrounging a meal from Kayla.

A screech of wood-on-wood floated down from the third floor. Someone was up there. She considered checking, but in case it was Rex, she didn't want to see him. It was highly unlikely that anyone else would be up there…unless, of course, the rather nefarious Uncle Henri had slunk back for something.

Earlier in the afternoon, she and Kayla had talked. About the future. About disappointment. And about family—loved and hated them at the same time. Tonight would be her last performance at Arceneau's until Kayla and Rex worked things out. Kayla had urged her to sign a new contract, but Nola resisted. Until the partnership and the roles of its members were determined, she couldn't in good faith sign on the dotted line. And she had no intention of working for

Rex. It wasn't the kind of relationship she wanted with him.

But what did she want?

Nola stepped to the microphone at ten p.m. She'd selected the saddest blues songs for the set, fighting back tears during each number. Her heart grieved for Rex, and he hadn't yet left the city.

During the break between sets, she mingled with customers and signed autographs. A few had purchased her CD when they paid for their dinner. One man waved a waitress over and asked for more napkins.

"She's breaking my heart," the older man sniffed. "I don't know who broke hers, but they ought to be dropped off the Crescent City Connection over the Mississippi River and hit by a passing barge."

As midnight arrived, Nola sang the last note, and the drummer ended the session with a quick *tat* of a cymbal, then clamped down on the shimmering sound to mute it. Her heart had been muted the same way by Rex. Thoughts of him left her more emotionally tattered than before.

He never made an appearance.

She had hoped he might ask her to stay on at the restaurant. In doing so, she planned to use the opportunity to pull him and Kayla closer together to resolve the chasm of personal and professional differences they faced—including the one that impacted her. Her job.

Silly girl. You want him to stay for you.

But no Rex. She'd listened for further sounds upstairs in the office. Nothing more had come. Maybe she'd imagined the noises earlier.

Heading downstairs to the now empty restaurant,

Nola met Kayla as she came from the kitchen.

"Hey girlfriend, you look like you've lost your last friend. But that ain't true, cuz I'm standing right here."

"Drink," Nola demanded, then picked a chair at a table in the corner of the darkened restaurant.

"Since when do you drink?"

"Now seems like a reasonable time to start."

Kayla shrugged. "What ya want?"

"Something that will put me to sleep forever...or at least until you and Rex work things out, he's gone, and I can work for you. Not him." When would her wish come true? Kayla could be so stubborn. Not mulish. Or even jackass-ish, but stuck-in-quicksand-up-to-her-nose kind of stubborn. Rex had offered an olive branch, and Kayla had swatted it away.

"How about The Obituary?"

"That's a drink? Kayla, I don't really want to die. I just want something to take the edge off so I can sleep. The whole night through."

"To forget Rex? Just because I'm pissed at him, doesn't mean you have to be. I'll make you a drink. Something more to your liking." She headed for the bar on the other side of the dining room.

"I have my own reasons for being angry as hell at him," Nola called out across the expanse of room.

"Did I just hear you cuss?" Kayla did an about face. Eyes wide. Mouth agape.

"Shit. Shit. Shit." Nola pounded the table. The silverware bounced and clanked together.

Kayla grabbed a bottle and a container from the bar and raced back to the table.

"What am I going to do?" Nola plunked her elbows on the table and rested her chin in her hands.

"Well, for starters, don't break my table. Then drink this." Kayla poured tequila into a water glass and pulled a wedge of lime from the container.

Nola swallowed hard. Anger and hurt twined together in a noose for her heart. It was death by hanging...of a sort. Could alcohol sufficiently dull the pain?

"Salt!" Kayla jumped up and ran to the kitchen.

Nola swirled the liquid in the glass as she waited. When her friend returned a moment later, Kayla plopped into a chair, sliding the tablecloth with her. Nola grabbed the bottle and her glass to keep it from toppling over.

"Good save." Kayla grabbed Nola's thumb and smeared the lime across the side of her hand. After sprinkling salt over the dampened area, she released her grip.

"What do we drink to?" Nola asked.

"Us."

"Why us? Why not men, broken hearts, and betrayal?"

"Who the fuck wants to celebrate that? A toast is to honor someone. Something. So here's to you, Nola Dutrey. The best friend a girl could ever have." Kayla licked the salt from her hand, flipped the glass up, downing the alcohol, and sucked on the lime. Drumming on the table, she bounced silverware onto the floor.

"Shit." Nola bent to pick it up.

"Leave it."

Nola sat up. "What?"

"Leave it. The silverware and the cussing. It's just not you."

"Maybe you don't know me as well as you think."

"Ever kill anyone?" Kayla smiled so wide her eyes squinted shut.

"No." Indignant, she eyed her friend. "Have you?"

"Not really, but I wanted to. And if I get drunk enough tonight, I just might do it."

"Kill who?"

"Uncle Henri."

Nola poured a double shot for Kayla. If she got drunk, she'd call Marquis to pick them up and Kayla could go home with her. There she'd have no chance to do anyone harm, most of all herself.

"Why him?"

"He stole my life away." Kayla's sober expression pierced Nola's heart. "Rex has always been everything to me. Mother. Father. Protector. Big brother. But now I learn he's only my half brother." Kayla knocked back the shot without a lick of salt and grabbed another lime to suck.

"But Kayla," Nola said softly, as she reached across to grasp her friend's wrist. "He's known since he was a ten-year-old little boy. And still he played those roles for you. He's loyal and devoted to you. Can't ask for a better brother, half or whole."

She was making a very good case for Kayla, but why couldn't she conjure up the same forgiveness and acceptance for Rex? Had his interference been so heinous?

Pain squeezed her battered heart as though trying to pry out the last drop of blood. Kayla still had her brother, whereas she had no lasting connection to the man she wanted to share her life with. Just a future of unfulfilled love.

Grabbing the bottle, she poured herself a double. Licked her hand. Sprinkled salt over the wet spot. Licked the grains. Then knocked the tequila back.

"Whoa, slow down, girl."

Going down, the alcohol warmed her insides. It hit her stomach. The burn made her scrunch her face tightly. She opened one eye.

"Suck! Suck!" Kayla shoved a quarter of a lime at her.

Nola bit into the fruit as ordered.

"Suck like your life depends on it." Kayla pounded the table.

Grabbing the container, Nola took another lime. The sucking sound rang loudly in her ears. Her mouth hurt from drawing out the juice of the fruit.

"Okay. Okay. Enough!" Kayla cried.

"That was painful." She sighed. "Kayla, what do you want? What do you want Rex to do? What do you want *for* him?"

"Too damn philosophical. I'll go to Mass in the morning and contemplate the answers to those questions—not."

Anger sparked in Nola. Kayla didn't understand what a wonderful brother she had. Yes, he'd crossed the line with her, but his sister—he'd only done good by her. Why couldn't she see she was hurting herself and him, too? "Talk to Rex."

"I will."

"When?"

"When I'm f'ing ready."

"But what if he goes away and never comes back? What if he'll only talk with you through an attorney? What if he gives you his share of the business, like he's offered? Don't you care about his pain?"

Kayla grabbed the bottle and drank. After wiping her mouth with the back of her hand, her eyes turned cold. "You're a fine one to talk. He's in love with you. You're breaking his heart because there's no future with you."

"What do you mean?" A nervous pulse skittered through her.

"My brother, *my* brother, has never loved a woman like he loves you. I doubt he can even admit it to himself. But you're so stubborn, you can't throw him a crumb of hope. You're standing on your pillar of ethics and integrity. But I know."

Nola's heartbeat quickened. "What do you know?"

"Have...another drink, Nola Belle. *I'll* tell you alllll about Nola Dutrey." The cadence of Kayla's words suggested the effects of alcohol had kicked in. But she wasn't alone. Nola fanned herself as a flush rose from her neck to her face.

Pouring another splash in each glass, Nola *thunked* the tequila bottle on the table, then she handed a lime to Kayla, and took one for herself.

"Take...take the"—Kayla motioned with her hand for her to drink—"then, I'll tell you...what I know."

The fear that Kayla might repeat untrue gossip sobered her some. Nola paused. What could Kayla possibly know about her?

Picking up the glass, Nola licked the remaining salt on her hand, downed the pale liquid, and squeezed the wedge of fruit so the juice dribbled into her mouth.

"There. Now tell me."

Kayla pursed her lips and stared. Her eyes narrowed. "You're so dammmmn independent. Won't take help. From anyone. *Anyone*. You're afraiddd…afraid…of real success. You give lip service to wanting to help kids. Do the band thingy. No New York. Only summer tours. You live in a cracker box. Work three jobs. You're fucking great. But you hide. Chickenshit. Why?"

Nola stood, pushing back the chair. The back of it crashed against the wall. "Who the hell died and made you judge and jury of me?"

"Ohhh…the mighty Nola Belle is mad." Kayla bobbed her head.

"Checkmark. You get a gold star."

Kayla blinked. Her eyelids drooped. "Yay, me." Putting her arms on the table, she rested her head.

"Awww, crap." Nola took out her phone and texted Marquis, asking for a ride to deliver Kayla home. He advised he'd be there in a half hour.

Sitting in silence with her sleeping friend, Nola's lips formed a pout. Her bottom lip quivered. The ache in her heart was trying to burst from her chest.

"Owwwww," she moaned. Tears welled in her eyes. The bottle of tequila in the middle of the table stared at her. "I don't want another drink. I want Rex."

"I'm here."

Startled, she looked around. In the darkness, she could barely make out a silhouette in the opposite corner. It moved. When it started toward her, the light streaming in through the big picture windows allowed her to see. Rex. He looked stern and businesslike in his gray suit and crisp white shirt. But so handsome. Her gaze focused on his lips. She sucked in a breath, rose, and then moved away from the table and Kayla, stepping into the center aisle. Rex drew closer. He pulled her in for a crushing hug, cupped her face with his hands, kissing her hungrily, urgently. Everything about him soothed her aching soul. The scent of his cologne. The strength of his grip. The smoothness of his lips. His tongue traced the outline of her lips and then dipped between them. In opening for him, she was opening all of herself, her soul. She loved him.

His hands caressed her neck, sliding down her arms.

Their hands met, and she laced her fingers through his. All the while, their lips kept them locked together.

She broke the kiss, and he stroked her hair. "I love you, Nola Dutrey," he whispered. She wrapped her arms around his neck and kissed him. His arms went around her lower back, and he hoisted her off the floor while peppering her lips with kisses.

Euphoria spread through her. Rex loved her. *Loved* her. He'd said it before, but not directly to her. He was a man declaring his love. Now she wanted to show him how much she loved him.

Urgently, she needed to feel all of him. Hating the constriction of clothing, she began to remove his jacket. She wanted more of him than his lips and his hands. Peeling his jacket off his shoulders, she tossed it on a table. She reached for his shirt. He'd already started with the top button. She moved to the bottom one. They would meet in the middle.

As his shirt opened, she smoothed her hands over his chest, soaking in the familiar warmth of him. He pulled her close again. Their bodies compressed together. His hardness pressing into her sent a thrill washing through her body. Moisture formed in her most private place. Building tension pushed at her with urgency.

Bang. Bang. Outside, Marquis pounded on the door. Rex let her go and stepped back. He scooped up his jacket.

"Oh. I forgot. I texted him to take Kayla home."

"Let him take her home. You go, too." Rex's voice was so low, it was barely audible. "Goodbye, Nola. I'll dream of what might have been."

"Wait. Don't go. Come home with me. Marquis can deliver Kayla home."

"Nola! You in there?" Marquis hollered, then pressed his face to the window of the front door.

"Yes! Coming!"

"What's the noise?" Kayla lifted her head from the table.

Nola looked at the door and Marquis, then back to Kayla. She hurried to give Marquis entry. When she turned back, Kayla was trying to stand, wobbling like a bobblehead doll.

Kayla's trumpet player pushed past her. "What took you so long to open the door?"

"I…I…was talking with Rex."

As Marquis scooped Kayla up, he glanced around. "How much did you have to drink?"

"Why?"

The man shrugged. "No Rex."

He was gone.

Chapter 21

The next morning, Rex dropped his bag in the foyer by the front door. He glanced back. His heart hurt to see his sister sitting on the couch stiff as a statue. "Kayla, I'm leaving. You're going to have to talk to me sooner or later. Why don't you ride with me to the airport?"

"I can't believe Marquis agreed to take you. Traitorous men, both of you."

"Look, I don't know how to reach you. I understand the revelation of our relationship is shocking, but it doesn't have to change anything."

Kayla pointed to the door. "Just go. I can't talk about it. You're walking out on me, just like when you left for college."

"I have to take care of business. I'll be back. I don't want to have to worry about operations on multiple fronts. You've got this. You can run Arceneau's. It's what you always wanted."

Standing, his sister turned around and pointed at him. "You're wrong," she said through clenched teeth. The dart of her anger hit him squarely in the chest. "I wanted *us* to work side by side. You thought I wasn't good enough to work with you in New York. You wanted to keep me here, keep me under Papa's thumb. You, like him, think that I'm only a woman, that pastry is all I can do. Papa wanted me to be a little girl until

259

the day he died."

"Not true. Think about it. I found out at ten, at ten years old, that I wasn't his son. I wanted him to favor you over me because I didn't feel like I belonged. I was half. Never whole. Can't you see how that would alter the world for a kid? I didn't take anything away from you. I worked to ensure you would always have what was rightfully yours. Which is why I'm willing to give you my share of the business."

"How dense is that male brain of yours? I want you. I told you that. You to teach me. Give me a year. I think you owe me that."

Rex shook his head. "There's no reasoning with you. I've got to go. I have to deal with the fires losses in New York. One of the restaurants and a barn at the farm burned."

Would the facts smooth the way? Would she relent? If he had any hope of discovering the truth behind the arson—he probably would never be able to prove his hunch that Henri was involved—he had to get there now.

Picking up his bags, he opened the front door. Before he crossed the threshold, he turned back. "Kayla, you're my sister. The only one I'll ever have. I love you."

As he closed the door behind him, he heard her shout, "I hate you!" Then sobbing reached his ears. His heart broke. He paused. Marquis waited by the limo. The crying continued. Sighing, he took another step away from the front door. He wanted to run. Run back inside the house, hug his sister, and convince her that everything would work out. But she needed time. He had a plane to catch. At least Kayla had Nola to look after her.

The ride to the airport stretched on forever. Heavy traffic on the interstate had them moving at less than a horse-trot pace. He shoved visions of Nola aside, but like the persistence of the woman he loved, his memories of her adamantly refused to dissipate. Would they have made love last night? She was spontaneous. Loved that about her, but he harbored wishes of treating her to a romantic night in a five-star hotel with all the luxuries of a bed, room service, and a view.

"Take care of her," Rex said, shaking hands with Marquis.

"No worries about Kayla. But man, what about Nola?"

"It would never work."

"Figure it out. I'm tellin' you, don't let that woman slip away." Marquis chuckled. "The two of you are two halves of the same whole. She's the feminine version of you with her do-gooder ways. You're the male version of her with all the responsibility you take on. Yin and yang. I'm not wrong about this."

"She won't move to New York," Rex said flatly. "She believes I betrayed her by trying to get her an audition. Her principles were trampled. Plus, I'm letting her down by leaving. Her parents' anniversary party. The fundraiser for her band."

"Okay, but when a man loves a woman, he's gotta do everything to keep her, or he becomes an empty shell. Life is about love. Love of music. Love of food. Love of others—especially that one special person who makes life worth sharing."

Rex shook his head. "Yeah, well, anyway…" He turned and walked into the airport, walking away from the nearest and dearest to his heart—Nola Bridgette Dutrey.

****

Nola stood in the one p.m. sunshine checking the buttons on her charcoal-gray suit jacket after exiting the cab. She'd paid for the ride to the councilwoman's office instead of asking Marquis to drive her. He was too painful a reminder of Rex.

Her palms began to sweat. She clutched her purse tighter. Her heels clicked on the granite steps as she climbed the stairs to the office. Pushing open a tall, carved wooden door, she entered a tiled foyer. Closing the doors shut out the traffic and noise of the city. It was as though she were encased in a hush.

Nola scanned the names stenciled on the doors and found the one she sought.

Pushing it open, she discovered the door to a wood-paneled antechamber and crossed the planked floor. The *tat-tat* of her footsteps stopped when she reached the carpet. A secretary seated behind a large desk with a monitor to one side greeted her. "May I help you?"

"I'm Nola Dutrey. I have an appointment with Mr. Sharp and the councilwoman." She approached closer. Trepidation rattled her as she stopped at the desk. It was much like when she was a kid and called before the principal back in grade school. She tried to shake off the nervousness. Today, she hoped to resolve the issue about the community center once and for all.

The secretary frowned. "I'm sorry. The councilwoman is at a luncheon today. That meeting has been on her calendar for weeks. Let me look to see if the appointment for you was set at a different date and time." She typed away on a keyboard. "I don't see you listed anywhere."

"What about Mr. Marc Sharp? Maybe he forgot to say that I was attending. He was the one who confirmed the date and time of this appointment."

"Mr. Sharp from that magazine?" The woman raised one eyebrow.

"Yes, that's him."

"Ms. Dutrey, I can assure you Mr. Sharp doesn't have an appointment."

"Hey," a voice called out.

Nola turned. "Mr. Sharp. This lady says we don't have an appointment. In fact, the councilwoman isn't even here."

"I know." He moved toward her, stopping only a foot away.

Anger flared. Nola swallowed against it. If she didn't get ahold of herself, her response to the situation would combust into a fireball—her purse connecting with the side of his head.

The day had started out poorly. She'd been at the airport to catch a last glimpse of Rex as he departed. Last night, he'd said he loved her. How could he just walk away? She'd never begged a man to stay before, but this time, she imagined throwing herself at him and him whisking her off on the plane with him. But of course, she couldn't do it. His responsibilities had a tighter rein over him than his heart. Watching him leave left her raw. Her nerves were like heart of pine kindling igniting into a raging fire. She'd wanted to tell him how much she loved him, but that alone couldn't be reason enough for him to change his entire life and stay.

Marc Sharp didn't know how lucky he was she

didn't channel Kayla and open a can of whoop-ass on him. She'd watched the man she loved leave her life. She wasn't about to allow another one to ruin the future for her kids.

"You got a fire extinguisher here?" Marc leaned around Nola, addressing the secretary.

"How may I help the two of you?" the woman asked.

"I'll tell you." Nola made an about-face and stared down at the receptionist. "I'm trying to keep the kids' community band running."

"Oh, yes. The councilwoman has you on her list of people to contact. I should've recognized your name, but I think of you as Nola Belle, not Nola Dutrey." She smiled.

"I'm in crisis mode. I want to keep the space. For my kids. For our kids. This is our community. They're our responsibility. In the meantime, Mr. Broussard, I'm told, has given the space to another group. I want it back. I want the councilwoman to help me negotiate with her staffer for Constituent Relations."

The secretary nodded.

"Then, this guy"—Nola thumbs over her shoulder—"barges into my life with nasty accusations. Tell her what you asked me yesterday. He's writing an article that includes me."

"Well…" Marc stuttered.

"Yes, well, what questions did you have for Miss Nola, Mr. Sharp?" the secretary asked.

He pulled a small pad from his back pocket. "Question one. Is it true that you had a little slap and tickle with Emile Broussard at the Carousel? Question two. Did he give you the key to his hotel room?

Question three. And *after that*, you received the exclusive contract on the community center."

"It sounds sordid and clandestine, but it's anything but." Nola placed her purse on the corner of the desk. "I met Mr. Broussard, at his direction, to discuss the contract at the Carousel Bar. It was the first time we met to talk about the lease. The second time"—she held up two of her fingers—"he lured me there with the belief that we were going to discuss a fundraiser *after* I signed the contract for the community center. Then he slipped me a room key and made it clear where he wanted the real conversation to take place. I left. With no contract. No visit to his room. A few days later, a courier delivered the contract to me at the private school where I teach." Nola paused and took a deep breath, then let it out. "I tell this so you are my witness to the accounting of the story, in the event Mr. Sharp libels me in his article."

"Hmm… I see." The secretary scribbled on the notepad on her desk. When she finished, she tapped the pen against the pad. "Miss Nola, while I cannot guarantee it, I have it on fairly good authority you will be meeting with the councilwoman in the immediate future." The woman clicked on the computer. She ran her finger down the screen. "I'll pencil you in, and you can meet her at the nail shop while she's getting a manicure. Next Friday. She likes to be out and about the community showing support for families and businesses. I want you to leave here knowing I believe she will throw her support your way."

Nola tingled down to her toes. She forced herself to not get on her hands and knees and bow before the woman. She maintained a professional decorum on the outside. Inside she was jumping up and down like she did at Mardi Gras eager to catch some beads. "May I come around and hug you?"

The receptionist stood. "It's not every day we have a happy constituent come through the door." She stepped to the side of the desk, and Nola hugged her.

"Thank you. Thank you." Nola waved goodbye, pushed past Marc Sharp, and left the office.

On the sidewalk, she twirled. One less worry. A big one. Her kids could continue with the band. Hopefully, she'd seen the last of Emile. And Marc Sharp.

"We are family."

Slightly dizzy, Nola stopped, staggered, then sat down on a granite step. Her phone ceased ringing, but then started again.

"Hello, sister dearest." Her sister's voice came through the phone.

"Hello, Biloxi. What's up?"

"I got a call from *the* Rex Arceneau. What's going on?"

"About?" She wasn't about to offer information her sister didn't need to know.

"He's *not* going to help with the catering for Momma and Daddy's party?" It was more an accusation than a question. Something her sister was famous for.

"Oh. Right. But no worries, Kayla's got it under control."

"She makes beautiful cakes, but…"

"Trust. Sister. Trust. Everything will work out just fine."

"What about you?" The tone of Biloxi's voice

changed to sincere.

"Me?"

"Will everything work out fine if he's in New York and you're down here? Remember, I was with you when you first laid eyes on him. He hooked you before 'hello.'" The worrying edge flittering in her sister's voice when she wanted to play older sister and offer unsolicited advice pushed Nola to the edge.

That's none of your business.

"Biloxi, everything will work out—just like it's supposed to. That's all I've got to say. See you before the party."

Nola stared at her phone after her sister ended the call. If only she could convince herself of the words she'd spoken...

"New York." She sighed. She had to come to terms with the fact that New York was his home, New Orleans only a stopover from time to time. As much as she might want to, she didn't have it in her to be a "stopover" kind of woman. That's the reason she refused to tour all the time. And she wanted a man who would be there when she woke each morning and put her head on the pillow each night. Life wasn't lived in minutes scheduled between airline flights. And that's all she could ever hope for from him.

"Life will go on."

But forever with a sad refrain.

Chapter 22

Nola dragged herself out of bed and shuffled to the kitchen to start the coffee machine at eight a.m. The plant on the table had withered and browned. Picking up the flowerpot, she chucked it in the garbage can.

"What a resume I have. Plant killer. Murderer of love," she muttered. "Perfect way to start the week."

Shoulders slumped, she unplugged the coffeemaker, then set an alarm on her phone. She could sleep the rest of the morning and half of the afternoon. It would take less than an hour to dress and then appear at band practice. She crawled back into bed.

Knock. Knock. Knock.

Nola ignored the knocking, rolled over, and pulled a pillow over her head.

Bang. Bang. Bang.

"What?" she yelled, throwing back the covers and stomping to the front door. She yanked open the door. Kayla and Marquis stood grinning at her.

"See," Kayla said. "Got to put some *oomph* into it."

"Knocking is politer." Marquis rolled his eyes.

"Like I have time for your commentary," Nola snapped. "You"—she pointed at Kayla—"never answered my text."

"Peace offering." Kayla held up a white paper cup like she was dangling a diamond in front of a New

Orleans socialite. "Decaf coffee. But don't you think you need to dress first? I'm not the jealous type. But this is my man. He's all man. And a tank top and panties was not the way you were raised to welcome guests at your door."

"Frick-frack. Who are you? What have you done with my friend?" Kayla not cursing was like a bowl of gumbo with no rice. Nola looked down at her scant attire, hugged her chest, and crossed her legs.

Marquis chuckled. "We're working on our relationship. I want her to swear less. She wants to make love at least once a day." He winked. "I got the better end of this deal."

"Come in. Close the door," Nola instructed as she headed to the bedroom to change. After pulling on black yoga pants and a purple sweatshirt, she returned to the living room.

The light from the lamp hurt her eyes. She turned it off, then joined her friends, flopping onto the couch. She pulled her knees to the side and tucked her feet close. Her apartment no longer felt like a sanctuary. The room reminded her of Rex.

"Here." Kayla, sitting on the other end of the couch, pushed the coffee cup at her. She turned on the lamp next to her.

"Turn off the light."

"No. And you can thank me for the coffee."

"Yes. And thank you." Nola closed her eyes against the brightness. Her world was dark with Rex gone. Adding artificial light didn't change reality.

"Since when don't you want coffee?"

"Since today. Is this a social call or what?" Nola set the cup on the side table.

"When did you eat last?" Kayla frowned.

"Before Rex left."

"Woman, you got to take care of yourself." Marquis seated himself in the chair, crossed his foot over his knee, and shook his finger at her.

Kayla rose and went to the fridge. "There's not sh—stuff in here," she complained.

"I'm not hungry."

"Nola, let's grab some breakfast." Marquis grinned. "I'll drive."

Kayla plopped down next to her and draped an arm over her shoulder. "Look, sister, we gotta talk. As in, you must listen to me. Pleeease come back and sing in the lounge. We'll get a contract worked out."

"You talked to Rex yet?"

Kayla squirmed. She folded her hands in her lap.

"No singing until you work things out with Rex."

"I can't work things out with Rex until *you* talk to him."

"You want to puncture my heart more? I can't talk to him."

"You really love him?" Marquis asked quietly.

Nola planted her feet on the floor and threw up her hands. "No, I'm crazy sick about the man. But…" The wind in her argument dissipated. "Leave me alone. Go away." She curled up on the couch into a tight ball.

"You taught me about positive possibilities," Kayla accused. "So where's your *oomph*? You want him here. I want him here. Let's work on this together."

"Just for the record, I want him in New York for the summer while I'm there," Marquis interjected.

Nola narrowed her eyes at him. "Well, you got your wish, didn't you? Both of you, please just go.

Leave me alone."

Kayla sighed. "I can't. I need you to help me get him back. I want to share Arceneau's with him. Buy Henri out. Rex can buy a farm here, if that's what he thinks it will take to make the restaurant stand out more. Besides..." Kayla looked down at her hands folded in prayer. "You asked me what I wanted for him. I want him to have the love of his life—you."

Tears welled in Nola's eyes. "I want him, too."

"So help me help you."

"I can't ask him to give up New York. I won't give up my life here. There's no hope."

"It's called compromise. It's called working on a relationship." Marquis stood. "Nola, you have to talk to Rex. You don't want to sing melody the rest of your life. Harmony is better. Decide on a tempo and work out the rhythm."

"It's a 12/8 beat." Her chin quivered.

"The blues?" Kayla asked.

"Find your bridge," Marquis continued. "Or this sad shit will be the coda of your life." He motioned for Kayla and headed toward the door.

Kayla hugged her, then left shaking her head.

"Get out!" Nola shouted. "Leave me alone. If I want help, I'll ask for it."

Nola flipped off the light. In the darkness, she hugged her chest. "I'll get used to him being gone," she whispered. "Someday."

****

Rex sat in the office at the farm and stared out the window at the Pennsylvania scenery. It wasn't yet time to plant in the field, but thankfully the arsonist hadn't torched the greenhouse where their organic lettuces and kale grew.

He rubbed around the large burn on his forearm. Trying to throw himself into work, he'd manned the grill rather than running the line. His concentration was off, resulting in the ugly wound. He'd lost his focus. Hell, it wasn't missing. It stayed behind in New Orleans. He couldn't get into the rhythm of the kitchen. And in his frustration, he broke nearly every rule he ever set for himself about how to treat employees. The evening host had stepped into the kitchen, cautioning him to keep his voice down as the customers could hear his swearing. If he was going to fight with anyone over anything, he wanted it to be with Nola. That would mean they were together and working on a future.

"Yo, Rex." Carter, one of his business partners, walked through the door, slapped Rex's boot-clad feet off the desktop, and parked in the spot. "What's the deal?"

Straightening, Rex handed over spreadsheets from a stack of papers on the desk. "We make enough to hire a full-time farm manager."

"I'm not asking about the numbers. What's with you? It's like you burned with the building. Your mood is scorched. You're as much an eyesore as that crumbling building."

"It's coming down tomorrow."

"Do you need to be going down, too?"

"Down?" Rex looked over at Carter and shook his head.

"You've been back for a few days. Yet it's like your body arrived, but your heart and mind are someplace else. What gives?"

Nola. Every waking moment I think of her.

Dreaming is the only time I can touch her.

Rex shrugged. "Nothing. Doing my job."

"Phillip and I had a meeting last night when the restaurant closed."

"Where was I?"

"Don't know. You left before we could tell you we wanted to talk."

Rex sighed. "I gave you what you came for. I'll see you back in the city later. I'll be at the restaurant on time."

"Phillip and I think you need to go home. Go back to New Orleans. Something changed you on this last trip. You won't say what, but we're betting there are loose ends still needing some closure. We've always worked as a team for the good of all. You've been outvoted this time. Dude, you lost your father less than two months ago. We think you need some time off."

Rex narrowed his eyes at his business partner and friend. They'd met in culinary school and competed to out-create each other with new dishes. "Are the two of you conspiring behind my back?" But could this be the answer he'd been looking for?

"Hell, yes. But for the good of all of us. You're dragging down morale at work. Can't have that. When you're ready to come back—"

"What if I don't?"

"Not return?"

"Yeah, what if I go and can't return?"

"It's not like planes are going to stop flying between here and there. What do you mean, *can't?*"

Nola. I need to be with her. Otherwise, I'm existing, not living.

"My father left the books in a mess. My sister

273

needs my help." Rex sighed. "New Orleans always has been, always will be, my home." Conjuring up images of the city, recalling scents of brackish water and frying grease, remembering the notes played by the students in Nola's band—that he could handle. But being denied the opportunity to ever hold her again. Kiss her lips. Make love to her. That wasn't a life. He needed her the same way he needed New Orleans.

Carter shrugged. "Do what you got to do. I'm your friend. You got to be happy. The business part—it's just business. If it isn't working for you, Phillip and I will offer to buy you out, or work out a compromise that suits everyone."

"Compromise…" Rex muttered. Why couldn't he and Nola find a compromise? "Let me think about it."

"You do that. And until you make a decision, Phillip and I have decided to relieve you from your management duties."

Carter rose from his spot and slugged Rex in the arm. "Dude, just keep us in the loop."

Through the window, Rex watched him climb into his SUV and drive away. Somehow he'd just gotten fired. Well, not exactly since he owned a third of the company, but the net result was pretty damn close.

He glanced around the room. Everything was just as it was the last time he'd been there. As though his coming and going had no real impact on anything. The business would carry on with or without him.

Did Nola feel the same way?

Ring. Ring.

"Hello, Mrs. Trahan. How may I help you?"

"Mr. X. Rex Arceneau, we have a problem that you need to fix." Biloxi's tone snapped at him.

"My sister, bless her heart, has dragged herself here. My family is very concerned. She looks like death warmed over. Her hair is barely combed. Her eyes sunken in. Your sister tells me Nola called in sick on Monday and Tuesday at Harbor House. The only thing she's done all week is take care of that blasted community band."

Was Nola sick? Rex rubbed his chin. Had something happened to her? "What do you want with me, Mrs. Trahan?"

"I want to know if you're in love with my sister. Kayla says you are."

He'd told Nola he loved her. She hadn't said it back. "I don't see what my feelings for your sister have to do with anything. I'm here. She's there."

"Mr. Arceneau, I know a little about family feuds. My husband can fill you in on all the details, if you'd like. But I can't think you'd want one between ours. A Dutrey-Arceneau feud doesn't have a nice ring to it."

"Noooo, can't say I see a benefit to that."

"Then I'll expect you tomorrow evening at my parents' anniversary party. Be prepared to crawl on glass to win my sister back. I know you're a fabulous chef. I hear you play a good horn. And I hear you have near perfect baritone pitch. You're accomplished in many of the arts."

What did he say to that? "Thanks, Mrs. Trahan, I think."

"Compromise. It's an art, too. One I suggest you start practicing right now. See you tomorrow, X. Rex Arceneau." Mrs. Trahan ended the call before he could try to make her understand and practice his compromising skills with her.

Rex raked his fingers through his hair and leaned back in the chair, lifting his feet to the desktop. "Nola," he whispered into the silence of the room. "I'm coming home. It's time I put my efforts into my next dream."

But did Nola's feelings match his? He sensed she did, though she'd never said.

It was time to find out.

Chapter 23

Saturday morning dawned, promising perfect weather. Nola had risen early to practice yoga on the upstairs gallery at Fleur de Lis to find some peace from missing Rex. Thankfully, Mother Nature cooperated. Throughout the morning, the humidity remained low, only rising slightly during the early afternoon.

The start of the party was still a few hours away. So far, everything was running smoothly, thanks to Biloxi. Nola brushed her hair as she watched the activity on the front lawn from her bedroom window. A rented van arrived for the second time that day. Her brother Linc directed it to a spot on the backside of the tent. It was the place designated for Kayla to unload and start her setup for dinner service. Her stunning anniversary cake had been delivered on the first run to Fleur de Lis early that morning.

Her brother had pitched in, along with her cousin Carson, Branna's brother, to set up tables, then covered them with turquoise tablecloths and beachy accessories Biloxi had selected. Chairs were unfolded, one for every guest. Her brother even oversaw the placement of the flowers and candles for each table, though he did have some help from Sophie, Biloxi's French sister-in-law. Whispers among the family hinted that a romance was budding between Linc and sweet Sophie.

Nola smiled when the pair appeared together

leaving the tent. Linc placed a flower in Sophie's hair.

"They make a cute couple, but she's so headstrong, like Nick. I don't think it can last," Biloxi said.

Nola turned. "Don't you believe in knocking before entering someone's bedroom?"

"The door was ajar. It's not like you're hiding a man in here."

True. However, she'd willingly break the house rules if she could have some time with Rex. What was he doing that moment in New York?

Biloxi ran her finger over the screen of her electronic notepad, then looked at her watch. "We're completely on schedule. Let's go down and make sure Kayla has everything."

Nola smiled. "I'm going to check on Camilla. I haven't seen her since I arrived." She didn't want to explain that she hadn't spoken to Kayla since she tossed her and Marquis out of her apartment. Her only contact had been a curt text to say she hadn't resolved the issues with Rex.

"Is something wrong?" Biloxi's forehead wrinkled with concern.

"Nothing. Now go. You'll be able to settle any nerves Kayla is having. I'll be down in a bit." And she would, but when she came face-to-face with Kayla again, she wanted their conversation to be private. No eavesdropping by well-meaning family who'd want to fix the problems in her life.

After Biloxi left, Nola went down the hall to Camila and Jared's room. "Hey there," she said, knocking on the open door. "May I come in?"

"Yes! I need the company." Camilla winced as she scooted in the bed.

"I mean this in a good way, you are *so* big. And you're glowing. You look radiant." Nola took the chair beside the bed.

"Greta comes and plays games to keep me company. Your sister is so wonderful to me. She set up a camera so I can watch the party tonight." Camilla pointed to the computer monitor on the antique chest of drawers.

"Are you sure you're not a spy? We're not using the real silver, so it's not like anyone will steal anything."

Camilla playfully slapped at her. "No, Boo, but it will make me feel a part of all that's going on. Have you seen Aunt Deidre's dress? Woo-hoo!"

"Momma is a fashion bee. She casts a long shadow. But, I hope I've inherited her genes. I want to look that good when I'm her age."

"And have a marriage as happy as hers."

Nola eyed her. "Not you, too!"

"It's a curse. You're next in line. When are you going to lasso that Rex and get him to the altar?"

"What do you know about Rex?"

Camilla smiled. "Darlin', what *don't* I know. X is for Xavier. Rex is his middle name. He's a king, all right. And from the look on your face, you've got it bad. I'm telling you—you got to do what it takes if you want true love. It's work. It's a full-time job, but a complete labor of love."

Nola blinked. Her vision blurred as her eyes misted. "There's just no way. He's New York. I'm New Orleans."

"You both share the 'New' part," she joked. "Jared and I are northwestern and southern. We live here, but spend our summers at the ranch. Nola, I'm telling you, find a compromise with Rex. Otherwise, darlin', you'll be existing, not living, with a broken heart."

Camilla offered a tissue. Nola snatched it from her hand. "Dang you. I miss him so bad. I haven't heard a word from him all week."

"Believe in miracles. Now, I need to rest."

Leaving the door slightly ajar, Nola left her cousin's room and headed back to her own. She pulled a cushion out from under her bed, lit a candle, and began to meditate. Something she'd practiced a couple of times a day since Rex left. It was the only thing that saved her sanity. That and her band kids. Lordy, she didn't even want to sing.

Instead of moving her mind into a peaceful place of rolling hills, babbling brooks, and chirping birds, her mind kept jerking back to the last kiss she'd shared with Rex.

At the restaurant.

In the dark.

She was beginning to believe she'd imagined it through a tequila haze. However, once her mind locked onto the image, her body took over, experiencing all the tingling sensations his touch aroused in her. She settled into the feelings and savored the experience—it would be all she ever had of him. Would it sustain her in the future? After a few minutes, she blew out the candle, watching the smoke curl upward and wishing it could carry her love to Rex.

She slid into a dress that had set her back over a hundred dollars at a secondhand store—the original price nearly five hundred. The large expenditure, she hoped, would stop Biloxi from teasing her about being so stingy with money. And stop her sister from picking out clothes for her.

"Momma will be proud." She glanced in the mirror at her reflection in the elegant purple tea-length gown with a lace bodice and long sleeves. It accentuated the narrowness of her waist. The full tulle skirt made it appear as though she glided rather than walked as she moved. The detail she loved the most about the dress were the tiny rhinestones sparkling around her waist.

Nola braided her hair, then wrapped the long length into a bun on top of her head, securing it with pins. The dangling diamond earrings she borrowed from her sister made her smile. She looked good enough to walk a red carpet. The styling was complete when she slipped on purple, strappy, low-heeled shoes.

Making her way to the tent, she wanted to be there before the guests began arriving at five p.m. She nodded to Kayla, then joined Biloxi and Linc waiting at the door to greet the party's invitees. Her sister planned for their parents to make a grand entrance after all the guests had arrived.

The ballroom set up inside the tent twinkled with a magical ambiance. A partition serving as a backdrop for the band glowed with tiny white lights. Up above, over the tables, strings of lights hung from tent supports like icicles. Balloons covered the ceiling and glittering stars dangled from their streamers, making them appear as though the stars twinkled.

"Ready?" she called to the bandleader.

"Let's get this party started!"

The combo played the first song on the music set list she'd carefully selected. She'd sung with these same musicians many times over the last ten years at nearly every event they played at Fleur de Lis. Their timing always hit perfectly.

When her parents, Deidre and Sean Dutrey, appeared in the doorway, the band played a contemporary anniversary song written by a New Orleans musician who'd relocated to Dallas after Hurricane Katrina.

All the guests rose and applauded. Nola tingled with excitement. She kissed Momma, then Daddy, as they paused to greet each of their children.

Biloxi stepped to the microphone. "Thank you for coming tonight to help us celebrate the thirty-fifth anniversary of our parents. We hope you'll enjoy the evening. The buffet is now open, courtesy of Arceneau's in New Orleans. And, Daddy, all your favorites are there, plus some salad just for Momma." Biloxi stepped off the stage. The band continued to play, and then she stepped back up. "Oh, one more thing. Our cousin Camilla is on bed rest due to her pregnancy. This camera over here is a way for her to witness the party. Please pass by and give her a wave. Everyone, enjoy."

On the way to the stage for her first song, Nola passed the five-tier cake perched on a round table in the middle of the tent. The turquoise cake covered in fondant matched the turquoise of the tablecloths. Each tier had been meticulously decorated with a band of lace that looked so real that Nola wanted to touch it to be certain it was edible. Seed pearls accented the lacey look. Kayla had topped the cake with handmade fondant flowers. The numbers 3 and 5 glittered in the middle. She had outdone herself. It was the most beautiful creation Nola's artistic friend had ever made.

Nola detoured to Kayla. "I'm sorry about what happened at my apartment. I'll apologize appropriately later, but know that your cake is stunning. Thank you."

Kayla winked. "I plan to make one for you. I can't wait until you're Fleur de Lis' next bride."

Nola tilted her head, uncertain what her friend meant, then continued to the microphone stand on stage.

She applauded as the musicians finished their number. "This first song I'm going to sing is one of Momma's favorites. Growing up, my sister and brother and I heard the stories of how our parents met. I'm sure most of your parents have stories like that." She counted down for the band. "One. Two. Three." Then she sang the song Roberta Flack made famous before Nola was born, "The First Time Ever I Saw Your Face."

Singing, she wandered near the first row of tables and poured her heart out. Her mother beamed. Her father's focus was glued to her mother.

All the while, she was singing about Rex. The first time she saw his face was forever permanently etched in her mind. It still made her heart beat at 12/8 time, and that which remained of her shredded heart trembled for him.

After finishing the song, she blew a kiss to her parents, then followed her sister's lead and mingled with guests, greeting and smiling. As she stood next to an elderly neighbor from Bayou Petite, her stomach growled. She covered her belly with her hands as though that would silence the noise.

"Beautiful song. Here, you need this bowl more than me." The elderly gentleman showed his plate covered in fried chicken, mashed potatoes, and collard greens. "I'm leaving room for crawfish étouffée. That'll be my dessert."

"What? No cake?" Nola pointed to the beautiful confection on the center table, then downed a spoonful of gumbo. She recalled the man had helped in the gardens at Fleur de Lis after Katrina.

"That's a cake? Gawd! That's too pretty to eat."

She winked at the man and moved on while the other guests teased him.

When it came time to cut the cake, Biloxi took the spotlight. "Ladies and gentlemen, well, ladies and guys…" The crowd laughed at her joke. "This fabulous creation of a cake was made by Kayla Arceneau of the Arceneau's of New Orleans. She's a genius with pastries."

"Excellent chef, too," Sean Dutrey called out.

"That she is, Daddy." Biloxi nodded. "Thank you, Kayla."

Nola looked on as her friend took a bow, then came forward with a knife almost as long as a sword. The handle was made of pearl and tied with a turquoise silk ribbon. "For the bride and groom. Cake-cutting time."

On cue, Nola's cousins, Evie and Melody, stood near the band. Sophie appeared with a camera and snapped photos. Obviously, Biloxi was grooming her in that art. Momma and Daddy rose from their seats and stood by the cake.

"Before we cut the cake, Linc has a toast. Please raise your glasses." Biloxi lifted a champagne flute. Nola snagged one from a passing server and lifted hers, too.

"Life without the one you love must be a prison or

hell. Congratulations to our parents who've made loving look so easy." Linc raised his glass higher. His words pierced Nola's heart. Is that what she had to look forward to? A week without Rex had been hell. True, she adored all of her students, but wanted someone to share the highs and lows of her day, to spend evenings listening to music they enjoyed, to cuddle and fall asleep wrapped together. To have him look at her with a look of love.

Rex. Oh, Rex.

Her heart skittered, crashed, and burned, tumbling over a cliff. Pain oozed. Intractable, that's what she was. Stubborn, so much so she was in competition with Kayla for being bullheaded. Which one of them took top billing?

For shame. As if that's a prize to battle over.

Momma and Daddy cut the cake. Cousins delivered the sweet treat to the guests as Nola picked up the microphone. "This next song continues the journey of Momma and Daddy's life. It appears, Momma, though completely smitten with Daddy, played hard to get. This song is one of Daddy's favorites. Thank you, Marvin Gaye, for recording "I Want You to Want Me." And everyone, please feel free to get up and dance."

Daddy tugged Momma away from the cake. They moved in unison on the dance floor. Daddy twirled her. Halfway through the song, Daddy belted out a line of the lyrics, then turned Momma and led her into a dip. The crowd cheered.

From her vantage point, Nola looked on. Love for her parents swelled in her heart. At the same time, each beat was a beat without Rex in her life. If her heart beat sixty times a minute, how many beats in an hour? A day? A week? What a waste. Linc was right. Without Rex, life was prison or hell.

She finished her song and ducked outside to feed her sorrow and to escape the joyfulness of the party. Couldn't have the party's headline singer be a downer for all.

The last rays of the setting sun blazed through the trees in orange, red, and pink. By seven thirty it would be dark.

What's Rex doing now?

Saturday night in New York. Probably working at one of his restaurants. Did he meet models, musicians, and socialites? Did any of them have their eyes on him?

As a car moved up the long driveway toward the tent, Nola ducked back inside. Whoever arrived had come late, but better late than never.

A few minutes later, Nola waved away a slice of cake, happy to wait and eat leftovers at midnight. Too much going on. Too much nervous energy. She joined the band for her last song, and she noticed Marquis pulling Kayla into a hug, then draping his arm over her shoulder. He waved. Nola waved back. She had considered caravanning back to New Orleans with Kayla tonight, but now that Marquis was there, the two might have other plans.

"Ladies and gentlemen, I hope you're enjoying yourselves." Nola pulled the microphone from its stand and stepped onto the dance floor. "My last song for the evening says it all with the title, "The Look of Love." It was written by Dusty Springfield."

The crowd applauded, and she turned to the band. "One. Two. Three."

As she sang, she crossed the dance floor. The

hauntingly beautiful song was perfect for her voice. She continued singing as she walked to the long table at the far end of the tent where her parents sat. There she serenaded them. They beamed.

Finishing the song, she bent and kissed each of her parents on the cheek. "I love you so."

Unable to blink back the mist forming in her eyes, she headed to the stage to return the microphone. Fighting tears, she had to escape the party before she broke down into a sobbing mess. As Nola made her way to the exit, Kayla snagged her arm.

"Whoa, Nola Belle, this next song is just for you." Kayla handed her a tissue.

Confused, Nola stopped and dabbed the leaking tears. Marquis stepped up to the stage and belted out the first few notes on his trumpet. The combo joined in, adding depth to the music. The crowd quieted.

From the far opposite corner of the tent, a single voice rang out, "When a Man Loves a Woman."

Nola blinked. Then swallowed. The baritone voice captivated her. Her heart lurched.

The smile on the face of the man who sang his heart out—to her—sent her heart orbiting. Choking back a sob, she fanned herself. Kayla shoved a chair beneath her. She sat, then folded her hands in her lap, never breaking eye contact with Rex.

Her heart soared.

Her mind blocked out everything—but Rex.

It was as though the two of them were in an empty room.

Crossing the expanse of space, weaving between tables, with each word of the song, Rex drew closer to her. As the song neared conclusion, he reached her and held out his hand. She put hers in his. Rex tugged her to standing. Spinning her around, he pulled her close with her back against his torso. They faced all of the guests when he ended the song and the band stopped playing.

A hush settled over the crowd.

"Mr. and Mrs. Dutrey, it's very nice to meet you. Happy Anniversary," Rex said. "Thanks for allowing me to be here and to crash your party."

Then the band began to play softly. Rex swayed side to side, and she followed his lead. He continued, "I told this woman I loved her, but she never told me if she loved me, too. So, I've come for my answer."

Rex twirled her around to face him.

"Nola Bridgette Dutrey. I love you. We're too smart not to find a way to make this work." Rex grinned wide. His eyes softened. His head cocked to one side.

Mesmerized, Nola stared at him.

The look of love!

"Yes!" She hugged him. "I love you, too."

The crowd cheered. The drummer shimmered the cymbals. Marquis busted out several notes on his trumpet that sounded like a cheer.

Heat rose from her neck to her cheeks. All of her family gathered around them. Handshakes. Hugs. Thumps on the back. Introductions were made all around.

It was *déjà vu*.

After a few minutes, she tugged on Rex's hand to pull him from the clutches of her family. There was plenty of time for them to get to know him. Together, they'd work on that. Right now, she needed him all to herself. Leading him out of the tent, she stopped beside the fountain in the circular drive and wrapped her arms around him, peppering his face with kisses—just to be sure he wasn't a dream.

Her vulnerable heart pinged with hope. No situation lasted forever, but her parents were proof that love was enduring.

"I'm sick without you, Nola," he whispered in her ear. "I want to offer you a contract, but not the musical kind. The kind that binds my heart and my life with yours forever."

"Shh. Just kiss me more. Silly man, we'll talk contracts later. Right now, we have more important business to attend to."

She smiled and hoped her grin appeared as wicked as she intended. "Come with me." She led him through the front door of Fleur de Lis. Picking up her full skirt, she ascended the staircase to her bedroom on the second floor.

G.G. Grace, I am going to be the next bride at Fleur de Lis, so forgive me for what I'm about to do. I know you'll love Rex, just as I do.

Inside the room, she closed the door, then opened the tall window. Music from the band filtered in.

"Come here." She crooked her finger at Rex. "Dance with me, please."

He raised an eyebrow. "I'm not sure it's proper for me to be here."

"Xavier Rex Arceneau. Are you telling me you won't dance with me?"

"No, sweetheart, I'm not saying that at all." She didn't miss when he cut his eyes to her bed. "But there's many ways to experience music. And in here, my want of you is rising like a crescendo."

She giggled and wiggled her eyebrows. Needing to feel the warmth of him, she wrapped her arms around his neck, swaying with him to the music. His hands rested on her hips.

"I just met your family. I want to stay on their right side. There are so many of them. It's a bit intimidating. Should we return to the party? They might want an encore from you."

"My family, they're harmless, I promise."

Rex kissed her, tugging on her bottom lip. "A family feud was threatened by your sister."

Nola chuckled. "There was one, once."

Allowing the music to wrap her in a cocoon with Rex, Nola swayed. Love flowed through her as effortlessly as the music.

"I've never invited a man into my bedroom before," she cooed as they danced. "It's against the rules. But I'm breaking them because I want you so much."

"Nola Bridgett Dutrey, music is the language of love. We take it in through hearing. We experience it through our emotions. Music doesn't require sight. It invites us to use other senses."

"Hmm…Mr. Arceneau, you're talking too much."

Rex scooped her, full tulle skirt and all, and carried her to the bed. Gently, he placed her in the middle. "I'll be quiet now. I'm going to demonstrate to you how much I love you using another one of our senses—touch."

****

At midnight, Nola left a sleeping Rex and slowly descended the front stairs, watching for the steps that creaked. A cool brush of air move across her cheek.

Swans mate for life.

The words stopped Nola on the stairs. "G.G. Grace? If that's a prediction from the other side, I'll take it. Does it come with a guarantee?"

No further message came. She headed for the kitchen in search of a slice of Kayla's cake and a glass of milk. The light over the stove cast a small shadow. The sound of metal, like a utensil, clinked against a plate. It came from the far side of the kitchen. Nola peered into the dimness. "Hello?"

"Sister dearest," Biloxi whispered. "I wondered if you'd come down."

Her sister sat at the counter in the dark. "You can thank me later."

She hugged Biloxi. "I'm thanking you now. Rex told me you invited him to come."

"Hmm…that's what he said? I invited him? I like that. Rex is a polite man."

Nola pulled open the refrigerator. "I'm guessing you used your considerable influence to draw him to the party. After all, it's Saturday night. Busy time for any restaurant."

"He impressed Momma and Daddy. Momma's gushing about you being the next bride."

"Rex and I aren't quite there yet."

But I've got my fingers crossed. Right, G.G. Grace? He's mine for life.

"Well, all I can say is that I've done my duty as your big sister. When we set eyes on him, I told you to touch."

Nola giggled. Yes, she had to admit, that was exactly what her big sister had said.

"I'll deny ever saying this, but sometimes, big

sisters know best."

Grabbing up two slices of cake and a tall glass of milk, Nola turned back to her sister. "Night. Night, Biloxi. I'm going back upstairs and touch some more."

Chapter 24

Nine months later…

Nola descended the stairs as quickly as she dared, the train of her peacock-blue mermaid dress sweeping the floor behind her. The straps of her rhinestone-studded heels were hooked through her fingers. As she reached the foyer of Rex's Garden District home, she asked, "Do I look presentable?"

Kayla, dressed in a short, black cocktail dress that showed off her long legs, folded her arms over her chest and cocked her head from one side to the other. "Your hair looks like a work of art, something I saw in a video. Yeah, I think you'll do." She winked. "Lordy, woman, you took so looong getting ready, but stunning. I've never seen you glow so much. You nearly hurt my eyes."

"Everything has to be perfect tonight." Nola smoothed the front of her gown and continued into the living room. "I'm so nervous about the soft opening for the restaurant. All of my family is coming."

"Xavier's." Kayla unfolded her arms and stepped beside her. Once in the living room, she reached for two glasses on the sidebar and handed one to Nola, lifting it in a toast. "You and my brother have done well. Your new place is going to be the big splash in the restaurant scene throughout the holidays. Rex said reservations are

293

booked for the next two months. Though, I do have to say again, thank you for agreeing to continue to sing at *my* restaurant on Friday nights."

They clinked glasses and each sipped.

"I think I need something stronger to steady my nerves, Kayla."

"Naw. The last time we did shots, you got me drunk."

"I got you…" She shook her head and snorted. "Right. You keep telling yourself that." It was a night she remembered all too well. The night Rex disappeared after he kissed her. "I haven't had alcohol since then."

Nola sat, slipped on her shoes, then worked the buckles on them.

"Here, let me help." Kayla knelt and secured the straps on the shoes. "You're my BFF. No man, not even my brother, will come between us."

"Thanks, my fingers are all fumbles right now." Nola stood and glanced around for her purse. It was on the foyer table, where she'd left it earlier. "He's not so bad," Nola gently chided. "Rex wanted to be sure that the two of you wouldn't be in direct competition in the French Quarter. I have to say, I wasn't crazy about the idea of a Warehouse District location, but I think it's all going to work out."

"Fu—heck, yeah."

Nola giggled. Kayla had been working hard to stop cussing. Marquis almost had her completely broken of the habit. Almost. "Do you miss living here at all?"

"You mean in this mausoleum? Nope. I love the condo. Marquis and I are quite settled there now."

"I look forward to invitations to Sunday night

dinners at your place. Now, where is that man of yours? Or did the plans change? He's still taking us to the restaurant, right?"

Clasping her hands together to keep her excitement from levitating her off the floor, Nola rushed to the door when the doorbell rang. Kayla was right behind her.

"Hey there!" She hugged Marquis.

"Oooh la la. You ladies look hot!"

"You clean up really nice yourself," she told him. "Come on, Kayla. Let's go. I can't wait to see what's on the menu for dinner tonight. Rex has kept it a secret. Wouldn't tell me. Did he tell you?" Gleeful and giddy, Nola tingled. She couldn't wait for Rex to see her in the custom-made dress. She'd never purchased a garment that cost so much money. But tonight was a special night...and she'd flatly refused her sister's help to select an outfit.

Marquis, dressed in a tux, held out both of his arms. Nola took one, Kayla took the other. He escorted them to the limo where a driver waited for them.

"I know everything about tonight, but one tiny detail," Marquis said, taking Kayla's hand in his.

Kayla beamed back at him, then planted a kiss on his cheek, promptly wiping away the stain of her lipstick.

Nola eyed the couple. They'd made their relationship work. Marquis had spent the summer in New York. Kayla had visited him every other Sunday and Monday. She'd mentioned the in-between times, but Nola had shut her down, not wanting to hear the details about long-distance sex via video chats on the internet.

Is Marquis going to propose to Kayla? Does Rex know? Tonight, we're all going to celebrate!

Images of Kayla as a bride at Fleur de Lis brought a smile to Nola's lips. That would make Momma very happy. She'd adopted Kayla after the anniversary party. Her tall, blonde, leggy friend blossomed under Momma's tutelage, and that took pressure off Nola. Momma had actually called her this morning and not once did she mention if Nola would be the next Fleur de Lis bride.

****

Rex checked his watch. He flipped the switch for the lights, then went outside to check the neon sign. He swelled with pride every time the sign glowed at night. He had fulfilled most of his dream. A restaurant—farm to table—that focused on freshness of ingredients, not so heavily in Cajun and Creole seasonings as Arceneau's, with Nola singing on Saturday nights as headliner. They intended to become a venue for introducing new musicians to New Orleans, and so far, it looked promising. Nola auditioned and managed the bookings, though she still sang for his sister every Friday night. Maybe that would change once...

A sign on the door notified people to knock for entrance to the invitation-only dinner. He intended to thoroughly wow Nola's family. He'd made a cheat sheet nine months ago to ensure he not only remembered all their names, but which side of the family they came from. Between the Dutreys on her father's side and Mrs. Dutrey's Beaudreau family, the family head count hit a hundred. The guest list also included his and Nola's mutual friends, some of whom were patrons of her community band. Rex had only invited a couple of his cousins. But Henri had not made the list. He still couldn't prove his uncle's involvement in the arson up north, but interestingly enough, the gold cuff links had been mysteriously delivered to the Garden District house and left on the porch.

Back inside Xavier's, he scanned the exposed brick walls of the dining room. The long, white opaque drapes covering the tall windows at Xavier's were closed, giving the industrial space with its high ceilings and visible ductwork a more intimate feel. Most nights, the place wouldn't be dressed so formally. Tonight was special. The opening to introduce the place to family and friends. Next week, Xavier's would start serving the public.

"Flowers, check. Candles, check. By the way, Leon did a good job with them. Wine for each course is ready." Kevin recounted the task list as he approached Rex. He'd come to work at Xavier's at Kayla's insistence. Rex was thankful to have a seasoned right-hand man.

"You've done a splendid job, Kevin. Thank you."

"The musicians are ready, too."

"Good. Have them go ahead and begin."

A bell rang and Rex went to the door. "Mr. and Mrs. Dutrey! You're the first guests to arrive. Let me welcome you to Xavier's."

Sean shook his hand. Rex kissed the air beside Deidre's cheeks.

"You know, Rex, when you're officially part of the family, you're going to have to stop being so formal with us." Deidre gave him a pointed look. Rex caught the hint.

Nick had warned him how Mrs. Dutrey had a way

of getting what she wanted. She hadn't pushed him, though, and said after he and Biloxi married, she'd become quite respectful of his place in the family. Of course, giving her grandchildren had mellowed her more.

"When?" Rex asked.

She narrowed her eyes at him. "Six months ago, you asked for our daughter's hand in marriage. Sean and I agreed. You swore us to secrecy. You've had me on pins and needles. Every time I talk with her, I expect her to tell me you got down on one knee. What's the holdup? Are you going to ask Nola to marry you? Tonight?"

Grinning, Rex shook his head. "Tonight is about introducing the dream that Nola and I share to all of you. I'll know the perfect time to propose. Maybe I'll let you know in advance." He winked. "Or maybe not. In the meantime, I have your seats reserved at a table near the stage. Nola will be singing tonight. You get front row seats."

One of the four hosts Rex had working that night ushered Mrs. and Mr. Dutrey away. No sooner had Rex turned back toward the door did the bell ring again.

"Biloxi and Nick! Welcome."

"Nine months is time enough to have a baby, X. Rex Arceneau. Not of the restaurant kind." Biloxi kissed his cheek. "Are you going to make an honest woman of my sister? My children need cousins, you know."

"Nick," Rex said. "Help me out. What is it with these Dutrey women?"

Chuckling, Nick said, "Believe me, surrendering will make you a much happier man." He slapped Rex on the back.

"Well, we'll see. In the meantime, your parents are up front. This gentleman will usher you to your seats."

"Where is she?" Rex muttered. He'd left his phone in the office. "Kevin," he called the man over. "Please monitor the door. You have the seating chart, correct?"

"All under control. I've got this covered."

Stalking toward the office, he passed his sister and Marquis in the hall.

"We came through the kitchen," Kayla said. "I had to be sure your new chef had everything under control." She elbowed him. "Wagyu beef. Excellent choice for tonight."

"Where's my girl?" he snapped at Marquis. "It was your job to get her here on time."

"Oh, Nola? She's waiting for you in the office."

"We were just on our way to find you and let you know." Kayla smiled sweetly.

Rex sniffed. Narrowed his eyes. Something was up.

As he reached the office and opened the door, light spilled across the floor and into the dark room. He opened the door wider. Illumination shone on Nola. She leaned, her back against the antique desk, her arms stretched out and bracing her body, her chest thrust upward. Her beautiful neck was exposed, as were her shoulders, in the sweetheart neckline. The soft blue tone of the fabric made her skin glow as though covered in opal dust. His breath hitched. His heart stopped. Never had she looked as lovely fully clothed as she did now, though his preference was to gaze at her naked.

Lowering her chin, she winked at him. "Hey, big boy." She stood and shimmied her shoulders. "I hear you have a great singer taking the stage tonight. Want to wish her good luck?"

Closing the space between them, he went to her and kissed her cheek. "You'll kill 'em. I know."

"Is that all I get?" She pouted.

"Gorgeous, the house is filling up. Let's go greet our guests. I promise to devour you later. I'm the one who needs luck tonight. It's resting in your hands." But she didn't understand the truth of that just yet.

"Are my parents here?"

"Up front. Biloxi and Nick, too. Kevin is making sure everyone is seated. We need to go greet our guests. They're waiting for us."

Rex led Nola down a hall which allowed them to enter the restaurant to the left of the stage. Applause sounded when they came into view. Rex held Nola's hand and escorted her front and center. Most of the seats were filled. All eyes focused on them. For the first time, uncertainty rattled him.

"Ah…ladies and gentlemen. Family and friends. Thank you for sharing this exciting night with Nola and me." Beside him, she gave a small curtsey. "Now, to make this special for all of us, Nola doesn't know the menu, and I don't know which songs she'll be singing. This way, she and I both get to experience some anticipation, along with all of you. That's what makes an evening special, right? Not knowing everything that's going to happen?"

"Lead the way," Sean Dutrey called out.

"Wine is being served now along with the appetizers. Onion tart with goat cheese, crab toast, and cranberry crostini. I'd be pleased if you'd take the cards by your plates and rate each dish. Add comments.

Feedback will be helpful. And to begin the evening's entertainment, I'm turning the stage over to Miss Nola Belle. She needs no introduction with this crowd."

Rex offered the mic to Nola. He stepped off to the side to watch the woman he loved do what she was most passionate about—bringing musical joy to others.

The lights dimmed slightly.

"Good evening. This is truly a special night." Nola glanced and smiled at him, then faced the audience. "I've selected some of my most favorite songs, hopefully for your enjoyment. This first song, the first time I heard it was on a turntable. Anyone remember them?"

A sprinkling of laughter was heard.

"Thank you, Great-Grandmother Grace. The song I'm about to sing, the music written by Isham Jones, lyrics by Gus Kahn, was published in 1924. Billie Holiday recorded her version of it in 1955. "It Had To Be You." I am dedicating this song to my man, Xavier Rex Arceneau."

Rex drew in a breath when she mentioned his name. His body thrummed as she sang the first line. Love filled him. He'd never been much of the praying sort, but just in case, every night when he laid his head on a pillow next to Nola's and woke to find her beside him the next morning, he gave thanks. His occasional trips to New York to unwind his business dealings had taken him away from her a few days at a time now and again, but she understood that those days apart were a means to an end. Now, he had her, the house in the Garden District, which Kayla had signed over ownership to him, and Xavier's. He'd given his shares of the restaurant to Kayla. Uncle Henri caved and was paid a reasonable price for his ten percent.

The roots of his dream had grown and now bloomed into a beautiful life.

Rex put his hands in his pockets and rocked on his heels. Every word Nola sang was just for him. The most special person in the world loved him. How had he gotten so lucky?

Just before Nola finished the song, Rex walked to the very edge of the stage. His palms were dampening. His breathing turned shallow. He forced a deep breath, then took a step toward her.

By the time she sang the last word, he was standing beside her. His heart pounded in his chest. His very stubborn, very independent woman had a mind of her own. It was now or never, but would she agree?

Nola bowed.

The audience applauded.

Her father rose and clapped, giving her a standing ovation. The rest of the crowd followed. A cacophony of clapping and whistling filled the space. The drummer shimmered the cymbals.

Rex beamed at her. She smiled back, but her eyes grew round as if to say, what's going on?

He took the mic from her hands. Bent and knelt down. Reaching in his pocket, he pulled out a small red leather box. "Nola Bridgette Dutrey. I love you. Only you. Will you marry me?"

****

Nola gasped. Her hands flew to her mouth. Her body thrummed with joy. She glanced at her mother and caught her grin stretching from ear to ear. She looked back at Rex gazing up lovingly at her.

"It has to be you, Nola. What do you say?" Rex

opened the box. White velvet set off a beautiful engagement ring.

"Yes!" she squealed. "Yes. Yes. Yes."

Rising, Rex plucked the ring from the box. Nola danced in place on her toes. Her hand trembled as he reached for it and slid the ring on her finger. "Yes, Rex. I will most definitely marry you."

She launched herself at him, and as she fully expected, he caught her. "I love you. Only you. Xavier Rex Arceneau." Having him with her forever was her dream come true. In his arms was the place she wanted to be. She'd been right to wait, not to be pressured by family and friends. She followed her heart to that 12/8 beat. Only Rex did that to her.

Around them, people stirred. Kevin motioned and plates were cleared. The next food course was delivered. The next wine was poured.

"Let's show everyone." Rex took her hand.

Nola resisted. "Oh, wait. Attention, everyone." Nola spoke into the mic. "I know my family feared I'd never find someone I could totally share my life with. Now I have. There's going to be a wedding at Fleur de Lis. *I'm* going to be a bride!"

Later, after everyone had left for the night, Nola sat next to Rex at the bar of Xavier's, and they sipped the last of the champagne. He traced a finger from her bare shoulder down her arm. "You know, the color of that dress looks very similar to a suit I have."

"It's the exact shade. The dress is custom-made."

"Biloxi didn't force you into that?"

She shook her head. "Do you think it was fate that brought us together? After all, we met at a bridal show put on by my sister and cousin."

Rex chuckled. "I thought it was Kayla's bullheadedness that brought us together. She lied to me, and I hunted her down at Fleur de Lis."

"Did I ever tell you that I thought you looked like a pimp in that suit?"

"What?"

"Never mind." She giggled.

"Let me get you home." Rex removed the glass from in front of her and set it on the side. "You've had enough to drink."

"I think I'm going to move home to Fleur de Lis until we get married. The wedding will be there. That's all right by you, yes?"

He cupped her chin and drew her closer to him. Gently he pressed his lips to hers. "Gorgeous, I'll marry you anywhere. Just make it soon. And just keep looking at me with love in your eyes."

Her heart sang. Passion. Love. Joy lifted her so high she could touch heaven. "I'm really going to be Mrs. Xavier Rex Arceneau."

And her heart continued that 12/8 beat.

A word about the author...

Amazon Best Selling author and multiple RONE Award Finalist, Linda Joyce writes about assertive females and the men who can't resist them.

A big fan of jazz and blues, Linda attributes her love of music to her southern roots, which run deep in Louisiana. Courtesy of her father's Air Force career, she has lived coast to coast in the U.S. and wrote her first manuscript when she was twelve while living in Japan.

In addition to being a book addict, Linda's a foodie, an RVer, loves to kayak, and binge watch movies. Now she lives in Atlanta with her husband and General Beauregard, their four-legged boy who thinks Linda is his pet.

Please visit her at www.linda-joyce.com